KIDNAPPED

A Romantic Suspense Novel

Suzanne Ferrell

**Ferrell, Suzanne (2012). Kidnapped. A Romantic
Suspense Novel. Suzanne Ferrell.**

ACKNOWLEDGMENTS

Thank you doesn't begin to cover the appreciation I have for those who have supported me in my writing endeavors.

Thank you to my husband and children who have graciously understood my obsession with the writing process and assumed when I talked to myself it was just me doing characterization and not schizophrenia.

To my wonderful editor, Jillian Bell. Thank you for loving my voice enough to take a chance on a new author. One of these days I might write a short story.

To the Writer Foxes; Alice, Sandy, Julie, Jo, Addison, Tracy, Jane, Lorraine and Kay, thank you for the laughter, the wine and all the support. I wouldn't be here without each of you behind me.

To the Romance Bandits, 19 of the best supporters a writer could have. I was blessed to have finaled in 2006 with y'all and even more blessed when we formed our blog.

To my critique partners. Julie Benson who taught me to fear the word "why?", Jo Davis whose timeless advice "write fearlessly" haunts me daily, and Sandy Blair who has been my rock and sounding board throughout the publication process. Thank you all for being there for me.

Finally, my mother, Mary Willis, who taught me to read and love books. Thank you, Mom, for loving me and this story from the beginning. I'll never forget your words when I told you I was writing my first romance story. You said, "I was wondering what took you so long to decide to write."

Suzanne Ferrell

.

CHAPTER ONE

Jake Carlisle needed help. He needed it now.

In the dark night the fluorescent emergency room lights called to the injured and sick like a lighthouse beacon on a stormy shore. The promise of medical aide lay one hundred yards away. It might as well be a thousand.

A cutting wind whipped around the cars in the deserted parking lot, blowing late autumn leaves past Jake's feet. Winter intended to visit Columbus, Ohio early this year. Two more weeks and Thanksgiving would arrive. Jake doubted he'd be around to give thanks for anything.

But for now the cold worked to his advantage. The security guards stuck close to the hospital entrances. Not one patrol passed where he and his witness sat hidden between two pickup trucks.

A soft moan drew his attention to the boy resting against the car beside him. Nicky was fading quickly. Jake pulled the blanket tighter around the boy's small frame, trying to protect him from the wind. The Kreshnin brothers had done a job on the kid. They'd sliced him like day old bread. Only God knew what other invisible damage they'd done.

Jake whispered an oath.

If he'd been earlier, even an hour, none of this would have happened. The minute he knew his case hinged on Nicky's testimony, he should've gotten him out of there.

From the amount of blood soaking his shirt, if the bleeding wasn't stopped soon, the kid would die. If Jake took him inside the emergency room, someone would report his injuries to the police, then he'd die for sure.

The light flashed out deeper into the night. Jake jerked around in time to see a woman exit the hospital emergency room, waving to those behind her. His sudden movement cost him dearly. Pain seared from the bullet wound in his shoulder down his back and arm.

Damn.

Through bleary eyes, he watched the woman swing a bag over her shoulder. The fluorescent parking lot light flashed on her dark hair, which she had pulled back off her face, as she passed beneath it. To ward off the night's chilling wind, she pulled her scrub jacket closed and headed out into the deserted parking lot--straight for Jake and his companion.

Please let her be a medical person and not housekeeping.

Nothing else has gone right tonight, just let her be a nurse or doctor.

With a downward motion of his open hand, Jake signaled Nicky to stay put and to remain silent. Though pain dulled his eyes, the boy motioned he understood.

Jake scooted into the shadows behind the car. Silently, he zigzagged his way behind the unsuspecting woman. When she paused two rows away from where he'd left the boy, Jake made his move.

She pressed the electronic key to unlock her door.

He slammed into her, pushing her into the side of her Suburban. In one quick move, his left hand covered her mouth while his other hand grabbed her keys.

Without warning, her head reared back and connected with the bullet wound in his shoulder.

"Damn," he hissed, pressing her harder into the metal car frame. He hadn't expected her to fight back.

The woman sank her teeth into the heel of his hand, tearing the callused flesh there. Instinctively, Jake pressed his other hand over her windpipe, just long enough for her to lose consciousness and slump against him. Then he opened the door, gently laying her on the floor. A frustrated grunt escaped him.For years he'd relied only on himself to get out of situations. Now, the one time he couldn't figure out a way to fix things on his own, his intended help puts up a fight.

He hadn't meant to render her unconscious, only subdue her long enough to get to a safe place and have her patch up Nicky. Tonight had turned into a series of choices. A combative conscious captive or a useless, unconscious one was just one more.

He searched the car, finding an old pair of pantyhose among the pile of compact discs, books, Tupperware and shoes. It took him a minute with his nearly useless left arm, but he managed to tie her hands behind her. As an added precaution, he stuffed a crumpled baseball cap into her mouth. In her pocket he found a roll of hospital tape to secure the gag.

He stared down at her for a moment. Her pale face was half hidden by the dark brown hairs that had escaped her braid during their struggle. With a gentle touch, he brushed them aside. Dark circles lay beneath dark lashes. She wasn't a big woman, probably about a hundred and thirty pounds, about five and a half feet tall. He rubbed his shoulder. His hand started to throb. Bruising had already started and two spots oozed blood where her teeth had broken the skin. For such a small woman, she sure could put up a fight.

One more disaster for this night. This keeps up and he might as well turn himself over to the hit squad.

He wiped the blood from his hand onto his shirt tail, then hurried to where he left Nicky. Gathering the boy against him, he half carried, half dragged him to the car. His two passengers safely inside, Jake climbed behind the steering wheel. Searching through the woman's things again, he located her driver's license.

Samantha Edgars, 5608 Morse Road.

Jake sighed in relief. Finally, something went his way.

That far beyond the city, her home sat squarely in the center of suburbia, but only thirty minutes drive from the heart of downtown at this time of night. If the woman lived alone, his luck might improve. He flipped through her wallet, past her credit cards and the picture of one small, dark-haired girl. He paused, then glanced around the truck. No hair barrettes, no dolls, not one sign that the little girl rode in this car. He looked at her hand. No wedding band, no tan line indicating she'd recently worn one either. No picture of a man in her wallet.

He relaxed slightly, then searched further in her wallet where he found the other thing he needed--a nurse's license.

Samantha was a registered nurse.

Classic rock blared from the radio when he started the engine. He liked the woman's taste in music. He put the car in gear, heading to Samantha Edgars' home.

He reached across the front seat and stroked Nicky's head to reassure himself as much as the little boy. "Nicky, hang on for a little while, man. We just might make it through this yet."

* * *

Something was in her mouth. Sami's tongue slid along the edges of something plastic. Flat, low ridges, holes--an adjustable strap. A baseball cap? Another taste. Hair spray. Gross. Someone had stuffed her baseball cap in her mouth, and from the feel of it they had taped it in place. Her arms were tied behind her and she lay face down on the floor--of what? Her car. The carpeting scraped her cheek every time they hit a bump.

Panic flooded Sami's senses. She came instantly awake. Inhaling deeply through her nose, she willed herself to calm down. Her working motto flashed through her

7

brain, panic never accomplished anything. Of course she had never been kidnapped and tied up before.

In the dim light of passing cars, she glimpsed things-- paper gum wrappers, an old straw, one whopper wrapper, a CD cover.

That's where Sting went. Been looking for that for days. Man did she need to vacuum this car out.

A metallic scent hit her nose. She'd recognize that smell until the day she died. Blood. And by the odor, someone had lost a great deal of it.

Panic welled inside her again. This time too much to dismiss. Her heart raced. *Breathe, dammit!* She couldn't. Oh God, who was this guy? Why did he pick her? Why hadn't she begged to stay and finish the shift, even if it was a slow night?

Calm down, Samantha. Think about something peaceful. You can't do anything right now. Maybe there's a simple explanation.

Get real. Nothing simple could explain away that much blood loss. She'd learned that the first time she'd stood by a gurney and watched her trauma victim's blood drip off the side to pool around her feet.

Even though she didn't do more than work, sleep and work some more, it was still her life. As much as she'd hated almost every waking moment since Aimee's death, she suddenly realized she wasn't ready to die. Not tonight. Certainly not like this.

A deep sigh bubbled out of her. Since the air rushed out her nose instead of her mouth, it sounded more like a snort. She scrunched her eyes and ignored the suddenly schizophrenic voices in her head.

She refused to panic. So far the only damage done was to her dignity. If she kept her wits about her, maybe she could escape. Isn't that what her brother had preached to her for years? They'd covered all the bases, from carjackings, to floods, tornadoes and any other natural disaster. In a crisis situation, remain calm and watch for an opportunity to act.

That same out of body experience she felt during an emergency flowed over her, allowing her to see the entire situation, and act accordingly. When everyone around her flew at break neck speed on an Adrenaline rush, Sami remained peacefully calm and organized.

Her body slumped into the carpeting. Quietly, she listened to the rhythm of the wheels beneath the floor. After a few minutes she almost fell asleep. Her near exhaustion, after working forty-eight of the last ninety-six hours, coupled with the mental and physical energy needed to fight her building hysteria, lulled her mind from the very real danger around her.

The car slowed, turned, then stopped.

Sami's eyes popped open.

"Damn, where does she keep the garage door opener?" the man in the driver's seat muttered. A chill crept up Sami's spine. That same deep baritone had rumbled over her ear earlier, just before something squeezed her throat and the lights went out.

A test swallow confirmed her tender throat. He'd cut off her air supply. This guy wasn't above controlling her by physical force.

A snap sounded above her head. Damn! He'd found the door opener's hiding place between the seats. A few minutes later, the Chevy inched forward. Motion sensor lights flooded the garage in a yellowish hue, casting eerie shadows inside the car. Sami thought she heard a moan. Then the garage door closed.

Breathe. Calm, just stay calm. Fight the panic.

The driver's door opened. The car's weight shifted, then rose. Heavy boots sounded on the cement garage floor. The front passenger door opened. A grunt and whoosh of air escaped the man. He sounded like an Olympic weight lifter going for the clean and jerk record. More boots thumping. Sami strained to lift her head, but couldn't see more than halfway up the seat in front of her. She rested her head on the floor once again, waiting.

Again, the boots thudded across the garage, drawing nearer.

Breathe. Stay calm. Count.

One-one thousand, two-two thousand.

The door swung open.

Sami clenched her eyes shut, pretending she was still out cold.

It seemed like minutes passed. Every second marked by the rapid beat of her pulse in her ears.

What was he waiting for?

Something soft and warm whispered across her cheek. The smell of cinnamon teased her nose.

She couldn't stand it.

Cautiously, she opened her eyes. Two clear blue eyes beneath the thickest black lashes this side of a movie star met her gaze—only upside down.

The rest of him was...shaggy. He reminded her of Robert Redford in that mountain man movie, Jeremiah something-or-other. Thick dishwater blonde hair hung to one side of his forehead and in layers down to his collar. A dark five-o'clock shadow covered the lower half of his face.

Her eyes traveled lower. Across the edge of his flannel shirt about an inch below his left collarbone, a circular pattern of dark crimson swirled outward from a hole, so full of old dried blood it bordered on black.

Whoever he was, he'd been shot tonight.

Her gaze flew to his.

He lifted his right eyebrow in a sardonic fashion. "Good, you're awake."

Both of his large hands grasped her by the shoulders. Carefully, he eased her into a sitting position.

"Let me make something perfectly clear. You are here only because I need you to patch up my friend. Got it?"

Sami nodded.

With one hand on top of her head, he guided her out of her car. Sami waited for the dizziness to clear her mind before taking a step forward. The garage door button next to the inside house door caught her eye.

An escape idea popped into her head.

Grasping her arm firmly, her captor nearly dragged her over to the door. Unsteady on her feet, she played it to her advantage and stumbled against him a step or two.

Timing was everything.

Just as they both stepped onto the bottom step leading into the house, Sami threw all her weight sideways into her captor. He grunted, falling to the side. His wounded shoulder hit the side of the house. Sami stumbled backward to the button, pressing the side of her head against it. Above her the w-h-i-r of the garage door opening sounded.

The panic she'd been fighting throughout her car trip surged through her once more. Fight or flight. She chose flight and suddenly propelled herself past his grasping hands toward the lifting garage door. Footsteps pounded behind her as she gained the driveway.

One step.

Two.

Three...

"Ooomph." She hit the grassy bank to the drive's side with what felt like a ton of bricks on top of her.

He swore as his arms wrapped around her and he rolled with her to the side.

Immediately, Sami began to squirm--legs thrashing, torso bucking into his.

"Damn it. Hold still!"

"Mmmph mmph!" *Like hell!*

He increased the pressure of his arms on her ribs, slowly purposefully squeezing the air out of her lungs. At the same time he trapped her flailing legs between his own. Very quickly Sami decided to give in, for now, rather than lose consciousness again. With a resigning snort she let her body go limp against him.

"Look!" He growled in her ear and Sami despised the

shiver of fear that coursed down her spine. "I don't have time to play games with you, lady. I tried to be nice. Now we'll do it the hard way."

He scrambled out from underneath her. Sami caught her breath. With great determination she struggled to her feet. But before she could completely straighten, he shoved his uninjured shoulder into her stomach. As the air left her lungs, she bent over his back. One strong arm wrapped around her thighs. Sami found herself looking at the dirty torn jeans stretched tightly across his hips.

Like a rolled up carpet he carried her unceremoniously into the garage, closing the door and proceeding into her house. Blood rushed into Sami's head, which bobbed up and down as her captor strode through to her living room. He dumped her onto the oversized chair in the corner. She shook her head to help it clear as the blood rushed out.

"Stay there!" he ordered. Something in his voice warned her that his patience had ended.

She nodded to him, but he already knelt by the couch, his attention focused away from her.

Only one table lamp lit the room. In the dim light, Sami studied him. His pale blue shirt stretched tight across the muscles of his shoulders and back as he leaned across something on her couch. She could still feel the warmth of his hands on her shoulders and the strength of his arm across the back of her legs as he'd effortlessly hauled her into her own house.

The man ran his hand through the thick mane of dark

blonde hair, then he shifted to one side.

Sami saw a body slumped on her old black and grey print couch. Soft moans filled the room. The man whispered something indistinguishable to the other person. She leaned to one side, trying to see around the man to the person in front of him.

"Hold on, Nicky," she heard the man murmur. He turned to look at her. "Where are your towels?"

Sami pointed to the left with her head, sort of shaking it toward the bathroom. Her captor hurried off in that direction. Now, she had a clear view of the body on the couch.

Sami sucked air in through her nose. Her stomach clenched.

He appeared to be a young boy, about eight or nine.

Sami's breath caught in her chest. *The same age Aimee would be now.* Tears welled in her eyes. Blinking them away, she fought hard to sniff in air. She couldn't lose it now. *Focus on the boy.*

Dark hair, flat nose, slight of frame--maybe four and a half feet tall, about eighty pounds soaking wet. That's what he was all right, soaking wet...with blood.

The trauma nurse inside her kicked into gear. The boy was hurt and needed her help. Her captor be damned. She wiggled to the edge of her seat. She'd just managed to stand when the man walked in carrying her new white towels.

"Sit!" the man ordered her—just like a dog.

Yeah, like she was about to obey *that* command. She slid to her knees and struggled over to the couch. The boy was pale, but his breathing didn't appear too labored. The man pressed a towel to the blood on his right chest, shoulder and arm. Sami wished she could get a better look at the boy's wounds.

She nudged the man's arm to get his attention.

"What?" he asked, distracted by his own actions.

Sami shoved her upper half into his side.

That got his attention! He moved sideways, just little enough to give her a closer view.

Sami leaned over the boy and pointed with her nose to what looked like the biggest wound. She sat back on her heels, repeating. "Mmph me mmph mmyph." *Show me his wounds.*

She could see the mental light bulb click on over the man's head. "You want to see them?"

Duh. She rolled her eyes, then nodded.

He dropped the towels and began unbuttoning the boy's shirt. With a gentleness that surprised her, he peeled the sticky material away from the boy's fair skin.

If she could have whistled, she would have. Instead she moaned deeply. Multiple lacerations crisscrossed the boy's chest. She couldn't tell how deep they ran with her hands tied behind her. Since his chest moved with ease and symmetry, she doubted a lung had been punctured.

"Mmph me mpph." *Let me help.* She turned to the side, wiggling her hands at her captor.

He looked at her hands, then her face.

"You want me to untie you?"

She nodded emphatically.

"And I am supposed to trust you not to run away? Even after your attempted escape in the garage?"

Sami shrugged, then nodded again. Though she wouldn't promise not to escape at some point.

He grabbed her chin in his hand—effectively holding her still. His intense blue eyes pinned her in place. He seemed to try reading her mind. "Listen to me very carefully, Samantha. I need your help, but will do without it if I need to. Nicky is in pretty bad shape. You are here only because I can't risk either of us being in the emergency room. Got that?"

Sami could only blink her eyes in agreement, since his grip prevented her from moving her head.

"You get one chance, lady. I have to tackle you again or you make any move to escape and I won't be held responsible for what happens to you. I don't have time to play around anymore. Understand my meaning?"

The barely veiled threat rang in Sami's ears. The reality of her situation finally hit her. She gulped hard, this time managing to nod her acquiescence.

He tore at the tape holding her baseball cap-gag in place. The tape stung as he pulled it off her skin. Once her face was free, Sami wiggled her jaw and lips. Her captor reached behind her to untie her hands. When his body leaned in close, Sami caught the metallic scent of blood mixed with something else—something decidedly masculine. Turning her head to the side, her cheek grazed against the rough hair covering his chin. To keep from giving into the urge to sigh, she coughed hard.

The man finished releasing her hands. He moved

away, his attention already on trying to stem the flow of blood on the boy's chest. To work out the stiffness and numbness that had settled into her joints and muscles, Sami rubbed her wrists and rolled her shoulders. She leaned in, grasping the towels. Gently she pulled them away from the man's hands. "Let me."

She blotted at the two largest wounds. The boy moaned as she worked. "Proklyatca."

"Etohrosho," the man replied in what sounded like some sort of Slavic language to Sami's straining ears. His reassuring tone eased the boy's tension.

Sami applied pressure, blotted, then looked at the wounds again. Her nurse's eye took over. There were a total of five gashes on the boy's chest and abdomen. Three looked like slashing cuts, the bleeding from them already stemmed and starting to clot over. Of the more dangerous looking ones, the largest kept oozing, but the smaller one had less of a blood flow.

"These two are going to need suturing. And he could do with some antibiotics too. You really need to get him to the emergency room."

He gave her a scathing look that questioned her mental state. "Didn't you hear me before? We *can't* go to the hospital."

"Why?"

"It's very complicated. Can you help him?"

Sami assessed the pale boy lying limp on her couch. She reached over and felt his pulse. Fast, but steady. The worst was probably over, but she had a feeling her immediate welfare might depend on their need of her nursing skills. Helping her own captors and not reporting the suspicious wounds to the police went against her personal beliefs, but staying alive seemed more important at this moment. Her mama always said compromise was a good thing.

"I have some suture in the laundry room off the kitchen back there." She nodded her head in the general direction. The question on his face almost made her smile. "I sometimes have it in my scrub jackets when I get home. It won't be a pretty suturing job, but I can probably close these. Lord knows I've seen it done enough."

"You're really going to help him?"

"That's what you want, isn't it?"

In all her life, Sami had rarely been intimidated like this man had done to her moments before, but growing up with three older brothers taught her never to let her fear show. She wasn't starting today, not even for this stranger. It was about time he realized she wasn't some helpless female. She'd dealt with obstinate men her whole life. What was one more?

"Unless you think you can stick a needle into flesh over and over to get these wounds closed effectively, I guess I'm the only candidate." She looked him directly in the eye, almost challenging. "Hold this towel in place and I'll go get the suture."

The scowl returned to his face. Instead of doing what she said, he gripped her arm just under her elbow and hauled her to her feet. "We'll go get it together."

He dragged her stumbling through the kitchen and into the laundry room. The box sat on the shelf over the dryer. If her luck held, maybe she could pocket the scissors and hemostats from the box without him knowing it. They might help her escape later.

"That all you need?" His grip on her arm tightened.

"A bowl of really hot water to wash the dirt away from his wounds wouldn't hurt."

He led her into the living room. To her dismay, he grabbed the box, rifled through it and withdrew the scissors and hemostats. "I'll hold on to these for you."

Her heart sank. "I'll need the scissors."

"You let me know when, and I'll give them to you. Until then, we'll all be safer with them in my care."

She lifted her chin defiantly. "The water?"

"You get started, and I'll get it. Remember, your job is to fix Nicky. I don't need you for anything else."

As he left the room to do her bidding, Sami knelt and held another towel on both wounds. "Shh, Nicky. It's going to be okay," she crooned to the boy.

She emptied the box's contents beside her. Suture packets. Bottle of peroxide. Band-Aids. Gauze pads. Sterile exam gloves—size six. Surgical tape.

Sami evaluated Nicky's overall condition. Even though none of his wounds looked life threatening to her, she wasn't about to tell the man that. As long as he believed he needed her, she was pretty sure he wouldn't harm her.

The child appeared underweight for his age, probably from malnourishment. Was the man holding her captive responsible for this child's injuries and neglect as well?

Her duty was first and foremost to get help. Somehow she needed to get the boy into protective care. If she could just get help on the way while she patched the boys wounds, the two of them might get away from their captor.

Desperately she glanced around her living room. The phone lying on the floor behind the chair caught her peripheral vision. If she hurried, she had one more opportunity to get some help.

Straining, she listened for sounds from the kitchen. Only the sound of water running met her ears.

Now was her chance, and as quick as this guy was, she might not get another one.

Without making any noise to alert her kidnapper, she eased herself off her knees and hurried over to the phone. The sound of running water continued in the kitchen.

Carefully, she lifted the receiver on the phone and punched 9-1...

Suddenly, the phone was jerked out of her hand. Sami gasped as her captor slammed it down. Then she watched, horrified, as he jerked the phone, line and jack from the wall with one giant pull.

He loomed over her.

Sami swallowed hard, but she refused to give him the satisfaction of watching her cower in front of him.

His jaw clenched. A muscle jerked rhythmically from his cheek to his neck.

His eyes narrowed with menace, his nares flared.

In that instant she knew her life expectancy just

dropped to one minute.

CHAPTER TWO

"I wondered how long it would take you to make a try for the phone." Jake held the phone in one hand, the cord stretched taut to the other one. He fought the urge to wrap it around the woman's neck. "No phone. No trying to escape. Not even a smoke signal!"

Samantha's eyes widened. Slowly, she nodded.

He dropped the phone, shoving her as gently as possible, but strong enough to show he meant business, in the couch's direction. "Now get your butt over there and fix Nicky."

Fear crossed her features, quickly replaced by anger. Damn, he had to give her credit, she might be scared, but she wasn't about to make this easy on him. It was as much for her safety as theirs that she not contact anyone, but he couldn't tell her that, yet. He followed her over to kneel next to Nicky.

"Onah seedekja ee boodyet pomooghat, moy droug." *This lady is going to help you, my friend.* He explained in Russian. Nicky knew English fairly well, but Jake was sure his own language would reassure him as much as the words.

The boy nodded, then turned to watch Samantha. He gave her a shaky smile.

She returned it with a more reassuring one of her own. "Nicky, this is going to hurt. There isn't anything I can give you to make it not hurt."

Jake laid his hand on the boy's shoulder, squeezing it firmly. "Nicholai, eto poveleetelnee-nedyelat ne zvook. Mne ne nada pleetzia eesledovat." *Nicholai, it is very important that you not make any noise. We must not bring the police here to investigate.*

Samantha pulled on a pair of medical gloves. She reached for the peroxide and some gauze pads. "This is going to sting, Nicky. But I need to clean the blood and wash away as much dirt as I can."

Jake grimaced as she poured the liquid onto the first wound. Nicky sucked in his breath when the peroxide bubbled and sizzled on his skin. Then his eyes rolled backward. His head fell against the pillows.

"Nicky." Jake tried to push Samantha aside to get closer to the boy.

She stopped him with a hand on his chest. "He only fainted. The pain was just too much for him."

"You're sure? You're sure he didn't lose too much blood?"

"Oh, I'm sure he lost a great deal of blood. But I doubt he lost enough to do more than make him weak at this point." Despite her words, she reached out a hand to feel the pulse in Nicky's neck. Then she nodded reassuringly.

Usually, he didn't trust complete strangers, and he was probably a fool for putting any faith in someone he'd coerced into helping him, but something in her calm confidence reassured him. He relaxed a little and moved back to give her room to work.

She opened the suture packet, taking out a curved needle with long purple string attached to it.

God, that was really going to hurt the kid.

She turned to look at him, holding out her hand. "I'm going to need those hemostats."

"I assume those are these?" Jake held the medical instrument in his hand. He slipped it into hers. "Just remember what you're using them for, lady."

For an instant she gave him a look that suggested she'd like to put those hemostats somewhere in his body. Dismissing him, she turned to probe at the first wound's edges. Jake squeezed Nicky's hand, even though the boy remained blissfully unconscious throughout the ordeal.

Samantha worked quickly, even though she stopped from time to time to whisper her apologies to Nicky. Every time she stuck the needle through a piece of skin, Jake fought his own need to look away.

Finally, the nurse had all the wounds that needed stitching closed. "I'll finish bandaging these and we can let him rest. Your friend is a very strong little boy."

"You don't know the half of it, lady."

Jake pulled a kitchen chair in to sit near her as she finished bandaging the boy. He gave himself a small mental pat on the back. One thing had gone right tonight. In kidnapping Samantha at least he'd gotten a nurse who knew her business. He was glad. Nicky had been through enough already in his young life. Jake wanted to try and keep him healthy and safe, at least the rest of this night. Who knew what trouble tomorrow would bring.

Samantha tucked a red and black wool afghan around Nicky, then sat back on her heels. "You're next."

She had the lightest green eyes, he'd ever seen. Something stirred deep inside him, something very inappropriate for the moment. Ignoring the feeling, he began unbuttoning his shirt.

"Just wiggle out of the right side," she instructed him. "I'll have to cut the shirt close to the edge of your wound, or else you'll just end up tearing the clots loose."

"You sound like you've done this before."

"More times than I can count. Gunshot wounds are all too common these days." She leaned forward on her knees and looked at the front, then the back of his shirt. "Lucky for you, the bullet passed straight through. At least I don't think it hit any bones."

"Yeah, I'm real lucky."

She reached over to the table where he had set the scissors. With his left hand, he grabbed her firmly around the wrist, trapping her where she knelt in front of him. "No funny stuff, Samantha. I haven't hurt you, yet. But if

I have to, believe me, I will."

Her eyes widened then she swallowed, slowly nodding once more. He released her wrist. Gingerly, he eased himself further into the chair. "Okay. I'm ready."

She pulled the shirt away, trimming to within an inch of the hole's center. When she had the front loose, Jake sat forward so she could work on his back. She set the blood-crusted material on the floor, then reached for the bottle of peroxide.

"The easiest way to loosen this is to soak it off." She smiled at him. Actually smiled at him, as she poured.

"Damn! Fuck!" Jake gripped the chair's side, as he muttered several more expletives. He gritted his teeth, sucking air inside in a low hiss. His vision blurred then went black. "Geeze, you actually liked doing that. Oh man."

He grabbed her by the wrist of the hand holding the bottle. Slowly his vision cleared. With great determination he looked her right in the eye. "You give sadistic nurses a bad name, Samantha."

He grasped her other wrist and drew her slowly closer, closer, until finally, only a breath separated their noses. "Don't do that again, without warning me."

Those fascinating, pale-green eyes of hers widened. Then she moved her head in the barest of nods. Half draped across his lap, he felt just the slightest tremors pass through her body. She was scared, but she didn't want to let him know how much. He had to give her credit. The woman had guts.

"Get on with it, then." This time he steeled himself for

her ministrations.

She pulled the last material piece away, whistling. "What caliber made this hole?"

"Thirty-eight."

She looked at him. "Police issue?"

"Yes, it is. Don't tell me you know that from working in the emergency room, too?"

"No. My brother's a cop."

He bit back another oath.

Great, all he needed now was to find out her brother was on the hit squad that had come after him and Nicky tonight. Could this night get any worse?

"You have a brother on the local force?"

"I should lie and tell you yes. But no. He's a cop down in Cincinnati."

Jake relaxed a bit. Maybe if his luck held, he and Nicky would be long gone before this brother-cop found out about her kidnapping. Right now, he didn't need someone else on his tail, especially an irate brother.

"So why are the local cops shooting you?" She finished cleaning the wound's edges by dabbing it with wet gauze. Then she picked up another suture packet. "And this is going to need a couple of sutures in it. Is that warning enough?"

"Go ahead." Jake grabbed the chair's edges tightly with both hands. "The cops weren't supposed to be firing at me." He kept talking to distract himself from what she was doing. "I wish I could say I just got caught in the cross fire, but..." Fire seared through his arm as she pulled the suture through the skin. "Damn woman! Are you trying to make it hurt more?"

"Actually, the pain is a good thing, Mr. Kidnapper. It means the nerve is still intact." She put in another suture.

"Jake." He grimaced, but this time refrained from commenting further.

Samantha paused, the needle an inch from his skin. "Excuse me?"

"The name's Jake. And I wish you'd stop talking and get finished."

Samantha didn't say another word until she closed both the front and back holes. Jake watched her as she worked. Her dark head bent slightly to the side, the low lamp light cast soft shadows to her skin. He wondered if it felt as soft as it looked. Despite the pain her efforts were causing him, he had to fight the urge to caress one of her cheeks.

It had been nearly three years since he'd been around a normal woman. Three long years or undercover work. His usual feminine company was the prostitutes that worked for the Kreshnins. Most were immigrant girls who'd come to America for a better life, only to find themselves trapped in a sex-slave ring to pay off their debt for transport from Europe. Although he'd felt sorry for the women and slept with a few to keep his cover intact, none had ever stirred any real sexual interest in him.

So why all of a sudden did this woman?

Samantha tilted her head further to the side, studying the wound. Concentrating on her work, she pulled her lower lip between her teeth.

Jake almost groaned. He reminded himself she served a purpose, and it wasn't to reawaken his own libido.

Finally, the torture of her ministrations ended, she had both holes sewn shut. To hold gauze pads in place as a clean dressing, she wrapped gauze around his chest and over his shoulder. Despite her professional actions, her fingers felt like soft, warm feathers caressing his skin.

Finished, she sat back on her heels once more. "So, Jake, this was an accidental police shooting?"

"No. It was no accident. Only I don't know exactly who had me targeted."

Samantha stopped in the midst of gathering her supplies to give him a puzzled look. "I thought you said it was the police that shot you."

"I did." Jake picked up the instruments, needles and gauze, carrying them into her kitchen. He searched through her trash.

"What are you looking for in there?" Samantha followed him, carrying her box of supplies. "I swear I don't keep any weapons in my trash. Although, after today, I just might start."

Jake pulled out a soup can and lid. "Give me your gloves."

"Why?" She held them out to him.

"Because I don't want anyone finding this stuff until it hits the city landfill." He stuffed the needles, bloody gauze, and gloves inside. Then he wedged the lid on top and buried the can deep into the bottom of her trash can.

Dizziness swamped over him. He fought to stay on his feet.

He clutched the counter to remain vertical, then hissed as the throbbing in his left hand began anew.

"Shit." He released his grip with that hand and shook it.

"What's wrong with your hand?" She reached for it and he pulled away. "Let me see it." With practiced patience, she reached again, her warm, soft hands grasping him firmly by the wrist.

How many reluctant patients had she gently manhandled in the same way working in the ER?

Slowly he opened his hand. A large circular bruise covered the heel's fleshy center. Small scabs covered several teeth marks marking the edge of his injury.

Samantha studied it a moment, then turned to look at him. "I did this, didn't I?"

He nodded.

A brief smile of pride crossed her lips. "Good."

Her pleasure in wounding him surprised him. He frowned and leaned closer. "I don't think you're in a position to gloat."

Her smile disappeared and she swallowed. She reached into her freezer and brought out a bag of frozen peas. "Hold that on it a while. It'll numb the pain some."

He held the frozen vegetables to his hand. Damn it felt good. He watched her finish putting away her supplies.

"What happened to Nicky?" she asked as she washed the blood from the towels in her sink. "He wasn't shot."

Once she'd squeezed the water from the towels, she set them on the counter. When she pumped liquid soap from the colorful dispenser next to the sink onto her hands a fresh lemony scent filled the air. With a circular, rolling motion, she worked the lather over and over her hands, squeezing it between her fingers. Then she dipped them under the hot water, working in the same circular motion.

Mesmerized by her professional hand-washing job, the dizziness hit him again. He needed to lie down before he fell down. No way could he leave her loose. He grabbed her by the gold and brown braid hanging down her back.

She gasped. Her eyes grew wide with fright once more.

"Enough questions. Where's your bedroom?"

"Please. I've done everything you've asked of me." She tried to struggle. He released her hair and grabbed one arm as much to hold himself up as to lead her through the house in the direction of the bedroom he'd seen earlier.

"Shut up and just move, Samantha."

Inside the bedroom, Jake closed the door behind them. With great will power he stood with his back pressed against it. "Climb onto the bed."

"No, I won't." Even though her words were a challenge the muscles in her jaw clenched and her eyes grew wide once more with fright. He knew he was being a jerk scaring her like this. For now, though, he needed her cooperation, not another discussion.

"Now, Samantha." He leaned heavy against the door.

Sheer determination kept him vertical. He dropped the bag of peas on her dresser next to the door, then reached down, pulling out the switchblade he carried in the lining of his boot. He clicked it open. It had saved his life in more than one tight spot. He narrowed his eyes menacingly at her. Tonight, he'd only use it to convince her to cooperate with him.

Eyes fixed on the gleaming stiletto blade Samantha inhaled deeply, her breasts rising and falling quickly. For a moment, Jake thought she meant to call his bluff. He flicked the knife at her. "Do it. Now!"

Resignation flitted across her face. Sitting on the edge of the bed, she pulled off her thin scrub jacket.

Jake reached into his pocket and pulled out the panty hose he'd used earlier to bind her in the car. "Lay down." He moved toward her, the knife blade glinting in the lamplight.

Samantha scooted backward onto the bed. "Please, I've done everything you have asked of me. Really, I have." She begged him, all the time squeezing her body tight against the headboard.

He hated seeing her that frightened of him. But if her fear gained him her cooperation, then he'd use it to his advantage.

"Hold out your hands."

She held them out, and he managed to loop one wrist then the other into the hose, never loosening his hold on the knife. "Hands up."

Samantha held her hands over her head.

He set the knife on the table to tie her hands to the

headboard's rails.

She was quick. With one swift move, her knee contacted with his thigh, inches from his groin.

His vision went black, then stars appeared. He managed to fall onto her, holding her in place. "Dammit."

"Get off me." She tried to wiggle.

His vision returned quick enough to let him finish tying her to the headboard. Then he pressed one hand over her mouth and nose. It took a moment for her to get the message, but she stilled quickly.

"Don't...ever...do...that...again," he gasped out.

She nodded beneath his hand. He moved it off her nose so she could breathe.

He lay on top of her for a few more minutes, while the pain subsided. The same clean citrus scent tickled his mind. Her soft body beneath his fit him in all the right places. The two soft mounds of her breasts pressed up against his chest. Her face felt soft against the curve of his neck and shoulder, and he inhaled the sweet scent of flowers off her hair.

Despite the kick that barely missed his genitals, his body responded to her instinctively. Her eyes grew wide, but with fright a new kind of fright. He knew she recognized his beginning erection for what it was. With a sigh, he pushed himself off of her.

He left her there, while he went to check on Nicky. The boy appeared to be sleeping soundly. Good.

Returning to the bedroom, he left the door open and turned off the light. He looked at Samantha. "Am I going to have to gag you again? Or are you going to be quiet."

"I won't be quiet while you rape me."

"Despite how enticing your body felt a moment ago, rape is not my modus operandi with women." Wearily, he climbed in behind her, curving his body to mold against hers. He draped one arm over her waist. Breathing deep of her scent, sultry woman and lemons, a deep sigh escaped him.

"I...just...need....to......sleep."

* * *

Sami struggled to climb out of the deep, dark, hot cave. Her arms ached from trying to climb up out of it. Hard tree roots entangled her legs and her waist.

Wait. That was an arm.

A man's arm lay heavily across her waist and abdomen. Now she knew she was dreaming. The only way a man had been in her bed in more than four years was in her dreams. She tried to clear some of the fuzziness out of her sleepy brain. There had been a man. One with a very nice butt.

Her eyes flew open.

She looked up. Yep, her hands were tied to the headboard. She looked down. Her kidnapper, no, wait he'd told her his name was Jake. His leg covered hers and his very masculine arm held her pressed back against him.

Warm breath flowed softly against her neck and ear. Tremors shot through her body. Sami's eyes rolled closed. So long. It had been so long. It would be so easy to give in to the sensations.

"You feel so good, Samantha."

She shivered as his sleep-roughened voice whispered into her ear.

"So soft. So warm."

Sami fought hard to smother the moan that wanted to escape her. Really, she did. It slipped out her lips anyway.

His hand slid across her belly. A finger slipped into her belly button, briefly. She trembled again. Then the hand pressed her tight against his body. She felt his erection against her buttocks.

That damn moan escaped again. Could it really be held against her if she let her body follow its own desire while he held her prisoner like this?

Then slowly he eased his body away from hers.

She felt his weight leave the bed. Her eyes popped open and she stared at the lavender and mint green print wallpaper she'd hung just last month.

The toilet flushed. Her bathroom drawers opened and closed one by one. Finally, she heard him come into the room. She closed her eyes tight. She couldn't believe she'd responded like that to a virtual stranger. And one that had invaded her life in such a violent way.

"Samantha?" He stood in front of her.

She swallowed hard and opened her eyes. He fixed those intense blue eyes on her once more.

"It's okay. Nicky and I'll be out of here later today. I promise." He untied her hands from the headboard, but left them tied together. He helped her sit. Then he rubbed her aching shoulders. "I'm going to let you clean up in the shower, but please, no more trying to get away."

The tender way he asked took her off guard. She feared if she answered him, she'd end up crying or begging him to come back to bed. Instead, she silently nodded.

"Good." He led her into the bathroom by the hose-rope around her wrists, then untied them, too. His lips rose in a half smile that sent her hormones soaring, then he closed the door and left her alone.

Sami locked the door and leaned against it. She groaned   loudly.

This was not good. She must be going crazy. The man had kidnapped her, tied her up, knocked her down, yelled at her, threatened her, tied her again and held her prisoner in her own home. Yet, for the first time in years she'd awakened warm and secure in a man's arms this morning. And she'd liked it.

How pathetic. Was she so isolated from her emotions that she'd welcome the physical contact of any man, even a possible criminal?

Through the door she heard him milling about her room. She didn't have time to contemplate the psychological implication of that question. He'd be back any minute for her.

Quickly, she stripped, jumped into the luke-warm shower and washed all the vital parts. She toweled off and pulled on her robe. When her eyes fell on the folded pair of blue panties and bra laying on top of a pair of faded jeans and dark blue T-shirt resting on the vanity, she sat down hard on the toilet.

When had he put those there? While she showered?

No, she'd locked the door. He'd brought them while she'd been tied up, anticipating what she'd need? What kind of man was this?

She considered everything she knew about him.

First, the police wanted him. Or at least he'd been shot by them. Secondly, he knew not to go to the emergency room for help. So he must be aware of the hospital's requirement to report any gunshots or stabbings to the police. Third, he hadn't really hurt her. Oh, he'd invaded her life, and tackled her. But other than threaten her, he had yet to do any real physical harm to her.

A laugh bubbled out of nowhere. He reminded her of her oldest brother. Dave liked to throw his weight around to prove how big and bad a lawman he was. Yet his wife, Judy, could turn him into a pussycat with just one look.

Sami looked at her folded clothes again. Jake had taken the time to anticipate her needs this morning. This was no ordinary kidnapper.

A knock on the door broke her reverie.

"Samantha? You aren't really going to make me come in there after you, are you?"

His tone suggested she shouldn't test him, not if she wanted to keep her door intact.

"Uhm, no. I'll be out in a minute."

She dressed in record time, running her brush through her hair and tying it in a ponytail.

What are you doing? You cannot trust this man! No matter how much your body wants you to surrender. Just because he didn't rape you last night, doesn't mean he won't attack you today.

The voice made sense this time.

A weapon. She needed something to use so she could escape.

She opened her vanity drawers. Scissors. She knew she had a pair of them in here, somewhere. Or a razor. Didn't she have one of those old fashioned, double-edged razor blades? Frantically she searched. Nothing. Where had they gone?

A louder knock on the door. "It's no use, Samantha. I got all the sharp items out earlier. Come out now.

She hung her head for a moment. Then she took a deep, steadying breath and opened the door.

Jake stood before her in his jeans, boots and a blue plaid shirt left by her ex-husband. Damn there wasn't an inch of fat on the man. He looked like the poster boy for hard, dangerous and sexy.

"Hope you don't mind me borrowing this shirt."

She shook her head. "No, I don't mind." What was she going to say? Yes? He filled it out better than her ex ever had.

His hand snaked out grabbing her by the arm. "Good girl. Now, come and look at Nicky."

He led her into her own living room.

She jerked to a stop at the foot of her couch. Seeing the small body tucked beneath her ancient afghan, the dark hair matted to the child's pale face, for a moment she thought it was Aimee.

Pain, so real she almost crumbled to her knees filled her chest. She'd avoided caring for children in the ER for the past four years just to keep the anguish and grief buried. It was the only way she could get through each day. Last night she'd thought of the child as another trauma patient, one she needed to keep alive to stay alive. She worked in automatic mode in the interest of self-preservation.

How was she supposed to care for him now? He reminded her so much of Aimee, lying there, pale and listless.

"What's the matter, Samantha?" Jake gripped her arm tighter and pulled her forward. "Is something wrong with Nicky?"

Jake's fingers digging into her arm and his harsh tone reminded her she had no choice but to care for the boy. Once again she shoved her pain and regret to the deepest part of her soul and forced herself into nurse mode.

"Hey there. Did you sleep well?" She leaned down, laying her hand on his forehead, then the back of his neck. "He's a little warm, but he doesn't feel like he has a temperature." She felt his pulse. She glanced at Jake. "It's a little fast. Could be the start of a temperature, or just because he lost so much blood."

"Can he travel today?"

"I don't know." She looked at the bandages across Nicky's chest and abdomen. The boy tensed, trying to cover them with his hands. "Shh. It's okay, Nicky, I just want to look. I promise not to make it hurt like last night."

Jake translated for her in that other language she now assumed was Russian. The way he called him Nicholai gave her a big hint. Whatever Jake said, the boy settled back against the couch, letting her look beneath his dressings.

"It's early, but there aren't any signs of a raging infection this morning." She smiled at Nicky. "Would you like something to drink?"

Nicky looked up at Jake, then back at Sami. "Yes, please."

Definitely a Russian accent.

Jake helped her stand, holding onto her elbow all the way into the kitchen. While she poured Nicky some water, he searched her cabinet drawers.

"What are you looking for?"

"Just checking which drawers have knives in them. As cute as you are this morning, I can't have you escaping before Nicky and I leave."

She ignored the cute comment. "So, you're leaving this morning?"

"That's my plan, but it hinges on one vital fact."

"Which is?" She carried the water to Nicky, helping him drink.

"Whether or not I can trust my boss." Jake leaned against the doorframe, she sensed his gaze following her movements.

She tried not to think about how they had awakened. Despite her efforts, her body warmed under his gaze. She tucked the afghan once more around Nicky, who drifted off to sleep. Then she took the glass to the kitchen. Jake barely moved to make room for her. Her arms grazed his as she passed, and the scent of Cinnamon tickled her nose once more.

"Where is the nearest payphone?"

"At the local drug store. Two blocks down to the left. Of course, if you hadn't disabled mine, you could have used it."

"It wouldn't have mattered. I need a secure, untraceable line."

Sami filed that comment away with the others. The man talked like some kind of secret agent.

"Back to the bedroom, Samantha."

Her heart started to pound. She dug her heels into the carpeting. "Why?"

"Because," he said as he pulled her along. "I need to leave and I am not about to allow you to run for help, that's why."

He shoved her onto the bed, wrapping the strip of nylon around her hands again. When he went to tie them over her head, she pulled away.

"Please not like that again. My shoulders already hurt from last night."

With a softening look, Jake lowered her hands. He tied them out in front of her. "Okay. It won't be for long this time, Samantha. But I don't need you crying out for help, either, so." He pulled out one of her ex-husband's old ties, and held it to her lips.

Sami clamped her jaw tight. No way would she let him gag her too.

"Now you don't want to do that, Samantha. Open up, or I'll have to make you."

She shook her head back and forth, refusing to open her mouth. No way was she making this easy on him. If he gagged her she wouldn't be able to use her teeth to untie the pantyhose, which was her plan the second he left the apartment

Jake heaved a heavy sigh. "Okay. Have it your way."

He reached forward, grasping her by the ponytail. With one swift yank, he pulled her upwards. At the same time he ground his mouth down on hers. It was a hard penetrating kiss. Sami fought and twisted, trying to get free. His hand gripped her hair tight. His lips pressed harder.

Then it changed. The pressure lightened. His tongue traced the outline of her lips, nudging, asking entrance. Heat suffused Sami from head to toe. The throbbing that woke her earlier in the day returned. He tasted like a sultry Cinnamon stick, all male and very spicy. Slowly, as if she had no control over them, her lips parted.

His tongue slipped inside. He tasted her like he was licking some stolen sweet. Stroking, sampling. Another moan escaped her.

Jake pulled away, ending the kiss as quickly as he started it. Before her mind cleared and she could close her mouth, he slid the tie in, securing it behind her head.

Reality snapped back into her mind, followed quickly by hot anger. She pulled on the ties to her hands. She tried to kick out at him. Quickly, he tied her to the bed once more, in such a way she couldn't get her mouth between the slats of the bed to her fingers and pull out the gag. Then he moved away, managing to dodge her feet.

"I warned you." He laughed as he scooted to the doorway.

"Mmpph mummph mouu!" *I hate you!* She shot hot daggers at his retreating back. His laughter filled her ears. Humiliation fanned her anger. How dare he!

The door closed. She slumped against the bed. Oh he would regret that kiss. Regret it as much as she was right now.

* * *

Jake dialed the number to Captain Bridges' office. God he hoped his boss was in and no one else picked up this line.

"Captain Bridges."

"Tom? It's Jake."

"Hold on a minute."

Jake heard him tell someone, "This is my daughter if you'll excuse me?" The door clicked shut in the background.

"Jake! Where the hell are you? And what happened last night? All hell's broken loose here because of that raid." Worry and anger filled his boss' voice, but Jake didn't have time to reassure him.

"Someone tipped off the Kreshnin brothers about me. They caught Nicky and tortured him. I managed to get him out, but by then the raid had started." He looked at his watch. Twenty seconds. "And the local police came gunning for me, not the Kreshnins like they were supposed to be."

"What?"

"The force has been compromised." Forty seconds.

"Who? How?"

"Look, Tom. Can you get Nicky and me into protective custody? And some medical aid? And can you meet me somewhere today?" Fifty seconds.

"Meet me at the Farmers market downtown."

"Make it for four this afternoon and we'll be there."

"Jake..."

Jake clicked the phone down. He hated to cut off Tom Bridges like that, but at this point the only person he could afford to trust was himself. The phone could be tapped. Or worse. Even his boss, whom he'd known nearly ten years, was suspect until he found out otherwise. Someone had informed the Kreshnins about Nicky working with him. The person who compromised his cover would live to regret it.

After checking that no one tailed him, Jake drove into town. His apartment was off limits, as well as the flop room he'd been using while undercover. He still had one totally secure place, the safety deposit box he leased in his maternal grandfather's name. He habitually concealed any personal papers there. Years of undercover work as a federal agent had honed his survival instincts to a sharp edge. He left nothing to chance when it came to hiding his identity.

The bank supervisor led him to the safety deposit vault, then left him to open his box in private. Jake slid the lid off the gray metal container. The room's dim central light gave the cubicle a surreal nineteen forties mystery feel. He laughed at his fantasy. His own personal film noir. One he would gladly not be featured in.

He lifted out the Glock and its holster. It felt good to hold it in his hand, comforting even. The cold metal gave him a sense of security he hadn't felt in the past three years.

Except for last night. Lying in Samantha's bed, her warm body pressed against his, he'd experienced the most relaxing sleep he'd had since this whole investigation fell into   his   lap.

He slipped off the jacket he'd found in her closet. The holster fit over his left shoulder, the support strap stretching across his back and over his right shoulder. A pair of steel police handcuffs lay on top of the papers in the box. Jake slipped them into his pants pocket.

He chuckled to himself. These could come in handy in dealing with Samantha. She had lots of gumption. Despite all his threats, she kept trying to find something to help her escape.

Finally he drew out the folded manila envelope. He didn't need to check its contents. It contained all the evidence he'd gathered against the Kreshnin brothers' black market weapons, sex slave prostitution houses, and strong arms deals, along with the information about how they ran their individual cells of underlings—complete with pictures. If he only had the cops' names that set him up, the puzzle would be complete. Once he got Nicky into protective custody with his people at the feds, the Kreshnins and their inside help would pay for the torture that kid had suffered.

Finished, he climbed into the Suburban, heading back to Samantha's place. She was another loose end he needed to do something about. He couldn't leave her tied up in the apartment when he left. She didn't deserve that. But until he had Nicky somewhere safe, he couldn't leave her free. No, he didn't trust her that much.

Maybe he could find the phone number of that cop brother of her's and get him to come get her as soon as they were safe. Yeah, he'd do that. Her brother would protect her.

As he pulled into the garage and cut the engine, he muttered another curse. Never in his life had he taken advantage of a woman. Despite his threats to her earlier, he didn't plan to start now.

"Nicky, I'm back," he called as he came though the kitchen.

Nicky didn't answer him.

He found the boy lying pale and shaking on the floor next to the couch. Gently, Jake lifted him back onto the couch and felt his head the same way he'd seen Samantha do earlier that morning. Dammit. The kid was burning up.

"Samantha," Jake pulled the switchblade out of his pocket and ran to the bedroom.

Samantha crawled onto the pillows, tugging wildly at her bindings. Fear deep in her wide eyes, she shook her head.

With one swift lunge of the blade, he sliced the ties holding her to the bed. Pulling the gag out of her mouth, he dragged her to the living room.

"Nicky is burning up with fever. You have to do something." He pointed the knife at her. "Do not let him die, lady."

CHAPTER THREE

Sami stared at the light gleaming off the blade in front of her. Once she raised her eyes to Jake's the panic that threatened to rear its ugly head in her once more, faded. In his eyes she read the anguish she'd seen so many times before in family members of critically ill patients. Desperate parents or guardians would do anything, say anything, promise anything, or threaten anyone to help save their child's life.

She knew, because once she'd done all those things, too. Even though she'd known there was no hope for her daughter, Aimee, she'd done them anyway. All the pleading had done nothing. Raging against heaven and earth yielded no miracles. Even searching every known treatment, no matter how bizarre, did not save her daughter.

She couldn't save Aimee, but she could help Nicky.

"Calm down, Jake. Let's see how bad it is." She felt the boy's head. Without a thermometer, it was hard to tell how high his temperature was. Sweat poured off the poor boy. "Nicky? Can you hear me?"

"He didn't answer me when I called him. Don't just sit there, do something."

Sami ignored the barely leashed anger in Jake's voice.

"Get me some cold water. A large pan full, and put ice in it." She lifted the boy's eyelids. His pupils reacted to the light. Good. "It's okay, Nicky. Jake and I are going to make you feel better soon. Hang in there."

She hurried to her bathroom closet, grabbing the bottle of rubbing alcohol, several wash cloths and three big towels. When she knelt beside Nicky, Jake returned with the pan of ice water.

Sami poured the alcohol into the water, soaked the wash cloths in the mixture, then opened Nicky's clothes. Squeezing out two cloths, she handed them to Jake. "Put these on any part of his skin not bandaged."

He dropped the towels back in the bowl. "That's damn cold. It'll make him shiver even more, See?" He pointed to Nicky.

"Yes, and if his temperature gets too high, his brain will literally cook. A cold alcohol bath is the quickest way to get his temp down and keep that from happening." She squeezed a small towel out once again and handed it to him. "I may not like you for barging into my life, but I certainly wouldn't do this boy any harm to get even with

49

you."

For a moment he studied her as if she might do just that. She waited patiently. Something, perhaps the calm way she spoke to him in the same voice she used for uncooperative patients or doctors, convinced him she knew what she was talking about.

"Okay, we'll do it your way," he said, laying the cloth on Nicky's forehead. "It just better work."

From the threat in his voice, she prayed it did, too.

While Jake did as she asked, Sami pulled off Nicky's drenched pants. She laid more wet cloths on his legs, then turned to repeat the process on his arms. She pulled off his shirt. The rope burn marks on his wrists stopped her short.

"They tied him up to torture him?"

Jake didn't even flinch. "I tried to protect the kid. He kept helping me, even when I asked him not to. They got to him before I could get him to safety."

"Who did? Why would anyone want to torture a little boy?" Sami could only stare at him.

Jake swept his hand over his face. "The less you know, the better off you'll be when we leave, Samantha."

"You know I have to report any form of child abuse to the child protection agency. I need to know exactly what they did to him." She laid her hand on Jake's. "What if something serious was damaged? Look, there is bruising near his ribs. I can't fix a lacerated spleen, kidney or liver, and I don't know that he does or doesn't have one. He may need to go to surgery. And I think he needs some antibiotics."

Jake pushed away from the couch. He strode to the window, resting his arm against the sill. Silence hung in the air like a kite waiting for a burst of wind. "Once I get him to my boss, he'll be okay. I really can't trust you to keep quiet, Samantha. You'll run right to the police to report this. And that could mean the death of all three of us."

His tense body signaled Sami that he'd made up his mind. Whatever had happened to Nicky, Jake intended to keep it to himself. Indignation flared hot inside her. "Look, you can't let your secrets endanger this boy any more than they already have. Until this fever comes down, he's at risk to have a seizure. You can't risk moving him."

"Look, lady! Maybe you don't understand English. He isn't safe here with you, neither am I. In fact you aren't safe with us here, either. And Nicky certainly isn't safe at any hospital." He ran his hands through his thick blonde hair again. Suddenly, he twirled around, slamming one hand against the wall. Sami winced at the sound.

"Damn. I can't believe this is happening. Just get Nicky well enough to travel, okay?"

Sami switched the warm cloths with cool ones. She needed to keep her own temper under control. "I don't know that I can. Alcohol baths are effective, but only for a short period of time."

"Don't you have some medicine he could take? Tylenol or something?" He headed for her bathroom, slamming through the pills she had in there.

"It's useless to look in there. I don't have children's Tylenol." Not for four years.

"Can't we give him some regular stuff?"

"I used the last of it the other day."

He strode back into the room, standing over her. "What kind of nurse are you, lady? You don't even keep Tylenol in the house?"

Sami stared at him with a look that had quelled more than one arrogant doctor during her career. "Excuse me. If I had known I was going to be kidnapped by a man with a sick child I would have run right out and bought some children's Tylenol."

"Okay. You made your point." He held up his hands in mock surrender. "So what do we do?"

"I could run out and get some." Sami smiled.

He sighed.

"If I get the Tylenol, how soon will it work? How soon can I move Nicky?"

"If I can get some down him, and if it has any effect, his fever might be lower in about an hour. But I still wouldn't recommend moving him, unless it's absolutely necessary."

"It's necessary." He grabbed her by the arm, literally hauling her to her feet.

"Hey!" Sami sputtered, as he dragged her back to the bedroom once more. "You can't tie me up again. Nicky needs me."

"I can't trust you not to take off for the neighbors."

What was this guy? A mind reader?

Sami tried to pull loose, but Jake gripped her too tight.

She dragged her feet, trying to slow him. "You can't leave him alone out there."

"Don't worry about, Nicky. I'll take care of him."

"You can't take him away. He needs me. You need me." Tears ran down her cheeks. She couldn't stand being tied again. Especially not with Nicky so sick and helpless. She had to convince Jake not to tie her up. "I'll do anything. Anything you want, just don't tie me up."

"Anything?" He held her arm tight. The bed pressed against the backs of her legs. Slowly, his gaze wandered from her head to her feet, then back again. Heat flooded her face. She refused to flinch. His smoldering look almost broke her resolve.

"Yes. Anything." She lifted her chin a little. Just a small challenge.

He moved closer. His free hand glided up her hip, over her side, gently across up her arm, to her face. He leaned over. She fought to remain upright. His hand caressed her neck, then went back into her hair. His fingers massaged the firm muscles of her neck, holding her in place.

Slowly his hand caressed her right arm. Shivers of delight ran across Sami's skin. His hand slid to hers, entwining it, pulling it outwards.

He leaned in closer, his body's heat flowing over hers, his chest touching her breasts with the slightest pressure.

"I'm sorry Samantha. I really am." He whispered, his breath warm and teasing against her ear. "I really don't have a choice this time."

Suddenly her left arm was released. A click sounded. Sami looked down.

She was cuffed to the side rail of her wrought iron bed.

* * *

Jake parked in the drug store lot.

Damn, the woman could cuss!

In fact, while he'd settled Nicky in the bed beside her, she called him every name he'd ever heard and a few inventive ones.

What was a pylonidal cyst on the butt of mankind, anyway?

He made a mental note to look that one up. Whatever it was, he was pretty sure it wasn't flattering.

Once he had Nicky tucked into bed beside her, Samantha calmed down enough to sooth the boy. He almost envied the kid. Being tucked in with her soft body and soothing voice, would make it almost worth getting wounded.

Memories of her body pressed against his as he awoke this morning, more aroused than he'd been in months, flashed into Jake's mind. He shook his head, trying to clear his brain. Despite what his body might think, he didn't have time right now for a repeat performance.

Inside the drug store he located both a thermometer and the children's Tylenol without too much difficulty. Success!

With any luck this medicine would make Nicky comfortable enough to move. His plans were to get out of Samantha Edgars' life as quick as possible. She'd become too much of a distraction. Besides, he truly believed the longer he and Nicky stayed with her the more likely she'd become a target for the people hunting them.

Jake carried his supplies to the counter. Trying to avoid making eye contact with the clerk, he stared at the television screen playing behind the check out stand.

Suddenly, his picture flashed on the television, with the words WANTED by the FBI. Thankfully, the clerk had the sound so low, neither he nor Jake could hear the reporter's commentary. Jake didn't need to.

The words kidnap victim and Nicky's immigration photo popped up next.

* * *

With one hand free, Sami switched warm cloths from Nicky's fevered body for cool ones from the alcohol bath. The boy lay snuggled against her. Through his clothes, and her own, heat radiated from his body. However, the shakes had finally stopped, and seemed less restless now. That meant the fever had stopped climbing. Now if it would only break.

She smoothed strands of his dark hair away from his pale face. Aimee's hair had been nearly the same deep black shade as Nicky's before she'd lost it to the ravishing affects of her chemo.

"Mommy, when I'm all better will my hair grow in long enough to wear piggy tails?" Aimee asked her one day. They'd tied a fancy scarf around her little bald head and let the ends fall down like purple and pink hanks of silken hair.

"It might." She'd been torn between trying to give her daughter

hope and not lying to her.

"If it does, can I have pretty hair ties like Miss Lucy?" Aimee loved her evening Candy Striper, Lucy and Lucy had felt the same about Aimee.

"We'll have to ask Lucy where she got hers. Which ones do you like the most?" She'd held Aimee close as they snuggled in her hospital bed among the monitor lines and IV tubes.

"I like the ones that look like glittery butterflies. They sparkle when she comes to see me, like they're gonna fly right off her hair."

She gently caressed her daughter's thin, bony shoulders and arms, marveling how such courage and hope could live in such a frail body. She'd blinked back her tears. "Then that's what we'll get you."

Two days later, Aimee had died. She'd told Lucy about Aimee's wish and Lucy had stood next to her tiny coffin, took her own barrettes out of her hair and tucked them into Aimee's tiny hands.

Grief so strong she thought she'd faint from it, filled her. Sami fought her tears, hugging Nicky closer, as much for her own comfort as his.

Aimee had been five years old the last time Sami held her. Had her daughter lived, she would've been Nicky's age now. The pneumonia that finally ended her battle with leukemia came upon her quickly. Aimee's poor, weakened immune system, just couldn't fight the strain of bacteria resistant to most antibiotics.

Sami had held her throughout the night, alternately soothing her child, praying to god, then railing at him for putting her tiny daughter through such hell. The priest, her mother and father had all tried to comfort her. In her anger and pain, Sami pushed them away. No one understood the despair she suffered for Aimee.

The one person who should have been there—Michael, her husband—could not find the courage to look at his dying daughter, or his desperate wife.

So she'd stayed with Aimee throughout that last long day. Never leaving her side. Not eating. Not drinking. Not sleeping. She bathed her daughter in the same alcohol bath she was using now on little Nicky. But nothing had helped her Aimee. Nothing. The fever just raged harder and hotter.

Sami slipped her hand behind Nicky's neck. He seemed a little cooler. Or maybe it was just wishful thinking. She couldn't tell if the alcohol bath was doing him any good without a thermometer. She never replaced the one Michael had thrown at her the week after Aimee died. Then he'd stomped out of the house, suitcase in hand, sending her divorce papers the next day by courier.

That was the last day a man other than her father and brothers had been in her house. Until Jake.

"Sergei...Lexus...don't hit me...nyet, nyet...pujyalsta"

"Shh, shh, Nicky." Sami smoothed her hand over his cheek, shoulder and down his back. "It's okay. No one is going to hurt you. Jake and I will protect you."

"Jake...police come now...must tell Jake...Petrov, Madson... He thrashed a little in the bed.

Sami pulled him closer, gently rocking him back and forth with her one free arm. She wished she knew some words of comfort in his native tongue. "Hush now,

Nicholai. Go to sleep. You are safe. I'll protect you."

"Andropov...three hundred. Baranov...four-fifty...," Nicky whispered more calmly.

"Nicky? What are you talking about?" She pulled back slightly to look at him.

His eyes were closed, and he seemed to be quoting a list in his sleep. "...Chernitsky...two-seventy-five. Dorogoi...three hundred. Dyakov...five hundred...Grachev..." His words started to slur off. "...three-fifty."

The little boy curled into her body. Finally his body relaxed, his breathing became less labored. What in the world did Nicky know? Jake called him a witness. His list sounded more like a financial ledger. Was that it? Did he have a list somewhere with all the Kreshnins' business listed? Had he memorized it? Just when she thought she knew what was going on, the puzzle changed.

Sami continued to rock his small body even after he'd fallen asleep. It felt good to hold a child once more. For so many years she'd avoided treating any children who came to the ER. Her coworkers, who understood how painful it was for her, always managed to volunteer to take them when it was her turn.

A heavy sigh escaped her. It wouldn't do to let herself get too attached to Nicky.

Her heart swelled with need. The need of a mother who has lost a child.

She called herself a fool. Already, she was attached.

With great determination, Sami forced herself to concentrate on something other than the small boy lying at her side. Sexy, kidnapper Jake popped up as first and foremost on her list of things to think about.

First, stop thinking of the man as sexy.

Well, he is.

You keep thinking like that and you're gonna have that Amsterdam syndrome.

Stockholm. It's called Stockholm Syndrome. It was named for a case where a hostage began to sympathize with her captors. It took place in Stockholm.

Okay, whatever. You keep thinking about how blue his eyes are, how sexy his voice is, the slightly off kilter way his nose looks, his big solid body pressed against yours and how great a kisser he is, you're gonna be one of those Stockholm syndrome people.

Sami gave herself a mental shake. This arguing with her inner self wasn't a good sign. Besides, that little voice just listed all the reasons why she was having trouble thinking of Jake as a big dangerous kidnapper anymore and more like the sexy man of her deepest dreams.

Face it. You need to have hot, hard sex and get it out of your system.

Shut up!

"Okay, what do I know about Jake?" Sami spoke aloud, hoping to keep the crazy voice from answering her. "First he's in trouble up to his sexy blue eyes. Second, he cares very much about what happens to Nicky. Nicky is Russian. Third, Jake knows police weapons and procedure. Either he's a rogue cop, ex-military or maybe even a federal agent. From his clothes, I'd guess undercover at least. Fourth, he's convinced the police are out to get him."

Considering he had a bullet hole in his shoulder, the man is proabably right.

Intent on ignoring the sarcasm in her own head, she shifted Nicky, then adjusted her own position. Her arm ached terribly even though Jake hadn't cuffed it over her head. Her face flushed when she thought about the kiss they'd shared today. Quickly, her anger flared to life.

How dare he use kisses to get me to cooperate? What a Neanderthal. Hadn't he heard of sexual harassment?

You didn't have to respond. And workplace etiquette is not in the kidnapper's handbook, babe.

This little voice was beginning to scare her. Any first year psych major knew hearing voices wasn't the sign of a stable person.

She looked at Nicky. "Somehow Jake either used Nicky in his surveillance or the kid got into trouble on his own. Either way, Jake rescued him after some really bad guys tortured him. Is Petrov a good guy to Nicky or a bad guy, or even family?"

Again, she pushed Nicky's dark damp hair off his face. "Where are your parents, Nicky?" she whispered to his unconscious body. "Is your mother worrying about where you are? Is she even in this country?"

If the woman was alive, Sami's heart went out to her. The anquish she must be feeling not knowing where her child was. No mother should have to do without her baby. She blinked back the stinging tears. And no mother should have to out live her child.

Sami pulled on the cuffs once more. The metal

clanged against the wrought iron post. The clock on the mantel chimed one.

Where the hell was Jake with the Tylenol?

* * *

Jake slipped into the Chevy's driver's side. He let out a deep breath. Luckily, he'd managed to distract the kid at the check out with idle talk about the football game long enough to keep him from seeing the news report. Hopefully, the kid would forget about him by the time it flashed on there again. The picture they'd flashed on the screen was from the fake arrest records his boss had planted in the local police files. He'd had a full beard. If he was lucky the kid wouldn't even figure out it was him.

He ran his hand over the three day-old growth of his beard. He'd need to get rid of it soon. Each time he'd been near the Kreshnins he'd had some sort of beard growing. Maybe now was the time to keep his face clean-shaven.

Fighting the urge to peel out and speed to Samantha's as fast he could, Jake headed to the gas station on the corner. There was a pay phone in the parking lot. He needed to get in touch with Captain Bridges again. No way could he wait until four to meet. If the Feds were looking for him, he needed to get Nicky hidden in protective custody until he could find out who was on the Kreshnin brothers' payroll.

He pulled up next to the pay phone. Stepping out to stand by the car, he dialed Bridges' private office number once more.

"Bridges here."

Jake looked at his watch. "Captain?"

"Jake? Have you seen the news?"

"Yeah, Tom. Someone pretty powerful wants my ass."

"Who?"

Twenty seconds.

"I don't know, Captain. But once I turn my witness over to you, I plan to find out. I need to meet you in an hour, not at four like we planned."

Forty seconds.

"An hour?" Jake heard the hesitation in his boss' voice. "Sure, sure. Same place?"

"Same place. And Captain?"

Fifty seconds.

"Yeah?"

"I would appreciate it if you can find out who sic'd the local authorities and the reporters on my ass so quickly."

"Have a seat, Sir," Tom said to someone in his office. "Will do, honey. No, I have to go, sweetheart. The DA is here."

Sixty seconds.

Jake hung up, chuckling softly. The captain had used "honey" and "sweetheart" to cover the call and warn him about the district attorney walking in on the conversation. Years ago Bridgers had run into a brick wall with a local DA's office in another town. The case full of political implications and media attention had blown up in his face. Now he never trusted the local prosecution team, almost to the point of paranoia

Pulling the baseball cap down to shade his face as a

police car drove past, Jake climbed into the Suburban. In the rearview mirror, he watched the squad car drive on down the road. He sighed with relief when it turned onto the freeway's entrance ramp.

"Damn, that was close." He leaned his forehead onto the steering wheel's cold leather for a minute. He forced himself to take several deep breaths to calm his racing heart and mind. Then he turned on the radio to the local news channel. He needed to know exactly what the public was being told.

The reporter's voice came on after the end of a song. "Again, our top story today, is...local police are searching for Jacob Carlisle. He is wanted in the alleged kidnapping of Nicholai Gregorian. Carlisle is presumed armed and dangerous. Do not attempt to apprehend or detain him. Anyone knowing the whereabouts of either Carlisle or Nicholai, please contact your local law enforcement department."

Jake muttered a few slanderous comments about the police department members' parents' marital status of the parents. He wasn't the one that was a threat to Nicky.

The local sports report came on. Ohio State managed to score a touchdown just before the half. He shook his head. At least something was going right somewhere in this   town.

Slowly, Jake pulled onto the highway and drove in the direction of Samantha's. With a glance at the Tylenol box sticking out of the paper bag, he let out another weary sigh. He hoped an hour would be enough time for the medicine to help Nicky feel better. If he could just get the kid to someplace where they could give him the antibiotics Samantha seemed to think he needed, then Nicky would be okay. Wouldn't he?

Samantha will know.

Damn, when did he start thinking of her as anything more than a means to an end? So far, she'd served the purpose he intended when he snatched her from the hospital parking lot. Nicky and he were patched up. At least he was back together enough to function, even though the kid was sick.

Maybe it was holding her throughout the long night, but somewhere along the way, Samantha's welfare had become just as important to him as Nicky's.

Jake shook his head. For a loaner who had no desire for strings, nothing to tie him down, he suddenly found himself with two people who's safety he needed to guard. If his brother Joe could see him now, the kid would laugh his ass off. When Jake had sent him off to California to medical school, years ago, Joe accused him of being part hermit. Joe hadn't understood then what Jake did. People close to an undercover cop were the ones whose lives were at the greatest risk. The scum he investigated wouldn't hesitate to use anyone he cared about to get even with him for betraying their trust.

Frustration nagged at him as he turned into Samantha's drive. Nicky and Samantha were now a liability. At least until he personally removed them from the picture. Protective custody for Nicky, a brother's custody for Samantha.

He doubted his pretty little captive would appreciate his plan.

He walked through the kitchen to the living room of her house. A soft sound came from the bedroom. Jake stopped and listened for a moment.

Singing?

He listened closer. It had rhythm so technically you could call the noise singing.

He inched his way to her bedroom door, pushing it slowly in. Samantha lay curled protectively around Nicky, one arm around his shoulder, her head on top of his, her eyes closed as she gently rocked him. She was singing an old Carole King classic—very much off key. But with lots of heart.

Smothering a chuckle and forcing all emotion from his face, he cleared his throat.

Samantha's eyes popped open, casting him a suspicious look. "How long have you been standing there?"

"Long enough to know you'll never make it as a singer."

She stuck her tongue out at him.

For the first time in months he laughed.

Her eyes narrowed. With gentle care, she edged Nicky onto the bed with her free arm. Then she pushed herself up to stand ramrod straight beside the bed her lips pressed in a thin line of indignation. "If you are finished picking on my vocal abilities, perhaps you could unfasten these so I can go to the bathroom?"

Jake bit back another laugh at her sudden primness. *Note to self, the lady takes her singing very seriously.*

"Yes, ma'am. I'd be happy to do that." He moved in close to her, reaching in front of her to the arm cuffed to the bed. She was just too tempting standing there. Devilishly, he pressed in a little more, just close enough for his chest to brush her breasts. He watched the blush fill her cheeks as he worked the key into the cuffs' lock. "You're free."

"I could only wish." She countered, slipping to the side and hurrying to the bathroom.

He shook his head. *Sassy woman.*

"How's Nicky?" He laid a hand on the little boy's head. Damn! He still burned with fever.

"Not much better than when you left. Not any worse though." Samantha entered the room, carrying a small ear dropper.

"What's that for?" Jake moved to giver her room beside Nicky. The scent of flowers teased him. She must've washed her hands. The woman seemed to have a different scented soap in every room.

She sat on the edge of the bed, gathering Nicky into her arms. "He's been out for a good while. I don't know if he can drink from the medicine cup that comes with the Tylenol. I may have to squirt it into his mouth to get enough in him to do any good." She held out her hand expectantly. "You did get the liquid kind, didn't you?"

He opened the box, handing her the bottle. "Yeah, I did. What kind of idiot do you think I am?"

"You don't really want an answer to that, do you?"

Jake leaned against the dresser, watching her work. After reading the directions, she poured the right amount into the cup. She tried to get Nicky to sip from the cup. But the kid was too listless to accomplish that. Next, Samantha filled the dropper with the red liquid, slipping it past Nicky's lips and into his mouth, tipping his head a bit backward. A little dribbled out the corner of his mouth. The rest managed to get far enough into his mouth for him to swallow. It was a slow process, but after a few minutes the medicine cup sat empty.

Gently, Samantha eased Nicky onto the bed. She stood, reaching both her arms over her head. She stretched from one side to the other, then backward and forward, molding her tee-shirt tightly over her breasts. The creamy flesh of her bare tummy peeked out the bottom edge

Jake gulped hard. "How long will it take to work?"

"The Tylenol?"

"Yeah." He knew exactly how long her stretching took to work on his body. Approximately one nano-second.

"I would say he'll be better in a couple of hours."

"We don't have a couple of hours."

She turned to look at him. "I thought you said you were leaving later this afternoon? He can't travel until his temperature is better."

"He's going to have to, Samantha. The police have put out an all-points-bulletin for me. I have to get Nicky into protective custody and my files to my boss, before some trigger happy cop decides to use me to further his career."

"Are you a rogue cop?" she asked him point blank, not blinking one eyelash.

He met her gaze unflinchingly. After all her help, he supposed he owed her some sort of explanation. Especially since she'd figured out so much on her own anyway. "No. I'm FBI. I've been undercover and caught in something pretty nasty."

With a slight nod of her head, she accepted his explanation without further question. "You shouldn't try to take Nicky into the car until he's less listless. You won't be able to drive and hold onto him."

"I know."

"What are you going to do?"

Her worry over Nicky touched Jake deep in his core. He'd invaded her life and forced her to help them. She should hate him. Instead, she had enough decency and compassion inside her to care about the small boy traveling with him.

"I have a simple solution."

She was really going to hate what he planned to do to her next.

"What?" her eyes narrowed slightly.

"You'll have to go along with us."

CHAPTER FOUR

"I'm not going anywhere with you, Jake." Sami backed up until the window prevented her from going any further. *Was the guy nuts?* No way was she going to this meeting with him. "You grab me in a dark parking lot, render me unconscious, which by the way, made my throat really hurt. Then you tie me up, hold me prisoner in my own home, force me to fix both your's and Nicky's wounds. And now you want to drag me to some clandestine meeting with someone you call your boss? What on God's green earth would possess you to think I would volunteer to go anywhere with you?"

Jake walked up to stand in front of her, completely invading her personal space.

Oh yeah, he projected intimidation at its best. That was too damn bad. No way would she let it work on her.

She didn't do submissiveness.

"You are going. You have no choice in the matter."

Sami lifted her chin. "That's your answer to everything? Just force the little woman to do what ever you want? Well this time I don't care what you do to me, I'm not leaving my home."

He reached up and tucked a loose strand of hair behind her ear. "I won't force you to do anything, Samantha. You'll go because you have no choice, but to go."

"And why is that?"

Jake moved a little to the side, looking at Nicky's listless body in the bed. Sami looked, too.

"Because, " his voice deepened, "whether or not you believe me, whether or not you want to help me, doesn't really matter now. He needs you, so you'll go."

Sami stared at the little boy in her bed.

He lay there so helpless, so defenseless. The wet rags she'd used to bring down his fever had plastered his black hair to his pale skin. His body looked so small snuggled in the quilt on her bed.

"I'll go." Her shoulders slumped in defeat. "What do you need me to do?"

He lifted her chin until she stared into those ice blue eyes again. "You could try believing me, when I tell you I care as much about what happens to Nicky as you do. It may not seem like it, but I'm not the bad guy here. If everything goes without any more glitches, Nicky will get the medical help you say he needs. I'll be out of your hair, and you'll be free to go back to your normal life. Okay?"

"Okay." Just the way Jake so fiercely demanded she take care of Nicky reassured her heart that the little boy's life meant a great deal to her kidnapper. She didn't trust herself to say as much.

Still she couldn't jump on the Jake-is-a-good-guy bandwagon, yet. The man had kidnapped her for goodness sakes. Part of her wanted to believe every word that came out of his mouth. Part of her wanted to see the police lock him up and throw away the key. And yet another part of her wanted to lock herself in with him.

"Do you have a small duffle bag, or suitcase?" Jake's words brought her thoughts back to the present situation.

"Uhm, yes. Why?" She hurried into the second bedroom and opened the closet. "I have a large camping backpack, and a medium sized carry-on suitcase." She dug around in boxes, finally retrieving both. She turned to take them to Jake, and nearly slammed right into his hard body. She jumped. "Don't do that."

He reached his hands out to hold her hips and steady her, a devilish grin on his face. "Do what?"

"Sneak up on me so quietly. It makes me jumpy."

"I noticed." The intensity of his gaze deepened. "It's about the only time you're nervous."

Sami let her tongue slide out to moisten her suddenly parched lips. "Uhm, it isn't good for someone in my line of work to panic easily."

"I can see why. A scared, nervous nurse might make a mistake that would cost a person their life, huh?"

Increasing the pressure of his hands on her hips, he started to draw her nearer, a serious gleam in his eyes.

Her breath caught in her throat.

The bags between them squished, letting out air like a whoopee cushion.

They both laughed. Jake released her and took the duffle bag from her. "This should do."

"What do you need it for?"

"I hoped you might have some clean clothes that Nicky might be able to wear. Nothing too fancy, t-shirts and pants. Maybe a sweatshirt or coat. The kid didn't have much to begin with, and now he literally has only the clothes on his back to wear." He moved to allow her to exit the closet. He tugged at the shirt he wore. "By the way, I hope you don't mind me borrowing your boyfriend's shirt."

"It belonged to my ex-husband," Sami bent and dragged a box from the same closet. "And no I don't mind. I had forgotten I still had it."

"What's in there?" He nodded in the box's direction.

"The last of Michael's clothes I packed. I hadn't decided whether to mail them to him, or make a neighborhood bonfire out of them. Maybe there is something in it Nicky could use, or you, too." She continued to dig through the box. "I think there is an old coat in here. It'll be huge on Nicky, but in Ohio you never know when bad weather will hit." She pulled out a couple of sweaters, a dark green flannel shirt, some old socks and then a big green jacket. Holding it, she looked at Jake. "What do you think?"

"It looked like snow on the horizon this afternoon." He pointed to the jacket's bottom. "That coat might work, except for the big hole down there."

"Damn, I forgot about that." Sami folded the coat and set it aside. "Michael loved this thing. He wore it to do everything on his days off, even to work on his antique El Dorado Cadillac." She sat back on her heels, laughing. "He spent so much time with that damn car, I ended up hating it. Then one day he set a hot battery on the coat. Burnt that hole clean through it." She laughed harder at the memory.

Jake chuckled along with her. Sami like the way his eyes crinkled, and his deep voice rumbled through the room. "Geeze, I haven't laughed like that in years." She wiped the tears from her eyes.

"Any other coat Nicky could use?" Jake took the sweaters, stuffing them and the socks into the bag.

Sami rummaged through the box again, retrieving several more long sleeved shirts. "No. No other coat in here."

"What's that back there?" He pointed into the closet, a gray sleeve stuck out of the back.

Standing, Sami reached for the item. Her heart beat faster. She pulled the Scarlet trimmed gray team jacket out and stared at it. She'd forgotten she still had this. Her brother Luke had bought the Ohio State jacket for Aimee the year she was diagnosed with cancer. He'd bought it too big so she could grow into it. Luke was a big believer in challenging people, giving them goals to live up to. The sad thing was this was one challenge her little daughter couldn't meet, no matter how much she'd wanted to.

Sami waited for the pain to hit her. It didn't. Only a sweet remembrance of how happy Aimee had been when she opened the box that Christmas. She never got to wear it. Tears sprang into Sami's eyes for the little life that had ended much too soon.

"Samantha?"

Startled, Sami blinked hard at the tears, then held the jacket up. "This should fit him, don't you think?"

"Yeah, I do." He gave her a quizzical look as she handed it to him.

"Did you get a thermometer? I'd like to know just how high Nicky's temp is before that Tylenol kicks in." She hurried past him. Suddenly feeling faint, she needed to escape the closet. She needed to do something. She needed air.

"It's in the bag on the dresser." He called after her.

In the bedroom, Sami stooped over and fought to take deep breaths. *Slow it down. You can handle this.* She concentrated hard and willed her breathing to return to normal. Her vision cleared.

On the dresser, she found the thermometer right where Jake said it would be. Slipping it in under Nicky's arm, she sat beside him. Waves of memories flooded her senses, finding out she was pregnant with Aimee; giving birth after the normal twelve hours for a first pregnancy; changing her daughter's diapers while the little baby cooed and grinned at her; the day in the doctor's office when he told her he suspected Aimee might have leukemia.

Pictures and scenes of her life she'd shoved into the dark corners of her memories, so she could function without the pain. Tonight the images rolled past her like the black and white images of a silent movie, almost as if she viewed someone else's life. Perhaps she did. The woman who'd experienced those things first hand had ceased to exist four years ago. Until last night when Jake forced himself and Nicky into her life, Sami Edgars hadn't lived since the day Aimee was taken from her.

Sami glanced at her scrub jacket crumpled on the floor where she'd dropped it the night before. Inside its pocket lay the duel sleeping pill prescriptions she'd conned from the docs at work. Her need for them now gone. Her will to live snapped back into place by her own brush with mortality.

A noise from the doorway thankfully brought her to the present.

"We need to leave, Samantha." Jake stood watching her. Wearing the canvas field coat her brother left at her apartment for emergencies open in front and the duffel bag slung over one shoulder, he looked like a model right out of a hunting magazine.

The very masculine way he leaned against the door jam, hands in his pockets, relaxed with one leg crossed in front of the other, pulled his jeans tight and accented his thighs. Her eyes traveled up over his hard body. Even in the loose, casual shirt and jacket, she knew how firm and conditioned his body was. She'd memorized every inch when he'd landed on her last night, then held her this morning.

Her body heated with the memory. No longer fearing he meant to kill her, this attraction to him scared her almost as much.

Forcing herself to concentrate, she removed the thermometer from under Nicky's arm. "One hundred and two, point eight. No wonder he feels so sick." She looked at Jake. "No way we can get him some antibiotics?"

Jake simply shook his head. "Do you need some help getting him dressed to go?"

"No. I can manage it."

"Okay." He laid the jacket on the corner of the bed. Striding down the hall, he left her alone to dress Nicky.

Sami lifted the pale blue cambric shirt, gently pushing first one of Nicky's arms then the other into the sleeves. Remembering the pair of khaki pants her nephew left the last time he went swimming at her apartment, she laid Nicky back against the pillows. She searched through her dresser, finding the pants in the bottom drawer. She had just slipped the jacket on Nicky when Jake returned. He thrust a piece of paper into his jeans pocket as he came into the room.

"Here, let me carry him," he said as she attempted to lift the listless boy.

"What? No handcuffs? No ropes to bind me this time?"

He flashed her a mischievous look. "Only if you want

them."

Sami ignored him as she folded Nicky's jeans. She thrust them into the duffel with the other clothes. She noted Jake had packed the bandage supplies, the last few packages of suture, more rubbing alcohol and peroxide, as well as the Tylenol. The man liked to be prepared. She added the thermometer.

"Ready?" Watching her, he held Nicky's limp body easily.

"Yes." She threw on her coat and started to follow him, then stopped. Running to her bedroom, she grabbed a quilt off the chair in the corner. She tucked it under her arm and snatched her purse on the way through the kitchen. Then she climbed into the Suburban's passenger seat. Jake laid Nicky on her lap, so the little boy's head rested on her shoulder. Sami tucked the quilt around him.

Jake climbed into the driver's side. He pushed the button for the garage door opener, then slowly pulled the big vehicle out into the late autumn day.

The steel grey skies did indeed predict a snow front coming into the area. Sami hoped she wouldn't get caught driving on icy roads on her way home.

The rural scenery turned more urban as they headed into the city limits of Columbus. For the last twelve years she'd lived here attending college at Ohio State to get her nursing degree, then as a married wife and mother. The city had grown a lot in that time. Like a sprawling giant, it slowly engulfed the surrounding towns and suburbs, then outlying farms as even the suburbs burst at the seams with yuppies during the eighties and nineties.

"Who did that jacket belong to, the one Nicky is wearing?" Jake's question drew her out of her reverie.

"Why do you ask?" A dull ache began around her heart. It had been years since she talked about Aimee with someone else.

He glanced at her, then looked at the road ahead. "You seemed a little upset about finding it in the closet. I just thought you might want to talk about it."

"My brother bought the jacket for my daughter several years ago."

"You have a daughter?" Jake glanced at her. Surprise registered on his face.

Sami bit her upper lip for a second. "Had. I had a daughter."

"Had?" He laid his hand on hers where it clutched the quilt tightly. "What happened to her?"

"She died from pneumonia complicated by her leukemia four years ago."

"Oh, man. I'm sorry to hear that." He squeezed her hand.

Sami blinked at the tears that suddenly filled her eyes. In one two-minute conversation, this virtual stranger had given her more comfort and compassion than her ex-husband had managed in all the years during and after Aimee's illness.

"Where are you meeting your boss?" She needed to change the subject quickly, before she embarrassed herself by dissolving into a flood of self-pitying tears.

Jake squeezed her hand once more, signaling he understood her desire not to continue the topic of Aimee. He lifted his hand, then stretched his arm over the back of the front seat. "We're meeting my captain at the farmers market."

"There will be lots of people there on a Saturday afternoon," she said as he turned the car onto the freeway.

"Yep. I wanted a crowd around. I figure the bad guys will be less likely to try and kidnap Nicky with thousands of witnesses."

"The Kreshnins?"

A shocked look on Jake's face rewarded her and she almost laughed. In the heavier city traffic he had to look back and forth from the road to her several times while trying to control the car on the freeway.

"How did you know about the Kreshnins?"

"Nicky mumbled the name in his sleep while you were away. I just put two and two together."

He sighed, turning onto the exit for the downtown farmers market. "I wish you didn't know anything about this. Until you are in a safe place the more you know, the more danger you are in. The wanted poster on the news report called me a kidnapper. It was true. Only I didn't kidnap Nicky. I kidnapped you. That might've been enough to protect you, as long as you didn't know anything."

"And it still may. Technically, I'm still your prisoner."

Their eyes met and held. Electricity filled the Suburban's closed confines for a moment. Then Jake pulled into the market place's parking lot.

"Okay. I'm supposed to take Nicky inside." He left the car idling in park and walked around the car to open the passenger side. He slung the duffel onto his shoulder, then scooped Nicky into his arms. "Listen carefully, Samantha. Once I'm inside, I want you to head to your place, pack a bag and drive directly to Cincinnati to your brother, the cop. Don't stop anywhere on the way. I have his number in my pocket. Once Nicky and I are safe, I'll call and explain to him the danger you're in. He can keep you safe until I get this mess all cleaned up. Okay?"

"You don't seriously think I need protection, do you?" she asked as she slid into the driver's seat, adjusting the seat forward for her shorter legs.

"Yes, I do." He grabbed her wrist as she fastened the seat belt in place. "Promise me."

Sami studied him for a moment. Concern etched his rugged features. He actually cared what happened to her. Oddly, her heart skipped a beat at the knowledge. "Okay. I promise."

The corners of his lips lifted in a half smile. "I'm sorry if I hurt you in any way. It would've been nice to meet you under other circumstances."

"You didn't really bruise anything more than my ego." She gave him a rueful smile. "Now get Nicky out of this cool weather."

"Yes, ma'am."

Sami sat behind the wheel, watching Jake swagger with

80

Nicky in his arms toward the market's front door. A few soft white flakes fell on the windshield. She sighed with regret. In one day, he'd filled her dull life with more excitement than she'd had in the past ten years combined. She'd never see either the man or boy again.

In front of him, the door to the market flew open. A balding man in jeans and a heavy sports-type windbreaker, hurried out. He waived frantically at Jake.

Jake halted.

The man yelled something.

Suddenly, several men ran out behind the older man. Without any warning, they took police stances, firing their weapons at Jake and the man. Jake turned, sprinting as fast as he could toward her.

In morbid fascination, fingers glued to the steering wheel, Sami watched as the balding man fell in slow motion. He sank to his knees. His hands flew upwards. He tipped forward like a felled tree in the forest. Finally, he sprawled, face down on the pavement.

The door to the suburban flew open. Jake jumped in, clutching Nicky tightly to him.

"Get us out of here, Samantha!"

Sami snapped to action at his orders. She threw the car in reverse. Gunning the engine, they flew backward. She laid on the horn hard. Innocent pedestrians in the path behind them scattered out of the way like startled pigeons at a public monument.

The men from the market ran toward them. Car

windows around them shattered. Bystanders dove for cover behind cars and light poles.

She maneuvered the car to the road entrance, turned the wheel sharply and backed into traffic. Ignoring the screeching tires and blaring horns of the other motorists around them, she slammed the car into first, and sped down the road.

"They killed him!" she yelled at Jake as she headed back to her house.

"Damn it, don't you think I know that?"

"They were police. You said you were police." She glanced at him, then turned onto the freeway. She let her foot lay heavily on the gas, maneuvering past cars and trucks. "Why would they kill him?"

"I don't know. And I don't know who, so don't ask me that, either." He ran his hand through his hair. "Slow down, Samantha. We don't want to draw the highway patrol's attention."

"What are we going to do?" She eased off the gas, panting from the fear and Adrenaline combination.

"Well, going to your house or your brother's is out of the question now."

Sami glanced at him. "Why?"

"Because I am sure they have your license plate number now, or at least enough to identify you." He leaned against the car door, giving her a worried look. "Like it or not, you're going to be named as my accomplice."

CHAPTER FIVE

"Your men missed, Petrov." The man's voice sounded abrupt and clipped even for him.

"We could not help that your FBI captain gave us away. But he will no longer be around to get in our way, no?"

"Don't sound so pleased with yourself, Petrov. Thanks to your little gun battle we now have a dead agent on our hands. I don't know how I can keep a lid on the investigation into a the killing of a federal agent."

A harsh laugh sounded on the line's other end. "Ah, but you will block any investigations, my friend. Convince them that Carlisle shot the other agent. You have as much to lose as I do if that little brat tells what he knows."

The hairs on the back of the man's neck slowly stood at attention. The Russian's threat hit close to home. He had quite a bit to lose should his involvement become known.

The day he'd joined forces with Petrov, his brother, and their band of exiled Russian thugs, he'd known the risks were high. He glanced at the Rolex on his arm, a symbol of the wealth he'd amassed over and above his trust fund. Until this fiasco with the kid and Carlisle, the benefits had far outweighed the risks.

Petrov might have the meanness of his Mongol ancestors, but he'd never underestimated the giant Russian's intelligence or ruthlessness. Only a fool would turn his back on the Kosak.

The image of a tightrope walker carrying a very wobbly pole flashed through his mind. If he didn't watch his step, a very large pigeon named Petrov Kreshnin would perch on that wire and knock him off balance, or Jake Carlisle and his little Russian witness would cut the wire right out from under him.

His mind added up all the possibilities as quick as an accountant's fingers on the keys of an adding machine. Perhaps he could use this fiasco to his benefit.

"I think it's time the Feds searched for our Mr. Carlisle and your ward, Nicholai, don't you, Petrov?"

"You expect the FBI to just hand them over to you, my friend?"

The hesitancy on the mafia leader's end of the conversation pleased the man. He picked up a pen, rolling it between his fingers. "You might be right, Petrov. It's time to let the feds do our hunting for us."

* * *

Jake watched the dawning of her situation settle on Samantha's shoulders. She slumped further into the leather seat, her fingers gripping the steering wheel so tight her knuckles blanched white.

Damn, he'd done nothing but turn her world upside down. Now he'd managed to put her life in danger, too. Somehow he needed to protect all of them and he didn't have a frickin clue who was pulling the local police division's strings. With Bridges dead, he didn't have a snowball's chance of finding out either.

He stared out the passenger window, the buildings speeding past as they drove away from the scene of Captain Bridges' death. Hot, stinging tears flooded Jake's eyes, blurring the scenery before him. Tom had been his lieutenant when he'd been a young rookie, and his captain for the past five years. More importantly, he'd been a friend. Now, he was gone. What would his wife and kids do without him?

"If we aren't going to my house, or to my brother's, where are we going?"

Samantha's question interrupted his grieving. With one hand he rubbed at his eyes. Damn he didn't have time for this. If he didn't get his act together and start thinking, they'd all be as dead as Tom.

"We need to ditch these plates." He scanned the access road up ahead. Snow flakes fell softly across the windows of the car. A service garage sign appeared, then flashed by. "Pull off at the next exit. We'll double back to that auto repair shop."

Samantha maneuvered the car at the exit he'd requested, turning to the right and heading back down the service road. "It looks like it's closed all ready."

"Good. Pull in back."

"What are you going to do?" she asked, following his directions.

Jake slid Nicky out of his arms to lay on the seat. "Do you have a screw driver in here?" He opened the car door, stepping out in the frigid Ohio air.

"I have a complete tool kit, thanks to my dad." Sami hopped out and opened the back of the Suburban. She pulled out the tool box, but held it away from him when he reached for it. "First, tell me what you plan on doing?"

The woman picked the most inconvenient times to show her stubborn streak. He might think her courage sexy as hell, but if they didn't get a move on it, they'd be behind bars or six feet under.

"First," he repeated the word back at her through clenched teeth, "I'm going to trade your tag with one of these cars in the lot. That will give us a little maneuvering room. The FBI and highway patrol will be looking for your plates, not the ones we'll be using. Then we have to find some safe place to hole up for the night, if not longer."

Satisfied with his explanation, Samantha handed him the tool kit. She stepped to the truck's front end to keep an eye on the road for any cars or police while Jake set about switching the plates. He glanced up once to see her seriously keeping lookout. She stood with her hands tucked in the pockets of her coat, her breath swirling in the cold air, snow flakes falling around her, landing on her dark hair.

The woman continued to amaze him. Any other woman, given the situation, would've gone hysterical at the sight of a man being murdered. True, shock froze her for the first few seconds, but she'd managed to get them all out of there fairly unscathed.

How had she learned to maneuver a car in reverse like a Hollywood stuntman?

Now, when his simple explanation about switching the plates appeased her curiosity, it also elicited her help. If only he could have met her under other circumstances.

"Almost finished?" She looked at him, rubbing her naked hands together in the cold air. The light was fading fast. It always did in Ohio in November.

"Just about." He gave the screw one last turn, replaced the screw driver in the kit, signaling her to get into the passenger seat. "You hold Nicky a while. I'll drive."

Once they were on the road, he crossed over the freeway, entered the southbound side, and headed back toward the downtown area.

"Where are you going? Downtown will be flooded with police, looking for us." Panic laced Sami's voice. Two squad cars with screaming sirens passed them, heading North in the direction they just left, emphasizing her words.

"That's why. By now, they'll have spread out,

searching for your car going in any direction but downtown. And some witness will have told them you got on the North bound side of the freeway." Two more cars flashed past them. "I want to head the opposite way. We'll get off at High Street and slowly work our way out of town to the South. We might find a motel to stay in."

"Won't they be searching those? I mean on all those cop shows you see them pulling the bad guys out of the motels. Isn't it like in the police handbook or something?" She grinned at him. "You know, step number one, have high speed chase through busiest intersections in town. Step number two, find sleaziest motels on the outskirts of town, handcuff anyone with fifty tattoos on their arms."

He laughed. The woman had spunk. In trouble up to their necks, and she managed to make him laugh. "Yeah, that's the chapter right before, how to chase your suspect through back alleys, over fences and deep forest ravines. Be sure to jump into every mud puddle, and pile of broken glass you can find."

"Seriously, though. Won't they be looking at all the motels tonight for my car?" she asked.

Jake slouched back in his seat, rubbing one hand over his face. "Yes."

"I don't know about you, but I know Nicky and I could use a good night's sleep."

A derisive laugh escaped him. "Lady, I don't know how to break this to you, but I don't know if any of us will ever have a good night's sleep, again."

"What if I told you I know a place for us to stay. Not

just for tonight but maybe long enough for you to decide how to get us out of this mess?"

Jake gazed at her for a moment in the fading evening light. God had finally answered one of his prayers when he'd been in that parking lot last night looking for some help. "Where?"

"When you get off on High street head south to Lancaster, then down into Logan and the Hocking Hills." She loosened the quilt around Nicky, her hand running over his head.

"How's he doing?"

"He seems cooler. His breathing is even, and his pulse isn't as fast. The Tylenol may be working."

"Poor kid. You're right. He needs to rest in one spot for a while. This place we're heading to, is it in your name?"

Sami shook her head. "No. It belongs to, my ex-husband's Uncle Victor. Victor never could stand Michael. So, when we divorced, Victor came to my house, gave me a key and told me to feel free to use it anytime I wanted. He said I had more right to it than Michael ever would."

Jake winked at her. "I think I like Uncle Victor."

The snow started to fall in earnest as they made their way through the rural farmland. It coated the road in a fine white layer.

Jake flipped on the radio to listen for the weather and news reports. Sami hummed to the classic rock songs, never quite finding the right key for any of them. He smiled to himself in the darkened interior of the car. Funny thing, when the Rolling Stones came on, she matched old Mick note for note.

As they drove through the small town of Logan, Sami pointed to a grocery store with a pharmacy. "Pull in there."

"We can't risk being seen out here, Samantha," he warned her, even as he did as she asked.

"There may not be much food out at the cabin, Jake. I think I should lay in some food stores." She slid Nicky off her lap, wiggling out the door. Jamming her baseball cap on her head, she pulled the brim just a little lower. "Besides, as far as we know, no one knows I'm traveling with you. I can sneak in and out probably unnoticed."

"Wait, do you have any cash?"

She fished out her ATM card. "No, I'll just use this."

"Hold on." He climbed out of his side, pulling out a bundle of cash he'd stashed in his jeans at the bank earlier in the day. "Don't use any credit cards, ATM or phone cards for now. We don't want to leave an electronic trail with them."

A charming blush crept over her face in the dim parking lot lights. "Oh God. I've become so accustomed to using the electronic cards, I didn't even consider they could trace us by them." She took the cash and headed inside.

Jake stood in the swirling snow, watching her walk away from him. He smiled as he watched her pony tail bounce on the back of her jacket and her hips gently sway with each step.

What a woman. How had he gotten so lucky last night? Despite the danger he knew he'd dragged her into, he had to admit he was glad she was to have her at his side. For the first time in a very long time, he didn't feel alone.

He climbed back into the truck, pulling Nicky up against his side. The little boy's lids fluttered open. Jake smiled into his deep blue eyes. "Svasvrashchnem, Nicholai. Ya fibya nadoaydiu." *Welcome back, Nicholai. You had me very worried.*

"Gdyay nahodetscia jenshina preyatna, Jake?" *Where is the nice lady, Jake?*

"Ona vosvrashchalla vscoray. Ona pashley nahodet ppeshcha. Nam nada skrivatz v Kreshnin-ya." *She will be right back. She went to get some food. We have to hide from the Kreshnins and the bad guys, little partner.*

"Mrye nravetsiz ona." *I like her.* He mumbled before drifting back to sleep.

"I like her, too." Jake watched the front of the store windows, absently stroking the little boy's arm and back.

The question remained, what to do with the lady? Part of him wanted to send her to her brother as fast as he could. Not to protect just her, but he had a feeling he needed some protection from her. At least his heart and soul did. She could be a very dangerous person to him. Then the other part of him wanted to tie her to the bed and keep her forever.

"Damn it! This is not a time for me to be thinking with the smaller of my brains. I can't even keep Samantha safe. How can I think of making love to her?" His lower body tightened in response to his words.

Yeah he knew how he could think of it. He'd been thinking about it off and on since he'd held the little brunette all through the night last night.

What did you call hair that was mostly shiny brown with hairs of red and gold spun in and out of it?

"Great, now I sound like some lovesick poet," he told himself with disgust.

Thankfully the news came on, saving him from slipping further into his maudlin thoughts. The snow was expected to accumulate to three inches in the city, heavier in the outlying areas, particularly those southeast of the mid-Ohio area.

That could be good news. If they got snowed in somewhere, whoever searched after them might get snowed in, too.

The news again called the kidnapping and FBI manhunt the most important news of the day. Jake groaned as the report went on to state that the FBI now believed he had a female accomplice. No description of their car was given, which gave him a little hope. And finally, the sports announced that the Buckeyes had beaten   Michigan.

"All right!"

"All right, what?" Sami asked as she opened the rear passenger door and dropped in several well loaded bags of groceries.

"The Buckeyes managed to beat Michigan.

She wiggled into the seat, pulling Nicky against her. "All right!"

"Find everything we need?" Jake asked, putting the car in gear. He pulled out onto the road.

Sami grinned at him. "Yes. Even something we needed that I didn't think we'd be able to get."

"What?"

"Antibiotics." Sami laughed at the surprised look on face.

"How did you manage that?"

She sat back smugly in her seat. "Turn left at the next intersection. That road will take us back into the Hocking Hills. After about twelve miles we'll come to a private camp resort. Victor's cabin is back in there."

"Yes, ma'am." He headed in the direction she gave, then glanced at her. "So, how did you get the antibiotics?"

"The pharmacist was a rather elderly gentleman. I simply played upon his kind nature."

Jake raised one brow at her in question.

She laughed. "I told him that my stupid husband had insisted on dragging us down from Cleveland to see his horrid mother. And now we were stuck here for the weekend, and our daughter was terribly sick. I asked him which over the counter medication would help her symptoms, fever, headache, wheezing and oh this awful green stuff she was coughing up."

"He bought it hook, line, and sinker?"

Sami waved the bottle of thick, pink liquid antibiotics in front of her face. "But of course!"

"That stuff will really make Nicky feel better?"

"It should do the trick." Sami slipped the bottle into her coat pocket. She hated deceiving the elderly man, but if it would make Nicky better, it was well worth the lie.

"Sweetheart, I could just kiss you."

Sami looked at Jake. For once he truly seemed happy. Her heart picked up its pace at the look on his face. *Oh hell, why not?* "I'll remind you of that later."

Jake gave her an intense stare that said he might just take her up on the challenge, all laugher gone from his face, then focused on the snow covered road they were driving down.

What in the world had possessed her to say that?

A severe case of horniness?

Oh, shut up!

For once the little voice wisely headed her command. The rhythm of the car slowly lulled her to sleep. She pulled Nicky a little closer to her, dreams of kissing Jake on her mind.

* * *

Someone shook her awake. Sami slowly opened her eyes to see Jake leaning over her. Her dreams still fresh in her mind, she smiled at him.

"Samantha, we're at the gate to the private cabins. It's padlocked."

Sami blinked once, then twice. Consciousness slowly oozed its way into her sleepy brain. "Padlocked?"

"The gate has a padlock on it, sweetheart. I could ram

it, but I don't want to cause any suspicions on anyone's part. Do you have a key?"

"Padlock. Key?" Sami sat up straight. "Oh the key, yes. Yes, Victor gave me a key to the gate and one to the cabin." She reached for her purse, searching until she found her keys. Holding them up to the light, she showed him which ones to use. "This is for the gate, and this other one on the same ring is for the cabin."

In the soft beam of the headlights she watched him slip and slide his way to the gate. Fat flakes of snow were now falling. Just what the forecaster had predicted earlier, the biggest early snowstorm the state had seen in the past seventy-five years.

And she was going to spend it in a cabin with a virtual stranger who introduced himself by rendering her unconscious and invading her life.

Nicky stirred in her arms. She looked down to see him staring up at her. "Hello there, Nicky. Feeling a bit better?"

"Da."

Jake opened the car door at that moment. "You must speak English, Nicholai. The lady does not understand Russian."

"Oo yahyo glaza graseevaya, Jake." *The lady has pretty eyes, Jake.*

"Yes, she does have pretty eyes, Nicholai. But use English. To speak in another language she cannot understand is rude."

The little boy looked at her again. "What is your name, lady?"

"My name is Samantha, Nicky. But my friends call me Sami. You can too, if you want."

He grinned and nodded. "It is snowing!"

Sami smiled at the excitement in his voice. Kids were universally the same. They all loved snow. "Maybe in a day or two if you are feeling better, we can play in it."

"Yes, please."

Sami and Jake laughed. He eased the car through the gate, then hopped out to close and lock it once more.

Like it or not, Sami was now locked in and about to be snowed in with her captor. Funny thing, she didn't seem to mind in the least.

CHAPTER SIX

Jake warmed his hands over the flames of the fire as it sparked to life in the stone fireplace. Looking around the cabin's big main room he admired the builder's eye for detail. The wood looked like milled pine with beam and post construction. Slate covered the floor of the kitchen area and the hearth. Hardwood floors filled the rest of the rooms. Two leather couches flanked the fire place and several old fashioned cane bottom chairs with quilted padding on the seats and backs made up the seating in the rustic family room. A dining table and chairs made of rough timber behind a couch could seat twelve easily in the dining area.

Uncle Victor had installed a little diesel-powered generator out back. Apparently, he had also stocked it for just such an emergency as this for there were several containers of fuel in the shed outside. If they kept their use to a minimum, they would have electricity for a few weeks if need be.

All in all, it was a very comfortable place to hide out in. If the circumstances were different, he could happily stay the winter out here away from their pursuers.

He watched Samantha move around in the kitchen area making them all grilled cheese sandwiches and tomato soup. She told him they were all too tired for any thing fancier. As she worked her hips swayed to the song she tried to sing. Her ponytail bounced from side to side. Given his choice of people to be snowed in with, he couldn't come up with anyone else he'd rather have here.

"Soup's on," she called, setting the last bowl on the table.

Jake helped Nicky from the couch to the table. "Smells awful good, huh, partner?"

"Da, real good, Jake." Nicky looked at the soup. "What is this called?"

"You've never had grilled cheese sandwiches and tomato soup, Nicky?" She tucked a napkin into the top of his shirt.

"No, Sami. It is good?"

Samantha looked quizzically at Jake, then sat next to Nicky. "Oh, it's the best food in the whole world. This is what all American kids eat for lunch on a snowy day."

Her enthusiasm didn't surprise Jake. Samantha apparently realized Nicky had never experienced the life of an ordinary American kid in the two years he'd lived in this country. Given this limited chance, the woman meant to give him as many pleasant memories as she could.

Nicky picked up the spoon. Leaning over his bowl, he sniffed. "Smells kharasho."

"What does that mean?" Samantha looked at Jake for an explanation.

"Good, delicious."

The little boy took a spoonful. His face lit up, his lips splitting in a gap-toothed grin. "Oozhasayoushchee. Wonderful. This is good, Sami."

She sat back in her chair, grinning at him. "Then eat up. It will help you get better."

"Ona gavareet tak moya babushka. Yaste! Yaste! Vee takzhe khudoy." Nicky whispered to Jake.

He laughed at the curious expression on Samantha's face. "He said you sound like his grandmother. Eat! Eat! You are too skinny!"

Samantha laughed, too, the sound low and sensual to Jake's ears. Her whole face lit up when she laughed. Her eyes crinkled at the corners, and a dimple appeared in her left cheek. However, dark circles remained beneath her eyes.

Had he caused those? Or had they been there long before he'd forced his way into her life? Jake shook his head and tried to fight the guilt eating at him. He'd done what he'd had to in order to ensure that Nicky survived. Given the chance to do it all again, he knew he'd make the same decision and kidnap Samantha

The remainder of the meal passed quickly, as no one had eaten much in the past twenty-four hours. Jake insisted that Nicky try to speak English, translating for Sami as the occasion arose. By the time he had finished his soup and sandwich, the effort had exhausted Nicky.

Finally, Jake carried the boy off to a double bed in the corner of the cabin's main room. Nicky, nearly toppled over when Jake helped him get out of his shoes and pants, then tucked him in. Samantha brought over the quilt to add extra warmth to his bed. Using the thermometer, she took his temperature once again, then insisted he take a spoonful of the antibiotics she'd procured, along with some more Tylenol. She fussed over him in a combination of motherly affection and the concern of a professional nurse.

Jake leaned against the wall, watching her. It amazed him how lucky he'd been in his choice of kidnap victims the previous night. He doubted he and Nicky would be alive had he picked anyone else. Now she gave Nicky something he had not had since arriving on the shores of America. Love and security.

The tender scene dredged up old fears inside Jake and he moved away to sit in front of the fireplace. Years ago he'd made the decision to battle on the side of the law. The guys he hunted down were the bad guys with no redeeming qualities. The baddest of the bad. They'd cut your throat without blinking an eye. Women and children were no exception. He'd taken care not to get involved in any relationship. The few women he'd even seen between assignments called him cold and heartless. They didn't realize he was doing them a favor. If they'd meant something to him, they'd wind up dead. For years he'd only had his own ass to worry about.

Staring into the flames, he wondered how to keep Nicky safe until he cleared up this mess. Hell, who was he kidding? He'd be lucky if he just kept them all alive. He needed to go on the offensive, dig around and find out who was pulling the Kreshnins' strings. Problem was he didn't have a clue where to start. Tom Bridges' death severed his link to any authority with the department. He'd been on one undercover assignment or another for the past five years. He rubbed his hand over his face and beard in frustration.

"Here," Samantha said, handing him a mug of hot chocolate as she sat beside him on the couch. "Drink this while you worry."

Jake raised an eyebrow at her with skepticism. "What makes you think I'm worrying?"

"Sure. Every time you get frustrated or worried, you run your hand over your face and beard." She took a sip of the hot chocolate in her mug. Her tongue slipped out to clean the foam off her lips.

The woman was starting to play havoc with his resolve. He took a drink of his own chocolate, fighting the urge to reach over and trace a finger over the path her tongue had taken. "You think you know me that well, do you?"

"Oh, I don't pretend to know much about you, Jake. But I'm paid to observe people—particularly people under stress. You have several habits, rubbing your face is just one."

"What else have you observed about me?"

"Well, you're fluent in Russian. Did you study it in college?"

"No, not in college. My grandmother came from Russia right after World War Two. From the time I started talking she spoke both English and Russian to me until I went to school."

Samantha smiled at him. "She must have been an interesting woman."

"Remarkable describes her better. She fought against Hitler in the battle of Leningrad. I don't mean she sat at home cooking and cleaning. Not Babushka. She picked up a rifle and fought as a sniper in the trenches with the men."

"Really?"

Jake grinned at the surprised look on her face. "Yep. Then when the troops headed west, she went right along with them. She was there for the capture of Berlin."

"How did she get to America?"

"Like I said, Nana just kept heading west. Since she wasn't a man the Russian Army sort of lost track of her. There she just wandered into the American side of Berlin one day. She met and married my grandfather, a captain in the Rangers. The rest is history."

"Ah, I didn't think Carlisle was a Russian name." Samantha drank the last of her hot chocolate. "Your grandmother sounds wonderful."

"She was. She taught my brother Joe and I to fire rifles. She took us camping and taught us to build camp fires and how to hunt."

"Your parents didn't do those things?"

The woman was tenacious with her quiet probing. Funny thing, for the first time in a long time he didn't mind telling someone about his past. Or maybe he just didn't mind telling Samantha.

"My mother died when I was twelve and Joe was about six. My dad worked long hours as a police detective. Nana came to live with us permanently then."

"So, you have a brother."

She curled her arm under her head, smiling at him. The firelight glowed around her. Jake slouched down in his seat, draining his mug.

He stared into the fire. "Yes, I have a younger brother. He's a doctor in Chicago. I call him a mechanic. He repairs broken bones for a living."

"Ah, an orthopedic guy."

"Sport medicine is his specialty. But not just for professionals. He works with inner city athletes, grade school through high school. Sometimes it's for free, based on the parent's income."

She grinned at him. "You're proud of him."

"Yeah. He's one of the good guys."

"Is the world divided like that for you? Good guys and bad guys?"

He leaned back, closing his eyes a moment. "In my line of work, I see a lot of the bad guys, Samantha. I have to rub elbows with some of the low-lifes in order to get to the really dangerous ones. Sometimes, I forget there are good people in the world."

"Like your brother."

Slowly, he opened his eyes. Turning his head, he stroked his hand against her cheek. "Like Joe. Like you."

Sami turned her face into his warm hand. He rubbed his thumb across her chin. Warmth spread through her body. Being alone with him, like this, was a romantic daydream come to life. A cold snowy night outside. A cozy cabin in the middle of nowhere. Only firelight with which to gaze into each others eyes. A very sexy man, sitting across from her, touching her, drawing her nearer with one hand on her neck.

She relaxed, opening herself for the fire she knew would burn inside her with his kiss. The pressure of his hand increased on her neck, drawing her nearer. His lips touched hers lightly. A sampling taste. Chocolate, cinnamon from the gum he always seemed to chew, and something decidedly masculine filled her senses, overflowed her mind, swirled around and though her.

The pressure on her lips suddenly changed. Jake's fingers gripped her hair tightly. She followed his directions, tipping her head to the side. Her lips parted under his more insistent ones.

A moan sounded in the room.

Sami didn't know who it came from. She reached for him. Her fingers frantically working at the buttons of his shirt. His free hand slipped under her T-shirt, caressing her ribs. Her fingers touched skin, sliding in to curl in the soft mat of hair on his chest. His hand found and cupped one breast encased in the soft lacy bra.

Jake pushed her backward on the couch. His body pressed down on hers, one leg sliding between her parted thighs. Sami instinctively thrust upwards, grinding against his firm thigh. With one swift move he had her T-shirt over her head. Her hands worked at the fly of his jeans.

"Mmm, yes," she murmured against his lips. Desperately she opened his pants, curling her fingers around the long hard length of him.

"Oh God, yes, baby." His deep voice whispered against her lips, his warm breath sending shivers over her pulsating body. He pushed up into her hands, his own freeing her breasts from the confining bra.

Another moan.

This time, she knew it came from her. She felt his big calloused hands stroking and kneading her breasts. Her hard aching nipples throbbed from the stimulating thumbs he rubbed over them.

His mouth trailed over her neck to her ears. Shivers ran through her body as his hot breath caressed the sensitive area behind her ear lobe. "That's it, baby. Stroke it."

Sami's whole world focused on the need to have this man inside her. She'd known him less than three days, however she knew one thing, at this moment her whole being depended on having this man—not just any man—but this particular man buried in the deepest part of her.

As his hands worked her jeans open, she thrust his

jeans down his hips. She slid her hands up the firm muscles of his back, pulling him closer. Cool air touched her hot skin as his hands pushed and pulled her own jeans downwards.

His hand cupped her mound.

"Yes, please yes." She heard the woman moaning again.

He parted her thighs, pushing her jeans off one leg. She drew him nearer.

Yes. Just another minute. He'll be inside.

"Nyet! Nyet! I won't tell you where Jake is. He is my friend."

They froze.

Sami's eyes popped open. They met his crystal blue ones. "Is he awake?" she whispered. "What if he heard us." Cold reason flooded her senses. She tried to push him off her.

"Wait. Don't." He gripped her arms, and held her in place. "I can't move just yet. Wait one second."

"We can't do this. Not here." She felt like crying. "Get off me!"

"Just one minute, Sami." He peeked over the couch. "He's thrashing in bed. I think he's asleep."

"His fever could be up." She lay beneath him, his chest rubbing her nipples with each labored breath they took. The tip of his erection teased her with its heat. "I need to get up. I need to go to him."

"Okay, okay." He rested his forehead against hers, his eyes closed. The muscles in his arms quivered from the effort to keep his upper body pushed away from hers. For a moment she feared he meant to push the issue.

He dragged in a deep breath. "God, how do married people do this?" Slowly, he released her hands, sliding backward. Gripping his pants in one hand, he eased himself back into them.

Sami struggled to sit with her back to the couch. He handed her T-shirt to her. A blush filled her cheeks as she slipped it on. Her eyes didn't meeting his as she mumbled, "Thank you."

Without another word to her, he stumbled to the door, letting himself out. He wasn't about to embarrass them both further by coming in his jeans in the house.

Outside, he took a deep breath, letting the cold air fill his lungs and cool his need. He couldn't believe what had almost happened! For the first time since he'd been a boy looking at his first playboy centerfold, he'd almost lost control.

Who was he kidding? If Nicky hadn't called out, he would have buried himself, unsheathed into Samantha's hot body.

Never had he been with a woman without protection. It was one of his personal rules. Wear a condom, no matter what. But with Samantha, a woman he respected greatly even though he'd known her for such a short time, he'd almost broken that rule.

Jake ran his hand over his face, then through his hair. His body still hummed with desire.

The door behind him opened.

"Jake?"

"Go to bed, Samantha."

"Are you okay?"

The hesitation in her voice, the concern it showed almost undid him. His manhood hardened further. "Find a bed behind a door and lock it," he growled out between clenched teeth. "Now!"

Silence filled the icy night air for several moments.

"Don't stay out in the cold too long. I don't need to nurse you with pneumonia, as well as Nicky." The hurt in her voice cut through him sharper than the Kreshnins' bullet had.

The door slammed behind him.

He leaned his head against the cold wooden porch beam.

This was not good!

* * *

Sami read the thermometer, one hundred degrees, even. The medicine seemed to be doing its job. Replacing the thermometer in the holder, she put it in her purse. Still shaking from her reactions both to Jake's touch and his rejection, she pulled off her shoes. Grabbing her quilt, she crawled into bed with Nicky, curling around him, like she had so many times with Aimee.

Go find a bed behind a locked door.

Well, she didn't need a locked door to protect her from him. A sick child could always be a barrier between a man and woman. She'd learned that from personal experience.

A few minutes passed. Her anger slowly eased. As her

eyes started to drift shut, the front door opened again. Sami's body and mind came instantly alert. She watched Jake bank the fire and turn all the lights down low. He stood by the bed, looking at her and Nicky.

"How is he?" Jake's deep voice re-ignited shivers of desire throughout her body.

"His fever is down, but not quite gone." For another few minutes he stood looking intently at her. Passion still smoldered in his eyes, but just like the fire, he'd banked it well. If he held out his hand, Sami knew she'd go with him without question or thought. Instead, he closed his eyes and backed away from the bed. Turning, he walked to the back bedroom.

He opened the door, gripping it so tightly his knuckles blanched. With his back to her he hesitated.

"Samantha, hiding behind a child, will not keep you safe from me. This thing is too strong between us. I can't promise to keep my hands off of you while we're here." He turned to gaze at her again in the dim moonlit cabin. "But I will promise to protect you."

Sami hugged Nicky's sleeping form close to her in the night as she watched the door close behind Jake. His words made her body hum as much as his hands had earlier. He promised to protect her, and she was sure he meant physically and sexually. But who was going to protect her heart from him?

Long after the bedroom door clicked close behind Jake, Sami finally relaxed. She pulled the quilt up and snuggled around Nicky. Instinctively she felt his head. Warm, but not feverish.

"My grandmother used to do that," Nicky murmured sleepily beside her.

Startled, Sami looked into his blue eyes. Oh God! How much had he heard? "Where is your grandmother, Nicky?"

"Boosha, died last winter. We just came here on train. She was housekeeper for Khazyaeen Kreshnin. But she got sick." He wiggled around to face Sami. "I think she missed our sello, villiage, in Russia. She was sick for homeland."

"Oh! You mean she was homesick?"

"Da!"

"Where are your parents?"

"Mama died having me. That is what grandmother said."

Sami smoothed the hair from his forehead. "And your father?"

"Grandmother said he was truce, coward. He ran far away from us."

Sami nodded. "Lots of truce fathers live in America, too. So there hasn't been anyone to protect you since your grandmother died?"

Nicky grinned. "Jake protects me. I am little partner."

"Oh? And what exactly does little partner do?"

"I watch. Sometimes I watch when I am working. I see the men coming and going away."

"What men, Nicky?"

"Lots of men. They come to the restaurant. Khaztaeen

Kreshnin, he is big man mafioso. They bring bags of money to him. Then it goes in the trunks of the cars out behind the restaurant."

"That sounds dangerous for you to be watching that, Nicky. Did Jake really ask you to do this?"

A frown settled on the boy's face. "No, he find me doing this. He very mad. He told me he was politzia, police. He told me I no watch anymore. Jake promised to get me away from Khazyaeen Kreshnin." His voice lowered to a whisper. "I don't like working for him."

"In America, little boys aren't supposed to work, Nicky. They're supposed to be in school."

"That what Jake say. He say he was going to send me away to school and Boss Kreshnin not be able to box my ears no more."

Sami pulled Nicky closer, wrapping her arms tightly around him. The cold winter wind rattled the windowpane above the bed they shared. Her heart ached for the little boy who had no family left to care about him.

She glanced at the closed bedroom door once more. By Nicky's admission Jake had tried to warn the boy away from the danger of helping him. Despite the cop's tough guy act, Nicky had known to trust him. A soft smile played on her lips. So had she.

"Sami?"

"Yes, Nicky?"

"Do you want to know secret?"

"Is it a secret you should be telling?"

Nicky shook his head. "Jake told me not to tell no one. Especially not Khazyaeen Kreshnin."

"Is that why they hurt you, Nicky? Because of the secret?"

He nodded.

"Then I think this once it would be a very good thing if you told it to me." She held her breath, waiting for Nicky's revelation.

"Khazyaeen Kreshnin hit a man on back of his head. Then he put man in his trunk, just like bags of money."

Sami's heart slammed into her stomach, beating double time. That was why Jake so desperately wanted to get the boy into protective custody. And why the Kreshnins wanted to find him.

Nicky was a material witness to a murder.

"Wow, that's some secret, Nicky."

When he didn't answer, she leaned closer. His steady breathing greeted her ears. His secret revealed, Nicky slept. However, her mind kicked into over-drive.

Somehow there had to be a way to protect Nicky. Jake's hands were pretty much tied after the shooting in the parking lot. Hugging Nicky close she had to admit she wanted to help both the boy and the man.

Her brothers had pounded it into her brain her whole life. You always trust the police. But they never told her what to do when the police were the ones chasing you.

She sighed with frustration. Her brothers weren't going to be happy with her. Dave, the oldest, was going to tell her she should've tried harder to get away. He would say she should've gotten the police to come help. Matt would get just as angry with her. He'd say if she was driving, she should've gone straight to the Highway Patrol. After all, he worked for them. They'd protect her.

Even Luke would put in his two cents.

Luke.

She sat straight up in the bed and gently pushed away from Nicky's body. The younger of her three big brothers might just be the answer. If he had his cell phone on. If he wasn't away on a case. Sami glanced at the clock. Two a.m. If he wasn't in bed with someone.

Padding over to the couch, she pulled the wool afghan off it. To ward off the chill of the cold cabin, she wrapped it around her shoulders like a giant shawl. She silently went to the bedroom door and listened. A light snoring sounded on the other side.

She smothered a giggle with her hand over her mouth. Jake snores.

Now, if only she remembered to charge her cell phone recently. She suppressed another giggle. Her inability to keep her phone charged drove her brothers nuts. Each one told her that the safety of having a cell phone lay in its constant readiness.

A board creaked under her foot.

She froze.

Every nerve fiber hummed with electricity. Her whole being focused on her hearing. Her breathing sounded like a tornado in the quiet room. Her heart beat thundered in her ears.

She listened for the door to open, expecting Jake to grab her from behind like he had so many times before. Surely he would come storming out, enraged that she would be sneaking around the cabin at night.

No sound came, but the crackling of the wood on the banked fired behind her. She inhaled and exhaled hard, forcing every ounce of air out of her lungs before filling them once more. Relaxed, she took another sock-covered step. No further creaks sounded beneath her feet as she inched her way to the kitchen area.

Kneeling, she pulled her backpack purse to her. In all the drama of the past twenty-four hours, she'd completely forgotten about her cell phone. She only carried it to appease her family, leaving it turned off almost all the time. Something about people calling her while she stood in the produce section feeling oranges really irked her.

In the dark she had to feel around in the depths of her pack. Her fingers came in contact with a pad of folded papers. She pulled them out and studied them a minute.

Three prescriptions. All for sleeping pills. All from different doctors.

She stared at them a moment, remembering she'd had a different plan for when she'd left work early. Ending her pain. A long sleep.

Funny how that hadn't entered her mind since Jake kidnapped her.

She thrust the papers back into the pack and hunted again until her fingers found the silky carrying case she kept the phone in. Flipping up the top, she covered the back to muffle the metallic sounding beep that filled the silence like a jumbo jet to her ears.

Her eyes darted to the door.

No movement.

Whew.

The messages light flashed in front of her eyes. Twenty-three messages. She just bet her family sent them all in the past twelve hours. You would think if she didn't answer them the first time, they'd get the idea she couldn't answer them at all.

Frustrated, she shook her head. She knew they were worried. Her parents must be frantic. But she couldn't risk more than one call, so she would just trust Luke to let the others know she was alive and okay.

Pressing the number four button, she auto-dialed Luke's cell phone number. This was one feature she liked about the phone. Her family swore she couldn't remember a phone number even if her life depended upon it. This time it might.

"Come on, Luke, pick up," she muttered quietly, her eyes riveted on the bedroom door. Out of everyone in the family, Luke slept the heaviest. Because of his job, he rarely slept in the same bed two nights in a row, so he always kept his cell phone right by the bed, in case someone at work or the family needed him.

"Hello?" His groggy voice rasped in Sami's ear.

"Luke?" she whispered.

"Sami? Is that you? I can hardly hear you." His voice

sounded instantly awake. "Where are you, sis? The family is worried sick. The feds are reporting you're helping a kidnapper. They're parked in front of Mom and Dad's house, hoping you'll show up."

That news didn't surprise her. Jake had been right. The moment she'd pulled out of that lot, whoever was behind this marked her as his accomplice. "Luke, listen, I don't have much time. Jake didn't kidnap, Nicky."

"Who's Nicky?"

"The little Russian boy. Just listen to me, don't ask questions, okay?"

"Okay."

"I need you to get me some information. I need to know how much the government knows about some Russian immigrants called the Kreshnins." She spelled the last name for him. "I also need to know if there are any records of money laundering or if the Kreshnins are under investigation by the feds. Also find out if the child protection agency is aware Nicky is an orphan. Got all that?"

"Sami?"

"What Luke?"

"Are you okay? Has this guy hurt you?"

"No, Luke. I'm okay. It's just...really complicated. If you can give me that information, it might help." Sami held the phone closer. "And Luke?"

"Yes?"

"Tell mom and dad that Jake's with the FBI. He's one of the good guys."

"Sami, where are you?"

"Someplace I feel very safe, Luke. Don't worry, okay?"

"You're asking the impossible, sis."

"I know. You guys always worry about me. But just this once, trust me to know what I'm doing, okay? "

"Sami, if this guy has hurt you, in any way..." the unfinished threat hung in the air, as Sami quietly clicked the phone off.

For years, she'd listened to her big brothers, always headed their advice no matter how much she resented their interference in her life. This time she wanted to do what she thought was right. Helping Nicky was the right thing to do. She also had a feeling helping Jake would be, too.

Quietly, she returned the phone to its hiding place, being sure to turn off the ringer. Jake didn't need to know about its existence yet. A day or two of rest would do both him and Nicky some good. She knew Jake would blow up when he found out she'd made that call. It was probably the coward's way to keep from facing his wrath a little longer. Hopefully the information Luke gave them would be worth enduring Jake's temper.

She bent over to set the bag down.

Behind   her   the   door   creaked Sami froze.

Oh, God. She was dead in the water.

Think! Why would you be digging around in your backpack at this time of night? Something innocent. Musn't let him search the bag.

Trying not to look panicked or suspicious, she stayed bent over, reaching her hand back in and feeling along the bottom of her bag with her fingers. They connected with something long and flat.

Thank, God. Gum!

"Samantha?"

Slipping a piece of the gum from its wrapper, she stood, folding it into her mouth. She tried to act nervous when she turned around. The sight of him standing in just his jeans, the only thing on him above the waist was the white bandage she'd taped on his wound, sent her heart racing like a speedometer on a formula one car. Nervous wasn't a difficult performance.

"Oh! You startled me."

"Is everything okay?"

She sauntered over to stand in front of him, blocking his view of her bag. Clutching the afghan in one hand, she held the pack of gum. "I hate not having a toothbrush. Thought a piece of gum might take the stale taste out of my mouth."

Jake smiled that killer smile again. His hand tucked a strand of her hair behind her ear. "You tasted just fine earlier."

Great! Now her heart jumped into a hyper-drive even Han Solo would appreciate.

Looking at Nicky, curled like a ball in the center of the bed, Jake's lips pressed into a thin line of worry. "Is he okay?"

"His fever is down for the moment. It will take another day of rest and antibiotics to really get control of the infection." She touched his shoulder. "How are you feeling?"

His hand wrapped around hers, where it caressed his bandage. "It's sore, but not too bad. Thanks for doing such a good job, fixing us both."

"Are you sleeping okay?"

"I was until I heard voices. Thought maybe Nicky was dreaming."

She gulped and thought fast. "He was awake for a few minutes. We talked about his grandmother."

"He misses her. She was the only family he had."

"I gathered that from our talk."

Jake held her gaze captive, and she could only stare at him. "We should get you in bed."

She blinked. Warmth surged through her body, settling low in her belly. Yes. Just what she wanted, him to take her to bed and let her snuggle against his body. She shivered more.

He pushed her toward the alcove. "You're freezing. You should climb in with Nicky."

"Oh. Yes. Bed. Nicky." Great now she sounded like a parrot. Her embarrassment complete, she climbed over Nicky to lay near the wall. She couldn't believe she thought he was suggesting she go to bed with him. God, how pathetic she must look!

Jake pulled the covers over them both. Leaning in, he rested one hand on the wall behind her. "Good night, Sami."

Before she knew what he intended, his lips came down on hers once more, for the softest, sexiest of kisses she could remember.

As he stood, he grinned at her. "Good flavor to that

gum."

Sami watched him go into the bedroom, then wrapped her arms around Nicky. Something about that man made her want to throw all her natural caution to the wind. If he knew about her cell phone, he'd be angry. But knowing he wouldn't trust her anymore scared her more than his wrath ever could.

CHAPTER SEVEN

The smell of baked cinnamon and coffee slowly penetrated the sleepy fog of Jake's brain. He'd been dreaming of being back at Bubushka Nana's kitchen, sitting at the table while she made breakfast. He could hear his mother in the next room laughing, probably at something his dad or Joey had said.

It wasn't just a dream, but a memory. One of the last Sunday mornings they'd all been together before his mother died.

Awake, Jake rolled over to stare out the cabin's window at the winter scene before him. Snow laden fir trees stood among the bare deciduous trees like quiet sentinels. Better these silent guards than the ones in the prison he'd end up if he didn't get out of the mess he'd managed to drag Nicky, Samantha and himself into. Assuming they all survived long enough for him to go to prison.

Thinking about Samantha, his mind and body flooded

with memories from last night. What to do with her?

He gave a harsh laugh.

Oh, he *knew* what he wanted to do with her. His hand slipped down to cup his growing arousal. He wanted to be buried deep inside her softness. If he thought about it long enough, he could chalk last night's instant combustion between them to nearly two years without a woman. Celibacy, even of his own making, could drive a guy to want sex with the closest female, he supposed.

He sat on the side of the bed and reached for his jeans, forcing his mind to be both honest and less carnal. He had to face facts. It wasn't just Samantha's hot soft body he lusted after.

Thrusting one leg, then the other into his jeans, he thought to himself, nope, he wanted the whole woman. Her raw courage, self-assuredness, efficient movements, logical thoughts, and her never panic attitude drew him as much as her round soft curves. Of course her sarcasm drove him a little bit over the edge.

He chuckled and shook his head. He suspected she used her sharp tongue as a way to push people away. Problem was, it had the opposite affect on him. All he wanted was to drag her close, kiss her into submission and show her he was stronger than even her anger.

Thinking about the power struggle pulling between him and her, he picked up his shirt and slipped it on. She wanted to use her words to sting him, he wanted to use his body to control her.

The smell of bacon wafted through the door. Apparently, Samantha planned on feeding them all a hearty breakfast. He grabbed the large gold envelope containing the files he'd secreted away on the Kreshnins. He might as well put his forced isolation to good use. Maybe somewhere in the papers he'd amassed would be a clue to who wanted them dead.

He'd better find the answer quick. The men hunting them had him in their cross hairs. It was part of his job and he'd been in this situation before. Only this time, Samantha and Nicky were targeted along with him. They'd both lost too much already in their lives. And he wasn't about to let anything more happen to either one.

Today, he'd become the hunter.

A very domestic scene greeted him when he stepped through the door into the cabin's main room. Sami stood at the stove, her back to him. Jake stopped and watched her as she cooked. He liked the way her faded blue jeans hugged her hips and thighs, not too tight, but enough to show her feminine curves. Today she had her dark hair pulled up in a ponytail. He'd love to taste the long column of her neck exposed beneath it.

That was just the kind of thought he shouldn't be having—the kind that only led to trouble.

He shook his head and focused his attention on the table where Nicky sat, scarfing down what appeared to be cinnamon rolls. Sticky white icing covered his lips. The kid was in sugar heaven.

Jake set the evidence envelope on the table, poured himself a cup of coffee and leaned against the counter next to the stove. Watching Samantha turn the bacon and beat several eggs in a bowl, he admired her efficient movements as he took a long sip of the coffee. Rich, dark, kick-you-in-the-ass-wake-up-coffee rolled across his tongue. He smiled. No foo-foo coffee for Samantha.

"He seems better this morning," he whispered, nodding toward Nicky.

Samantha cast a quick glance at Nicky. "I hope so. His fever broke in the middle of the night. Then he slept pretty sound, until about an hour ago."

"The kid is amazing."

"Yes, he's pretty resilient for all he's been through."

Jake took another big swallow of coffee. "What all did he tell you?"

"Not too much. Mostly I've read between the lines." She flipped the bacon slices one at a time with the fork. "He and his grandmother came here recently from Russia. Something happened to her, and Nicky ended up working for the Kreshnins, first in their restaurant, then running numbers. Something totally against the law, I might add."

"I know that, Samantha." Jake tried not to laugh. The mama lion in her was coming out full force. "I am not the one that forced the kid into working at his age."

"No, but what have you done about it?" She pointed the grease-splattered fork at him with each word.

Angrily, Jake grasped her wrist to stop the fork. "I had a job to do. I got him out as fast as I could."

"It wasn't fast enough, was it?"

Sparks flew between them like a welding torch to steel. His grip loosened. She was right. He was the first to break the visual contact. Releasing her hand, he inched further back against the counter. They both knew he was as much to blame for Nicky's poor treatment as the Kreshnins. Guilt gnawed at his nerves.

"No, it wasn't fast enough."

"Why?"

"Why did I let him stay in there one day longer than I should have?" Jake raked his hand through his hair. "Don't you think I've asked myself that all night? I could've gotten him away to childrens services two days ago. But I needed an airtight case--one that would keep them from ever hurting Nicky again. I should've taken him away the day I found him out huddling behind the garbage bin in the alley watching the money transfers into the limousine."

"You should have gotten him to the Childrens Protective Agency the minute you met him."

Her whispered words weighed heavily on Jake. Her aim was dead-on target this morning and it stung. His jaw clenched in an effort to control the anger surging through him. "You don't pull any punches, do you?"

"Not usually. Right is right, wrong is wrong."

Jake glanced at her to find her watching him. Even though her words were totalitarian, her face held little censure. "Not all things are so black and white. Sometimes there is a gray area, Samantha."

"But in the case of the welfare of children, there shouldn't be. Their lives are precious and we should protect them at all costs. Especially, if there is no one else to do it."

"Are we talking about Nicky now, or your daughter?" The minute the question was out of his mouth, he wished he could take it back. The pain that flashed across her features tore at his conscience, adding to the guilt he already felt because of Nicky's injuries. "Dammit, Samantha, I'm sorry. I shouldn't have said that."

She blinked a few times at the water gathering in her eyes, dropping her gaze to concentrate on removing the bacon from the pan. Jake refilled his coffee. Silence hung in the room, the sizzling of the grease in the pan and Nicky licking the sweet sugar from his fingers the only sounds.

"Eggs?" Her voice was shaky, but determined.

Apparently she didn't plan to let his anger or her own pain get her down. Good. She was one tough cookie. Rather than embarrass her more, he'd follow her lead and change the subject.

"Sure. How about you, little partner?" he asked Nicky. "Want some eggs?"

"Yesh pweash," he mumbled as he stuffed another piece of roll in his mouth.

Sami chuckled beside Jake. "Okay two orders of scrambled eggs coming up. Here take these." She handed him the plate of bacon and one of homemade biscuits to carry to the table.

"You've been busy this morning. Did you sleep at all?"

"A little, then when Nicky's fever finally broke, I decided just to get up." A blush filled her cheeks. "I tend to bake when I worry."

"Good thing Nicky and I are starving, huh, little

partner?" he asked as he sat across the table from him.

Nicky nodded.

Jake put two biscuits and a roll on his plate. "Is all this sugar good for the kid?"

"Given all the energy that fever used yesterday, and all the healing he needs, one morning of sugar overload probably won't hurt him. I just hope he doesn't bounce off the walls from the sugar rush like my nephew does."

Jake sampled the roll as he sipped his coffee. Better than any he'd eaten at any bakery. No wonder Nicky was pigging out on them.

Sami set a plate of soft fluffy eggs in front of Jake and one in front of Nicky. She brought her own to the table and sat next to Nicky, across the table from Jake. Right now she wanted to be as far away from him as possible. Since leaving wasn't an option, she'd just keep as much distance as available between them.

His question still stung. Not so much because he'd asked it, but because in his anger he'd zeroed in on her Achilles' heel and hadn't hesitated to use it. The man didn't take any prisoners.

As she scooped a forkful of eggs into her mouth, her eyes settled on the envelope at his elbow. Determinedly she forced herself to concentrate on eating her eggs and biscuits. Once she finished and set her fork aside, curiosity finally got the better of her. She propped her elbows on the table, her hands wrapped around her own mug of coffee. She nodded at the envelope. "What's that?"

Jake looked at her, then at Nicky. "Files," was her only answer before he reached for another biscuit.

Okay, that subject was off limits. For now.

Sami bit lightly on the inside of her cheek. She didn't want to upset Nicky anymore than Jake did, but if he thought for one second he could dismiss her questions, and keep her in the dark any longer, he had another think coming. Once before, she let someone isolate her in a time of crisis. On the day of Aimee's funeral she promised herself she wouldn't let it happen again. Ever.

She turned her attention to Nicky. Half a dozen giant cinnamon rolls and nearly all his eggs gone, he rested his head on his arm on the table, while he pushed the remaining eggs around his plate with his fork, completely stuffed.

"You need to at least try and eat, Aimee," she'd begged her daughter the last time she'd sat at the table for breakfast. Her favorite cinnamon rolls, sausage biscuits sandwiches and sliced strawberries littered the table.

"I don't know why you cooked all this, she hasn't eaten more than a few bites in weeks." Michael had said with condemnation as he kept his nose stuck in the financial papers of the daily paper.

She'd bitten her tongue not to tell him that at least she recognized their daughter wasn't dead and buried in the ground already. At least she hadn't given up hope. Even if that hope was all she had left to cling to. That same hope had her up at the crack of dawn, making foods she thought would tempt Aimee to at least eat something.

"I can't, Mommy. My tummy doesn't want anything."

"Please, sweetie, try just a little something?"

"I can't watch this." Michael threw his paper on the table and stormed out of the house to work.

"Can I go back to bed, Mommy?"

"I tell you what, sweetie. If you eat a little of the sausage buscuit and drink your juice, I'll tuck you in and read the princess story to you. How does that sound?"

Aimee had smiled that courageous I-can-do-anything smile she used to face every medical test and blood draw, then picked up her food and ate three whole bites.

It was the last time she'd cooked anything until last night's simple meal. Sami pinched the bridge of her nose to stop the tears that threatened. She couldn't change the past. Watching Nicky this morning eat until he couldn't hold anymore warmed her heart.

"Getting tired, little guy?" She gently felt his head. Not too warm. Good.

Nicky nodded.

"How about you go take a nap, and when you wake up, we can play checkers?"

"What is checkers?" he asked, as she helped him from the table.

Sami looked at Jake.

He simply shrugged. Big help he was.

"Checkers is a very old game in America, Nicky." She set him in the bed, and pulled the covers over him. "There's a board with red and black squares on it, and little round playing pieces like chips, or quarters."

"I have never played this, Sami."

She smiled at him, tousling his hair with her hand. "Then we'll have fun teaching you it later, okay?"

He grinned at her with one tooth missing. "Okay, Sami." He started to turn, then looked at her once more. "You are good cook."

She couldn't help it, she brushed a kiss on his cheek. "Thank you, Nicky. And you are a good eater."

He giggled, then yawned. Sami stood beside him a moment, listening to his breathing ease as he gently fell asleep.

Clattering and running water sounded in the kitchen. She turned to see Jake filling the sink with dish soap and the dirty dishes. The man does dishes? Without being asked? The man tempted her way too much. She'd better remember he lived life as a lone wolf. And he was just as dangerous and wild as one.

She inhaled, then exhaled hard.

Time to face the wolf in his den. He might not want to discuss what that envelope contained. Too bad. She did. Her game plan set, she carried her own plate to the sink.

"What's in the files?" she asked without warning. With three older brothers, she'd learned early on a frontal attack with the element of surprise on her side usually got her the results she wanted. Subtlety was lost on men.

Jake continued to soap and rinse a plate. For a minute, she thought he planned to ignore her.

"The envelope contains all the information I have on the Kreshnins' organization. I'm hoping somewhere in there is a clue to who the mole is in the police department."

"Maybe I can help." She took the plate he handed her, drying it and setting it on the counter.

He handed her another. "I don't want you involved any deeper in this, Samantha. The less you know, the better."

"Could you do me a favor?"

"Depends on the favor."

"Quit calling me Samantha. I prefer to go by Sami. When I was growing up the only time anyone called me Samantha was when I was in trouble."

He gave her a grin that would melt a popsicle at the North Pole. "Well, *Samantha*, in case you hadn't noticed, we are in trouble. Hip-deep-in-alligators trouble."

She glared at him.

"But if it will make you more comfortable, I'd be happy to call you Sami."

"Thank you." She stacked the dry plates in the cabinet and counted to ten to reign in her temper. "As for keeping me in the dark for my own good, the minute I drove you away from that gun battle yesterday, I got involved in this right up to my chin. If you don't mind, I'd like to know exactly who it is we're fighting."

Jake studied her a moment, then nodded. "I see your point. Let's get these finished, then you can look at the files."

"Really?"

He shrugged. "Yes. You're right, I dragged you into this. The least I can do is give you a good reason for it."

Sami looked at the bed in the alcove where Nicky slept. "You've already given me that, Jake. But information can be a powerful weapon."

He laid his soapy hand on hers. "I'm sorry for that

crack earlier about your daughter."

"It's okay. You're right. Nicky isn't Aimee. Her's was a losing battle, his isn't."

* * *

Jake watched Samantha study the papers on her lap. She hadn't said a word while she read each one.

After a few more minutes, she looked up from the files. "Oh my God. Nicky is the <u>only</u> witness to this murder?"

"Yep." Jake sat across the couch from her. "The minute he told me what he'd seen, I knew I had to get him out of there. Only I didn't count on the whole raid blowing up in my face. The only reason I can think for them not killing him immediately, is that they were trying to get out of him who he'd told about the murder and how much information he'd given about their organization."

"Why didn't they just torture you? Why go after Nicky?"

"My cover wasn't blown yet. As far as they knew I was a low level member, recruited because of my family's Russian background and my need for work."

"Did you ever hurt anyone?"

Might as well let her know he wasn't some kind of knight in shining armor. In order to be part of a criminal gang he'd had to act think like a criminal and act like one, too. He shrugged. "Depends on your definition of hurt. Did I kill anyone? No. Mostly I was a driver. I drove Petrov to meetings upon occasion. Other times I'd go with Ivan to make collections from their victims. If someone was short on what they owed, I'd rough them up a bit to remind them how their families back in Russia might be treated."

"You beat people up?"

He winced inside at the censure in her voice. For the first time in a long time, it mattered to him what someone thought of him. He hated disappointing her, but he kept his face void of any emotion. Best not to let her know how much her question and his answer hurt him.

"Yes, I beat people up. These are dangerous men and I was pretending to be one in order to move up in their organization. If I'd been a real thug, I would've done more than throw a few punches and bruise a few faces. Some enforcers cut off fingers or ears."

"And some kill."

"Yes. This isn't some Mickey Mouse group you see on TV, Samantha. If they catch us, they *will* kill us."

The words filled the silence of the cabin.

Samantha nodded and pulled her lower lip between her teeth. She focused on the packet in her lap and flipped though it until she came across the immigrations papers. "The Kreshnins came in on diplomatic papers twelve years ago, then got green cards?"

"Back then the rules were not enforced as much as they are now. Seems no one bothered to do a thorough background check on them at Immigration and Naturalization Services."

"They would've found out they were ex-KGB agents." Sami looked at him. "Bribes?"

"Probably. Sloppy paperwork and easy entrance smells

of   bribes   to   me."

"Is this what the media calls the Russian Mafia?"

Jake watched her flip through the papers once again. The lady didn't miss much. "There's no centralized group like with the Costa Nostra. It's more like a loosely woven web of small groups. Occasionally they work together, occasionally they work with others, such as cells from Japan, China, the Italians, even the Hispanics. The Kreshnins seem to be the most organized Russian clan this side of New York."

"They're money laundering for both the Japanese and the Sicilians?"

Jake nodded. "They're extorting bankers with ties to the old Russia. They deposit their drug money into the banks, the banks invest it, then deposit clean dividends into dummy companies. Everyone benefits from the system. The old mafia system has no ties to these bankers so they stay off the feds and IRS radar, the Kreshnins get a big cut, and the banker gets to keep his life."

She handed him the pile of papers. "I thought Nicky just worked in the restaurant the Kreshnins owned, like a bus boy or something."

"Right after his grandmother died, I think he did start out doing something like that. But after a while his duties changed and became more dangerous."

"What exactly did the Kreshnins have him doing?"

Jake fought the sudden rage that surged through him. "They had him carrying messages from the restaurant to their lieutenants. Sometimes into the ugliest parts of town. I'd go along as body guard."

"Weren't they worried that someone would find the message on him? That he might leave evidence in the wrong place? He's a child after all."

"It seems our little friend has a unique qualification for the job of messenger. Something that wouldn't leave a paper trail back to them." He watched the dawning light her eyes.

"Nicky has a photographic memory?"

Her response surprised him. "Yes. How did you figure it out?"

"When he was delirious from the fever he quoted a list of Russian names and numbers. At the time I didn't know what it meant. Now it makes sense. He knows everyone the Kreshnins were extorting money from."

"Yep." Not to mention each cell that traded drugs for them, the names and places of the sex-slave operations. The kid is a walking talking indictment for the prosecution. If they ever get to talk to him."

"So, they have more to fear from him than just the murder?"

"Oh yeah. Nicky can identify them as the leaders of the cell operating in the central Midwest area. He can also identify their under-chiefs, lieutenants, and the leaders of the other criminal groups who had dealings with them. He can list financial transactions for the past two years." The kid had more deadly secrets, but Jake wasn't going to tell her unless she figured it out on her own.

"The Kreshnins exploited him and his abilities to stay out of court?"

He nodded.

"Let me ask you something?" She pinned him in place with her clear innocent gaze.

Jake wasn't buying her act for a second. She had a point to make and he wasn't going to like it. His stomach clenched. "Shoot."

"What makes you different from these criminals? Aren't you willing to put Nicky in danger to serve your own purposes?"

"I'm not using him like the Kreshnins do." Jake's body tensed with anger. "I've never laid a finger on the kid. Remember, I'm the one who got Nicky away from them."

"But aren't you doing the same thing? Using his memory to put the Kreshnins behind bars?"

"You don't understand."

Samantha laid her hand on his arm. "Then explain it to me so I will."

The warm touch of her hand on his flesh calmed him. He ran a hand through his hair, glancing at where Nicky lay sleeping.

"The kid's life is hanging by a thread with this whole mess, Samantha. His testimony in the money laundering would only put the Kreshnins in prison. But since he witnessed the murder…"

"Since he witnessed the murder," she prodded.

"If I can't find out who on the force is helping the Kreshnins, the kid is as good as dead, no matter where or with whom I hide him."

His words hung in the air like the blade of a guillotine. Sami's hand tightened on his arm. He reached for her. Pulling her into his arms, he held her against his chest, breathing in the fresh scent of vanilla on her hair.

Visions of Nicky's bleeding, tortured body the night he rescued him from the Kreshnins flashed through his mind. If Nicky ever fell into their hands again, Jake knew the little boy's torture would seem like a birthday party compared to what they'd do to him. Jake forced his mind away from those dark thoughts to the day he met Nicky.

"The kid was so alone the first time I saw him." He continued to stroke Samantha's hair as the words poured out. "He was sitting in the corner of the kitchen of the Kreshnins' restaurant, KAPTOREB. All he had on was this ripped t-shirt and a pair of baggy pants. I don't think he'd had a bath in a month."

The same anger he felt then, overwhelmed him again. No kid should have to be that alone, that ignored by the world. Even when his own father lost himself in his job on the police force, he and his brother still had their grandmother there for them. Never once did they feel abandoned.

Setting Samantha away from him, he stood to poke at the logs in the fire. They sparked, cracked and flamed again. He leaned his arm on the mantel, pressing his forehead against his arm. Staring into the flames, he thought about how he'd treated Nicky.

When his chance came along to give someone that same feeling of belonging, that same safety factor he'd gotten from his grandmother, what had he done? Nothing.

Guilt welled up inside him. He growled with frustration. "You're right. I should have gotten him out of there the first day."

A soft hand settled on his shoulder. He looked around at her.

The censure was gone from her. Understanding and empathy filled her eyes, but no sign of pity.

"I shouldn't have come down so hard on you. If his life is in that much danger, perhaps your plan is the best. We find a way to put the Kreshins away so they can't ever hurt him. The question is, where do we go from here?"

He leaned his back against the mantel. A loose hair hung over her shoulder. He tucked it behind her ear, letting his fingers caress her cheek. "You're amazing. I pulled you into this mess, without thinking it would endanger you as much as Nicky and me. By all rights you should hate me. Instead, here you make my problem *our* problem. Why?"

She glanced at the small boy in the bed. "Because he needs us both. And because you need my help."

"I can't ask you to help me more than you have, Samantha. I think the best plan is to find a safe place for you and Nicky, then go after the Kreshnins myself."

"You do everything alone, don't you?"

"In my line of work it's best not to trust too many people with your secrets. Trust the wrong person and you wind up dead."

"This time you don't have to do it alone."

Tenderness filled her voice, tempting him to tell her more—to explain this gnawing fear that his job would cost him more than he'd ever thought before—her and Nicky. This wasn't the time or place to confess his inner demons. Their future was tenuous at best. Right now, he could think of something he'd much rather share with her than the burden of his soul.

His hand slid over her cheek and around her neck to grip the back of her head. He pulled her to him, his lips pressing against hers in the softest of kisses.

Just like paper in fire, it was sudden combustion. His lungs ached with lack of air. Her lips parted, and his tongue slid in to claim the taste of her. She wrapped her arms around him. He gripped her hair tight in one fist, reaching down the other hand to cup her bottom. Then the other joined it. He lifted her, pressing her into his now aching erection.

"Mmm," she moaned against him.

He released her lips, trailing kisses against the hot flesh of her exposed neck. At the juncture of her shoulder and neck he stopped to suck softly on the pulse point throbbing there. She lifted one leg to wind it around his hips and thigh, pressing so close he could feel her heat through their clothes.

"Sami, now honey, please."

"Mmm, yes, oh god yes."

Neither one wanted to break their embrace. He edged her backward to the bedroom door. Managing to maneuver them both into the bedroom, he kicked the door closed behind them.

When the door banged, they froze.

Over the pounding of blood in his ears, Jake strained to hear any movement in the cabin's main room. Releasing her, he eased the door open enough to peek at the bed. Nicky hadn't budged an inch. When he closed the door this time, he made sure it clicked softly.

"Is he still asleep?" Samantha whispered behind him.

He grinned at her. "Snug as a bug.

A giggle escaped her, followed by a sudden redness to her face. "I've never...done...Maybe," she mumbled, moving away from him.

With more patience than he felt, he leaned against the door, hands behind him. "Samantha?"

She stopped her retreat. "Jake?"

"I want you so much, I may just die from it, but..." He waited for his words to sink in. "This has to be what you want, too."

Sami stared across the small chasm of the room. There, pressed against the exit stood the man of her secret fantasies. His lean body, accented by his skintight jeans, slouched in his bad boy stance sent her heart racing a little faster. Her eyes traveled to his face, over the lips she knew would set her on fire, to the eyes that spoke of his need and promised her a passion she hadn't felt in years, if ever. Her body flushed with anticipation. Heat surged through her breasts, both nipples drawing taut in response to the primal need of a woman for her man. Liquid fire settled in the juncture of her thighs.

And he wanted her so much, he just might die from it.

For the first time in her life she knew the true power of a woman. Not breaking eye contact with those promises, she unzipped her jeans, shoving them over her hips, down her thighs, stepping out of them.

"Jake." She reached a hand out to him.

He descended on her like a mid-western tornado. He let his hands pull her close at the same time stripping her remaining clothes. Sami worked just as feverishly to reveal the feel of his skin against her own. A deep moan filled the room when her hand encircled him.

"Yes, sweetheart. Mmm…just like that."

The need in his voice filled her with confidence. She let her hands stroke him. The control lay entirely with her. Even as he moved her toward the bed, she felt him waiting for her directions. When he handed her the foil pack, she knew he still left the decision in her corner.

She pulled away, slowly stretching the latex condom on him. Where he had gotten it from, she didn't want to ask. The fact he thought to protect her fed her desire for him.

She cupped his face. "I need you, Jake. Now!" She whispered against his lips, as they landed on the bed.

With little grace, he surged deep inside her. "Sami…you feel…so good," he murmured between deep, soul wrenching kisses.

"Been…so…long," she murmured, thrusting to meet his hips as he drove them further and further back on the bed.

"Yes, baby." With a gentle tug he bit her lip.

She reached behind him, cupping his buttocks to pull him in tighter. Her legs wrapped around him, riding him as he drove deeper. "Mmm, yes Jake, please."

"Baby, now, please now." He reached between them, his fingers finding her and stroking her own desire further.

Sami's body arched, her head pressed into the pillows, every muscle tightening as her orgasm shot through her. "Jake!"

He smothered her moan with his mouth, claiming it for his own as his release shot through him.

It took eons for him come back to reality after his explosion. He realized he squished her into the mattress.

Carefully, he rolled to the side, pulling her up against him. He pushed the wet tendrils of dark hair off her face, bending to kiss her forehead. "I'm sorry it didn't last longer, sweetheart."

She shushed him with a finger to his lips. "I would've died if it had."

A rumble sounded in his chest. Lord the woman made him laugh more than anyone had in a long time. "So would I."

He held her in the waning afternoon light, his hand stroking her passion flushed skin. A peaceful contentment settled over him. If he could he'd stay like this with her forever.

"How are you going to go after the Kreshnins?" Her soft words floated through the sensual tide around them, breaking the spell and bringing them back to reality.

"That's a good question. I have a contact in the DA's office I could get in touch with. The local police department's leak limits how much I can depend on their help." He sighed in exasperation. "I really want to nail whoever set up the captain yesterday. The electric chair is too tame for what they deserve."

"Did he have family?"

Jake nodded. "A wife, a son in college and a daughter in high school. He took me under his wing when I got my first undercover assignment with the Bureau and has supported me ever since." He pinched the bridge of his nose to stop the stinging in his eyes. "Tom was a good friend as much as he was a boss."

"I'm sorry." She wrapped her arms around him. "Watching him go down like that, yesterday. It was so...so awful to see. It had to be even harder for you."

He pressed his lips to Samantha's hair. Her arms wrapped so tight around him, it felt like she wanted to protect him from the pain and grief over losing his friend.

When was the last time someone had tried to comfort him? Years? With all the pain she'd had in her life, how did she have anything left to give him, or Nicky?

"Tell me about your daughter. What was her name?"

"Aimee."

Samantha tensed in his arms. He ran his hand down her arm and up her back until she relaxed again.

"What was she like?"

"Little. That's the first thing anyone said about her when they met her. She looked just like a little china doll. She was always so petite. She never could gain enough weight, even as a baby."

"Did she look like you?"

"She had my hair, and nose. But she had these big brown eyes, like her dad. And a very good sense of humor. No matter how bad her disease or the treatments seemed to get—blood tests, radiation, chemo—she always tried to make her care-givers laugh."

A shudder ran through her.

With an open palm he softly stroked her back. "Tell me about her last day."

"She was so frail by then, lying in her bed at home. Michael, her father, wanted her to go to the hospital. But I'd promised her she could stay in her bed with her favorite animals around her, and the big clouds I'd painted on her walls so she could feel like she was outside again. He wouldn't listen to me. Against both our wishes he called the ambulance and whisked her away. I had to sit in the cold hospital room holding her hand while she gasped for every breath. In the one thing she ever asked of me, to die at home, I failed her."

The words came out in one big rush, as if she'd dammed them behind a wall that finally burst open.

Samantha's body shuddered against him. "Her last words to me were it's okay, Mommy." She hiccuped a harsh laugh. "She was the one dying and she wanted to make me feel better for disappointing her."

Hot tears fell onto his chest. Jake pulled her closer, holding her while she cried.

"I miss her so much," she said after a few minutes. "Funny, I should be talking to you about her last day. I haven't talked about it to anyone. Not once since that day four years ago."

"Thank you."

Sami leaned up on her elbow to study him in the fading evening light. "For what?"

"For trusting me with your memory of her. It must be

painful.

"Not as painful as I might've thought. Maybe the old adage is right. Time heals."

He gazed into her clear green eyes, his body stirring to life again. He gripped her hair in his hands, bringing her to him once more. He sampled her mouth, pulling first on her lower lip, then tugging on the upper one. His tongue lightly stroking them. She parted hers, offering him more. Still he nibbled, licked, sucked; feeding in his desire to taste and savor the essence of her.

A sound came through the door.

"Sami?" They both heard Nicky call her.

With great self-control, Jake released her.

Samantha rose off the bed. The early evening sun cast a golden glow over her creamy sex dampened flesh. She was the picture of feminity. He started to get up with her, she pushed him down. "You rest, I'll go to him. Besides I need to look at his wounds."

He watched her wiggle into her jeans. The urge to pull them off her washed over him. He didn't know why she made him want to touch her, kiss her, hold her, but if he wasn't careful he could get very used to having her around.

She slipped out the door, sending him a shy smile as she closed it behind her.

God, he wanted to trust her. It had been such a long time since he felt this close to someone, maybe the very first time since his mother died. It felt good these past two days having someone to share the load. But she was here under duress. How could he trust her?

Going against the Kreshnins alone was crazy. Even he knew that. If there were two of them, maybe they could divide and conquer. But how to keep her safe and still put the Kreshnins out of commission?

He closed his eyes, flopping one arm over them. Contemplating letting her help him without some other sort of back up, was even crazier. The loss of her daughter and abandonment by her husband had hurt her deep inside, but if he let her stay with him, the danger wouldn't just be emotional. Could he allow her to put her life on the line?

The light slowly faded, casting shadows throughout the room. Jake listened to the noises of Samantha and Nicky in the other room. He also listened to the quiet outside his window. The wind rustling the few leaves left on the trees.

Then the quiet changed.

It came so silently, he almost missed the sound of the snow and gravel crunching under the tires.

Jake surged off the bed, standing to the side of the window in time to see the gray vehicle pull up beside the house. Two men stepped out.

CHAPTER EIGHT

The bedroom door crashed open behind Sami. Jake stood in the threshold struggling to pull up his jeans, his gun in his hand. "Get down, Samantha."

"Why? What's going on?" She looked from him to the window, recognizing the two figures approaching the porch. "Oh God, what are *they* doing here?" She ran to the front door. She had to stop them before bullets started flying.

"Samantha, get down!" Jake stepped between the cabin entrance and where Nicky sat on the bed.

The instant Sami opened the door she was pulled into the arms of her brother, Luke. The two of them were shoved to the side, as Matt pushed his way into the cabin. She could only stare in horror as her older brother took a police stance with his weapon drawn with both hands. Her eyes followed his line of site to where Jake, looking sexy in his half-zipped jeans, naked chest and bare feet, took a similar position.

Great. His state of partial dress left little doubt to her brothers what had just occurred between them. Now they had more reason to put holes in him.

"Matt! Put down the gun." She struggled against Luke.

"Be quiet, Sami," Matt ordered her without taking his eyes off Jake. "This guy's dangerous." Matt moved to one side, giving Jake two targets, instead of one.

She pushed against Luke again. "Stop it. Someone is going to get hurt." Her eyes locked with Jake's. She read both betrayal and resignation written there. "Please, Jake. They're my brothers."

"I figured that out, sweetheart."

Sarcasm dripped from his cold voice. His anger flowed over her from across the room like a mental slap. Her heart froze with the pain of it. He thought she'd set him up. Desperation pushed her to fight Luke, harder.

"Sami, stay still," her brother whispered in her ear, grappling to hold her back.

She reached around and grabbed him in the one spot where her youngest brother was ticklish, and pinched. At the same time her heel came down on his instep. He released her.

Sami jumped into the center of the room, directly between Jake and her brothers. She faced two of her three brothers, the heros of her past, with her back to Jake. The man had just shown her pleasure like she'd never known. She'd be damned if she'd let these two idiots put another hole in him.

"Sami, get down!" Matt ordered.

"What are you doing?" Luke looked at her, then to

Matt.

"Samantha, get out of the way." Jake ordered her from behind.

Oh great, a room full of testosterone.

"I'm not moving, until you all," she paused to look at each of them, "put down your weapons."

"Sami, he's a criminal." Matt informed her with that by the book attitude he'd had long before becoming a law officer.

"He's dangerous." Luke just had to add his two cents.

"I'm not letting them arrest me, Samantha."

She cast Jake an angry look, then turned back to fix her meanest little sister look at her brothers. Hands on her hips, she glared at them. "Look, I realize you thought I needed rescuing. But I don't. Jake is no more dangerous to me than you guys."

She held her ground and her breath, while her brothers exchanged looks. Never mind talking sense to Jake right now.

"Sami?" A small, frightened voice from behind Jake drew everyone's attention to Nicky.

"Come here, Nicky." She wrapped her arms around him, turning to glare at her brothers. "See what you've done. You've scared him. Now put those things away. Either you help us, or get out."

Finally, her brothers looked sheepish enough. Matt slipped his weapon back in its holster. Sami, waited until they appeared calm, then turned to beseech Jake to lower his weapon, too. It took him a moment to take his focus off her brothers, but eventually he too lowered his gun.

"Now, if you guys will tell me what you're doing here?"

"Sweetheart, that's obvious," Jake snarled from behind her. "This little show of yours isn't necessary for my benefit. I haven't figured out where you hid the phone, but somehow you called them to come rescue you and Nicky from me. Too bad they were a few hours too late to save your virtue, too."

"Look you," Matt lurched across the room like a charging rhino, Luke right on his heels.

Sami, too stunned by Jake's outrageous comment, barely moved Nicky out of their path before they descended on Jake. She watched in horror as three sets of arms and legs scrambled on the floor in an all-out-battle.

They were going to tear out his stitches. Even if the big jerk deserved to have some sense knocked into him, she hated to see her work torn to shreds by their stupidity.

"Stop it." She grabbed Luke's belt and pulled back until his chin hit the floor. Dazed, he rolled to the side.

"Matt! Jake! I said stop...ooph," Matt's elbow clipped her on the head, sending her stumbling backward to land on her butt.

The two combatants froze. Jake managed to push Matt off him. He scooted across the floor, moving her hand from her forehead.

"Samantha? Are you okay?" The concern in his voice and his gentle touch as he searched her for injuries, gave her a little hope that her brothers' appearance hadn't completely destroyed the tenuous relationship they'd formed.

"Yes, no thanks to you guys." She batted his hand away, then looked at his shoulder. Splotches of fresh blood spattered the white gauze. "Dammit. I knew that was going to happen. Is the male bonding period finished now? Or would you like to go a second round until there isn't anything left of either of you for me to patch up?"

He had sense enough not to answer her question. Instead, he helped her to her feet, then over to the couch. She glared at her brothers, then held her hand out to Nicky to join them once more. Luke and Matt slumped on the opposite couch. Jake stood by the fireplace, buttoning his shirt.

"I will have to look under that bandage. Who knows what damage you did under there." She let her gaze linger on him a moment.

He nodded. "Later."

She switched her attention to her youngest brother. "You just had to call him didn't you?" she said, waving her hand in Matt's direction.

"What do you mean he just had to call me?" Matt jumped in. "You get kidnapped by this guy, the police and feds are looking for you, then in the middle of the night, *he's,*" he pointed to Luke, "the only one you contact? You're damn straight he had to call me."

"I didn't ask him to!" *There Jake, take that information and stuff it in your ear.* Sami pulled Nicky tighter into her arms. God save her from big brothers and their egos. She glanced at Jake. He looked like the poster boy for belligerence. *Make that all men.* "Look, I needed some

151

information that Luke could obtain. If there was some other way to get it, be assured I wouldn't have called him, either."

"What information could Luke give you, I couldn't get? *Police*," Matt emphasized the word, fixing his gaze on Jake, "can usually get anything you need, little sister."

"This is the cop?" Jake mumbled beside her.

Sami shook her head. "This one is highway patrol. The cop isn't here," she suddenly realized. "By the way, why isn't big brother with you two?"

"Dave's back in Cincinnati." Matt crossed one leg over the other, his ankle resting on a knee. "With Judy so close to delivery, Luke and I decided to leave him out of this for now."

Sami nodded her agreement. Their oldest brother would be highly irritated when he found out he'd been left out of the loop, but she felt he should stay with his wife and kids, too. Besides compared to Dave's take-no-prisoners attitude, Matt appeared levelheaded and calm.

"Great," Jake muttered, "a family full of cops."

"Yeah, we're cops. Apparently we take our oath to serve and protect a little more serious than you feds do."

Sami watched Matt bluster from his seat. He'd always hated when someone on his force went bad. If he believed Jake was dirty like the news reports said, her defense of Jake was the only thing keeping her brother from attacking again.

"What did you tell them about the investigation, sweetheart?"

Sami tried not to flinch at the sarcasm Jake continued

put into the endearment.

Matt surged off his chair. "One beating not enough for you, Carlisle?"

"Will you stop?" She glared at her brother, then swung around to fix the same look on Jake. "And you stop trying to antagonize them. I didn't tell them anything. I asked Luke to find out some information for us about the Kreshnins. I can't help it if he's a blabber mouth." Something she said registered positive in his brain. He smiled, actually smiled that melt-your-heart smile at her again. Would she ever understand this man?

With a soft growl, she switched her attention to Luke once more. "Besides telling this Neanderthal where I was, did you announce it to anyone else?"

Luke had the good sense to simply shake his head.

"Did you find out anything useful?"

"Who are the Kreshnins?" Matt asked.

"Boss Kreshnin, is a *chielovek ochen zloy*, very bad man." Nicky spat the words out with so much hatred Sami's brothers exchanged a curious look.

She wrapped her arm tighter around the little boy. "We are all going to protect you from Boss Kreshnin. You don't have anything to worry about anymore. Okay, sweetie?"

Nicky nodded.

"Obviously there's more going on here than we've been told, Sami." Matt leaned back in his seat, relaxed for the first time since arriving. "Maybe you and Carlisle would like to fill us in?"

Sami   glanced   at   Jake.

The look on his face suggested he'd rather die than explain things to her bothers. It also told her he didn't plan to forgive her anytime soon. Well. Fine. She handled the impossible on a daily basis. Earning his forgiveness would rank somewhere between a fractured pelvis and a ten-car pile-up on the hard-to-handle scale. Whether he wanted it or not, right now, she and her brothers were all the help the man had.

"They can help us. I know you think of yourself as The Lone Ranger, Jake. But you're going to need help this time. And right now, they're all we've got." She stood and took Nicky by the hand. "Now, I'm going to go change Nicky's bandages."

She slammed the door behind her.

"Are they going to kill, Jake, Sami?" Nicky's frightened question stopped her in her tracks.

She stooped and grabbed him into a fierce hug. "Oh no, Nicky. They're my stupid big brothers, but they wouldn't hurt Jake." At least she didn't think so. "Let's get those bandages off and see how things are healing."

Nicky climbed on the bed. "Will it hurt?"

"Will it hurt, Mommy?" Aimee lay on the narrow hospital table, nearly swallowed up by the thin cotton gown, surrounded by all the sterile hospital equimpent. The nurse busily prepared the equipment for the bone marrow tap—the very first one Aimee had ever had.

Her heart tore at the thought of the pain her delicate child was about to endure, but she'd never lied to a patient. She wouldn't start with her own daughter. She smoothed the hair from her forehead and kissed her softly. "I'm sorry, sweetie. It will hurt some."

"Worse than when I had to take the medicine?"

Aimee hated the chemo, but had taken it without question. She hadn't even flinched when the nurses had to replace her IVs.

"Yes, it probably will."

Aimee had stared at her with those big brown eyes of hers, then she smiled. "I bet it won't hurt me nearly as much as Mr. Bungles hurt when he had his arm torned off."

She'd laughed at the memory of Aimee's stuffed bear having his arm ripped off by her brother Dave's dog. Trust her daughter to find courage to face the ordeal ahead. "No, I'm sure it won't hurt that much. I promise."

Sami's heart jumped into her throat. She gave Nicky the most honest answer she could. "Not near as much as it did when the Kreshnins did this to you. I promise."

* * *

Jake watched Samantha march off to the bedroom. God she had a cute butt for a traitor. Despite his anger, his body remembered the soft warmth of her as he'd made love to her.

"Now, tell us about this mess you dragged our little sister into." Matt emphasized the words little sister. The guy believed in driving the point home.

Jake filled them in on his undercover roll in the newly emerging Russian mafia, the shooting that led to his kidnapping Samantha, and the death of his captain and mentor, Tom Bridges.

"How long were you under?" Matt asked.

"Almost three years. I had to slowly work my way in from the fringes. This new mafia has little structure."

Matt nodded. "That's what we've heard. Dave says

they're starting to see some of their kind in Cinci, too."

"Then you know they're ruthless."

"Not afraid to maim someone just to prove they can." Matt explained to his brother. "So what's these Kreshnins' game?" Matt asked. "Drugs?"

"Yes along with money laundering and extortion."

"Tax evasion," Luke added. His older brother stared at him. "That's why Sami called me. Seems Jake here, has stumbled into a tax evasion case, as well as immigration cover-up."

Jake sat back and studied the men across from him. Samantha *had* called for information, just like she claimed. She hadn't really sent out an APB on him. They came to her rescue even though she hadn't asked for it.

"Anything else?" Matt asked him.

Jake shrugged. "Just murder."

Matt eyed him with suspicion. "Who's murder?"

"A Russian immigrant who headed the local bank in the Russian-speaking community, Alexi Ivanovich." Jake relaxed into the leather couch. Damn his shoulder ached since his wrestling match with Samantha's brothers.

The younger brother, Luke, scooted to the edge of his seat, excitement shining on his face. "That's the guy who's been on all the local news shows the last two weeks. His family believes he's been kidnapped," he explained to his brother. "He's a celebrity among the immigrant community, guaranteeing stable loans and liberal pay-back conditions. He works through the state government to assure the people meet all the regulations and have ample housing, too. He's a model citizen."

"He was." Jake's statement hung like ice in the suddenly chilled room.

"You saw these Kreshnins kill him?" Matt continued to sound suspicious.

Jake shook his head. "Not me. Nicky."

"The kid told you he saw the murder go down?"

Again Jake shook his head. "I heard it through the gang the Kreshnins were laundering crack money for."

"Which gang?" Matt asked.

"Ever hear of the Haviers?"

Matt whistled. "Biggest cocaine-running cartel in the Eastern United States. Every State Trooper division in their path has lost at least one man to them, our unit included."

"Didn't they come out of Cuba?" Luke asked his brother.

"Yeah, in that wave of refugees Castro let out of prison during the Mariel boat lift in nineteen-eighty. They took over little Havana in Miami, managing to gain control of the cocaine pipeline one city at a time." He fixed his gaze on Jake. "Don't tell me they're mixed up in this mess, too."

Jake shrugged, immediately regretting the action as pain shot through his shoulder. Damn what he wouldn't give to feel Samantha's soothing touch on it right now. "According to the contacts I made with the Havier people, Boss Kreshnin tried every strong arm tactic he had to convince Ivanovich to let him launder money through his bank."

"And the old man wouldn't play ball." Matt nodded as he made the statement.

"Apparently Ivanovich was a true capitalist and something of a philanthropist among the people from the old country. No way would he let a group of thugs muscle into his business."

Matt retrieved a wet cloth to hold to his cut lip. "So Kreshnin decided to get rid of the obstacle."

Jake idly rubbed his shoulder. "My source in the Havier gang said that Boss Kreshnin was searching for the "memory kid". When I asked what for, he laughed and said, that Boss planned on getting rid of the evidence." Jake ran his hand across his face and chin. The minute he'd heard that, his heart had jumped into hyper-drive. There hadn't been a minute to waste trying to get Nicky out before the Kreshnins tired of torturing him. He'd called the captain and arranged a raid on the restaurant, hoping to get Nicky away.

Samantha's brothers once again exchanged curious looks. Matt voiced the question for them both. "The memory kid?"

"That's what they call Nicky. He has a photographic and phono-graphic memory." Jake tried not to laugh at the look on their faces. "The kid remembers every detail of things he hears or sees. Kreshnin used him as a messenger so there would be no..."

"...paper trail," Matt finished for him.

Jake nodded. "The night I called in the police raid to get the cops inside the place, I needed to get the kid out of there."

"That's why he's in danger."

Samantha stood in the doorway, arms folded under her breasts. Jake shook his head trying not to remember how they felt and tasted. He concentrated on her face instead. Anger etched the fine lines around her eyes.

"The only reason he's still alive is they chose to find out how much he had passed on to Jake. Come see how they tried to get the information out of him." She stepped aside so her brothers could get into the bedroom.

Nicky sat there, his chest exposed for them to see. One wicked looking jagged wound with stitches crossed his chest. A matching one stretched across his stomach. Dozens of other minor cuts covered his shoulders, chest, abdomen and back. Black and blue marks the shapes of fists covered his rib cage.

Luke bolted from the room.

Matt murmured several oaths, then marched into the living room, quiet rage written on his face.

Her own anger overwhelming her, Sami gathered Nicky's shirt closed with shaking fingers. She felt Jake watching her, then his hand closed over hers.

"Lady, you've got more guts than most men I know," he whispered in her ear. Blinking at the tears, she watched Jake rub Nicky's dark hair. "You do too, little partner."

"Sami's brati they are not bad men?" He looked at his hero with trust in his eyes. Sami swallowed hard.

Jake held his chin in his big hand. "Don't worry, little partner. Samantha and I aren't going to let anything happen to you. Her brothers are part of the cavalry."

Confusion crossed Nicky's features. "What is cavalry?"

"The good guys, Nicky." Jake laughed, releasing his face. "When this is all finished you and I are going to have a John Wayne movie marathon." He ruffled the small boy's hair again, then left the room.

Sami worked the over-sized flannel shirt closed over Nicky's wounds. To help the healing occur faster, she'd left all the bandages off, smearing them with antibiotic ointment. With the amount of healing that had already taken place, Nicky's immune system appeared strong and healthy.

While that knowledge thrilled Sami, she struggled to calm her own raging emotions. Nicky's situation brought out so many in her she couldn't begin to figure out how she felt. She grew angry every time she had to treat the evidence of his abuse. Then sadness filled her heart with every little piece of his young life he revealed to her. Each time she saw how resilient his body and spirit were, she rejoiced for him.

Yet, a small spark of anger slithered across her spine at the same time. Her Aimee had no such healthy immune system. That's what killed her. And this little boy, who by all standards should not be alive, managed to thrive under the harshest of conditions.

Life sucked sometimes.

Her gaze fell on the boy leaning around her, trying to see the man in the other room.

And sometimes, when you least expect it, miracles happen.

She kissed the top of Nicky's head, then sent him off into the other room. She watched him run out the bedroom door to where Jake stood speaking to her brothers. His hand went to rest behind Nicky's neck and he turned to listen to what the little boy said.

The man might believe he was a loan wolf, not needing anyone, but Nicky knew better. Jake had become the solid anchor in the boy's life. Nicky trusted and admired him. Given his patience and concern over Nicky, Jake felt the same. Like it or not Jake had formed an attachment.

So had she. And it scared her like hell.

Until Jake kidnapped her, she hadn't realized how deep into her own depression she'd sunk, completely isolating herself from life and those who wanted to help her the most.

In the past two days she'd felt more alive than she had since before Aimee's illness began. Both Jake and Nicky touched that spot inside her she thought long dead. If they couldn't stop the Kreshnins and whoever helped them on the police force, she risked having those budding emotions ripped from her again. She didn't know if she could survive it this time.

She swiped her hands at her eyes, sweeping away the tears that stung them. Well, the Kreshnins didn't know it yet, but they now had more to worry about than Nicky's testimony.

"Sami?"

Luke looking pale, stood near the door watching her. Out of her three brothers, he was the only one still naive about the darker side of life. She went to him, wrapping her arms around him for a hug. "Hey, Luke. You going to be okay?"

At twenty-nine, he could still blush like a teenager. "I'm not used to seeing something that...brutal."

"I know. I guess the rest of us have seen some pretty rotten things, so Nicky's torture didn't shock us as much." She stood hugging him a moment longer.

He leaned back to look at her. He always saw her more clearly than anyone. "The real question is, when all this is finished, are you going to be okay, sis?"

She stared at Jake once more. He caught her watching him. His face lost its smile, his features hardening. She knew he still thought she'd betrayed him. The knowledge that he didn't trust her cut deep. But his anger, gave her hope. He had to feel something for her to let her inside his wall of isolation and make him react so strongly to her phone call. Anger she could handle. It was apathy she feared.

"I'm going to be just fine, Luke. As long as we manage to get the bad guys behind bars." She hugged him again, then walked into the main room. "How about you show us what you managed to dig up on the Kreshnins."

* * *

Petrov threw his crystal tumbler at the wall. The glass shattered in a thousand directions. Growling low like a Siberian black bear, he stalked across the room and pounded both fists on his desk.

Ivan glanced up from his newspaper. "What is wrong now, Petrov?"

"Wrong? You ask me what is wrong? Why not ask me what is right?"

Petrov took out a second glass and filled it with Bourbon. He knew most Russians loved Vodka, but he preferred the Americans' Kentucky brewed whiskey. He took a long swallow, feeling it burn its way down his throat.

"How could one small boy cause so much trouble? He refuses to talk under Sergei's interrogation, something even our strongest KGB agents couldn't do. Then he escapes thanks to Carlisle, sending a message to our enemies that we are weak. If I don't find the pair of them and gut them like fish, no one will fear us."

"Everyone fears us, brother. You worry needlessly."

"Idiot." He turned to glare at his brother across the room. "How long do you think Juan Havier will keep the terms of our agreement if he knows I cannot stop one little boy from talking to the government? He'll have my balls in a vice or he'll get his money cleaned somewhere else. The stupid bankers will decide I can't hurt their families back home and refuse to launder the money. Our drug business will dry up on the streets. Even the whores will close their legs."

"The shadowman will find them. We took care of Carlisle's man with the FBI. There is no one left for him to turn to. The shadowman will bring him and the boy to us. You worry too much." Ivan turned the page of the racing form.

Petrov contemplated strangling his brother, but it would make him one man short. Right now he needed all the men from his own country he could trust. Besides, Ivan wasn't who he was really angry with. "I don't trust the shadowman. He is the reason we are in this mess."

"How so? Nicholai saw you kill Ivanovich, not the shadowman."

Petrov stomped across the room to lean over his brother. "I wanted to kill Nicholai straight out. The shadowman insisted we find out if he'd told anyone he'd been with me. That's why. It's all his fault we are even looking for the boy." He switched directions, striding back over the hardwood floors, until he stood at his desk again and swallowed more whiskey. "Fuck!"

Ivan arched an eyebrow at his use of the American word.

Petrov ignored him. Sometimes the slang word fit the moment. The boy knew everything. He forgot nothing. Every deal he'd made. Every amount of money that had traded hands. Locations. Names. Things his partner and even his brother didn't know about. If he didn't get Carlisle and the kid soon, he was so fucked.

He picked up the phone and dialed the shadowman's number. He didn't care if it was his work number. He wanted to talk to him now.

"Yes?"

The one word answer meant his partner wasn't pleased. Good. Let him feel his balls getting squeezed, too.

"Have you found Carlisle or the boy?" He finished the whiskey in his glass and stared out into the bleak landscape. The snow-covered streets almost reminded him of Russia. God he hated winter!

"There may be a lead in the case."

"Tell me."

"Seems our man has found some help."

"The lady in the truck?"

"Yes."

"Give me her address. We'll pay her little visit, sweet talk her, convince her to tell us where Carlisle took Nicholai."

"That may be a little difficult as they are all out of town."

"You've lost them."

"Yes, but there have been some inquires."

This sounded promising. "Inquiries?"

"Let me get back to you tonight. I'll have more time to talk then."

Petrov growled. "Tell me now."

"If you insist."

Petrov growled again under his breath. He hated the American's condescending tone.

"My guess is Carlisle has resources we weren't aware of."

"What happened?"

"Seems someone has been snooping around in confidential files. My contacts also report that whoever it is, they've also been asking some interesting questions."

"Questions? What kind of questions?" Petrov wanted to reach through the phone and tear the shadowman's throat out with his bare hands.

"Questions about you, your brother. The immigration department and IRS have been buzzing with talk. You, my friend, are now on the government's radar."

Petrov threw the phone at the stone fireplace. It landed on the floor in a thousand pieces among the glass shards.

CHAPTER NINE

"How did you convince my sister to bring you here?" Matt asked.

"I'd meant to leave her yesterday when she dropped Nicky and me off at the Farmers Market." Jake stared over Matt's shoulder and watched Samantha emerge from the bedroom. "When Bridges was gunned down in front of us, she drove us out of there like a demolition derby expert."

Matt laughed. "Dave taught her to do that. Said he didn't want her driving like a girl."

"I'd wondered where she'd learned it. She's one tough lady."

"Yep. We didn't cut her much slack growing up. She wanted to tag along. We tried everything to discourage her. It made her tenacious and she only tried harder to be one of us guys." Matt turned to study her a moment. His jaw tightened and his hands clenched into fists "There's not a challenge she won't try to overcome, even if it nearly kills her."

Jake nodded his understanding. Her brother was talking about her daughter dying. Jake felt the same rage that she'd ever had to endure such pain in her life. The woman he'd come to know deserved happiness and peace. He also hated himself at this moment because he'd dragged her into his fight with the Kreshnins.

Across the room her other brother wrapped her in his arms for comfort. Suspicious wetness glistened around her eyes.

I should be the one comforting her.

She belonged in his arms.

The thought slammed into his chest and gut at the same time. Despite the fact that she sneaked behind his back and called her family for help, essentially lying to him, he wanted to pull her into his arms and tell her brothers she belonged to him now.

How had this happened so fast, this need to be with her, to hold her, to want to trust her? When had this desire to claim her swept over him?

The need scared the shit out of him.

His whole life he'd avoided getting involved with anyone. It wasn't fair to form a bond with someone and not be around for months at a time or not be able to share with her information about his cases. Even if he could do those things, how could he put someone he cared for in harm's way? He'd learned early on a man in his line of work couldn't expect things the average man had like a wife and family.

Now he had a whole new problem. If the Kreshnins or whomever working for them on the force knew how much this one small woman and boy meant to him, there'd be no keeping them safe.

Rage surged through him.

Images of Samantha's soft body, bloodied and battered, as Nicky's had been when he found him flashed through Jake's mind. Let anyone touch one hair on either of their heads, and they were dead men.

As he watched her, pain and sadness crossed her face. He wondered what she was thinking as she pushed past her brother. His gaze followed her to the cabinet where she pulled out a cartoon movie.

"Nicky," she called him to her. "Why don't we let you watch something fun while Jake and I talk to my brothers?"

Nicky looked up at him, excitement in his eyes. "I go watch cartoons, Big Partner?"

Jake nodded and gave him a little nudge. "Go find out all about American cartoons."

"Is it Bugs the rabbit Sami?"

"Bugs Bunny? No. I thought you might like to watch Robin Hood." She glanced at Jake, then followed the little boy into the back room. "When we get you back to the city, we'll see if we can find some Bugs Bunny and Road Runner cartoons for you."

"Sami asked me to look into the tax records of the

Kreshnin outfit." Luke said as he sat at the kitchen table, pulling papers out of the thick file he'd brought with him. His brother flanked him.

Jake continued to watch Sami settle Nicky in the back room for a moment. Why couldn't this be his reality? A woman he wanted to spend time with. A child he wanted to see learn and grow. An isolated cabin in the country. Her two brothers.

Okay. Not everything about the situation was ideal, but even he could have a fantasy, couldn't he?

Shoving his daydream aside, he joined her brothers at the table. He sat across from them.

"She wanted to know what irregularities I could uncover. I checked on that and with the immigration office."

"And what did you find?" Samantha leaned over the table, between her brothers and Jake.

The urge to touch her rounded bottom, overwhelmed him. Oh hell, how long did he really have to enjoy her company? Brothers be damned.

He scooted his chair back. Slipping his hand over her bottom to her far hip, he edged her to perch on his knee. Her face registered her curiosity, but she didn't protest.

Matt glared at him. Jake let it fall off him like water off a duck.

God, she felt so good.

Rubbing his hand over her jean-clad thigh, Jake enjoyed the feel of Sami's rounded bottom on his lap. They all listened to Luke bring them up to date on what he'd learned about the Kreshnins activities since arriving in the United States.

Jake eyed Luke suspiciously. "How did you find this out?"

"Most information is available to the person with the right clearance codes."

Jake looked from Luke to Samantha. "Clearance codes? Don't tell me he works for the CIA."

"No. The Treasury Department and Homeland Security." She grinned at him. "Luke's an investigator stationed in the mid-west."

Jake closed his eyes and groaned. "Another cop."

Samantha laughed and wrapped her arms around his neck, hugging him. "Face it Mr. Kidnapper, the fates blessed you when they chose me as your victim."

Jake opened his eyes. She smiled at him. Even in the midst of this mess, she found a way to lighten his spirit. He glanced at her brothers. Angry glares stared at him. "Or cursed me, sweetheart."

Sami swallowed hard as Jake's words caused tears to fill her eyes. Did he really think she'd cursed him? If he only knew how much she already believed that about herself. She inched forward to leave his lap.

He tightened his grip on her waist, keeping her seated.

Okay, he wanted her to stay. She'd stay, for now. Not because he demanded it, but because she sensed he needed her. She'd always been a sucker for someone needing her.

When this was finished, she really needed to get therapy.

"Luke." Sami cringed inwardly at the shrill sound in her voice. She cleared her throat. "Did you find out about their tax returns?"

"The tax returns they file are on their restaurant's business and are completely on the up and up."

Sami's heart sank. "Damn it. I thought we could get them on something there."

"Those are the legitimate taxes, sweetheart." Jake emphasized his words with a squeeze to her hip. Her heart lightened a little at the gesture. "We're interested in what they're not paying taxes on."

"Like Al Capone?"

Luke nodded. "Just like him." He handed a paper to her. "Seems our friends the Kreshnins live way above their means. Homes in the richest part of town, summer homes in Florida. Mercedes for them and members of their crew. Given their opulent life style, I'm surprised no one has started an investigation before this."

Sami and Jake exchanged knowing looks. "Luke? Who could prevent a federal investigation by your department?"

"The Justice Department."

Jake muttered a few oaths that matched the same thing she was thinking.

Matt cleared his throat. "Who in your department knew you were in deep cover, Carlisle?"

Jake ran his hand over his face and beard. "Captain Bridges, his contact in the DA's office, and my old partner, Bill Doyle."

"Bridges is dead. This Doyle, how sure of him are you?"

"He turned in an old partner for taking bribe money,

about twelve years ago. I can't imagine the Russians turned him."

Matt back sat in his chair, tapping his fingers on the table.

Sami knew her brother well. She could almost see the wheels turning inside his head. His mind was working out a plan. She glanced at Jake. He matched her brother's look. Sadness and fear filled her. In another time, these two would probably have been good friends. Now, the fact they were thinking along the same lines scared her. Whatever plan they were formulating couldn't be good.

"The District Attorney contact? Any good?" Luke asked from across the table.

Jake shrugged. "Natalie Johnson, a lower level assistant. She doesn't have much juice, but I doubt she's given this to the higher ups. My assignment came through her. Natalie's mother is a third generation Russian. Her hairdresser's aunt complained about people from the old country threatening her husband's business. They were paying out half their profits. Seems this old lady didn't like sharing her hard-earned money. She told Natalie's mother, who in turn asked her to look into the allegations. Ms. Johnson approached Bridges who threw the assignment to me. I don't know if the girl learned how deep undercover I'd gotten."

"We'll keep her as a backup plan." Matt stared Jake right in the eye. "No need in getting someone with untainted hands in the middle of this, unless we have no other choice."

"Agreed. Enough innocents have been hurt already."

Sami turned to study Jake. "Did you ever hurt any innocent people while you worked for the Kreshnins?"

Those piercing blue eyes stared steadily at her. "Except for leaving Nicky in long enough to get tortured, no. The only people I had to rough up as part of my cover were low level hoods and drug dealers who worked for the gang, Samantha."

"Good." She gulped hard.

It mattered very much to her that he'd held onto his police ethics while undercover. For years she'd heard from her brothers about undercover cops who became as bad as the people they were supposed to be infiltrating. She didn't want to contemplate why it mattered so much to her that Jake hadn't crossed over that line, she just knew it did.

"The problem is that I have no idea who sold me out," Jake muttered. "It's the reason I couldn't take Nicky into the ER that first night. I couldn't risk someone calling the cops and bringing in the person on the Kreshnins payroll."

"That's why you took me." Sami grinned a little at him.

"Yes, it was." He gave her that smoldering, I-want-to-take-you-to-bed-right-now look again. Sami suddenly wished her brothers would disappear.

Luke tapped Sami on the shoulder, breaking the spell Jake held over her. "If I could find out from my end who is protecting the Kreshnins, we could get a federal task force to investigate them."

"That's a good long-term idea, Luke," Jake agreed. "I

have a feeling Petrov Kreshnin has tentacles that reach far into the government. He learned one thing from all his years working with the KGB and the Soviet's bureaucratic system. Low paid, over worked middle management people can be bought at a low price and the information they provide could be invaluable."

"As good as the idea is, Luke, we don't have the time or luxury to wait for some congressional committee to call for a special investigation." Matt shook his head. "We need something faster."

"Why?" Sami, asked, even though she already knew the answer.

"It's imperative we collapse our trap around the whole extortion ring at once, so no one who could be a threat to Nicky escapes." Jake pulled her farther back onto his lap, wrapping his arms around her.

Sami managed to smother the sigh that surged through her at the warmth and security his body offered.

"We need something to draw them out," Luke suggested.

"Something they won't be able to resist," Matt added, staring intently at Jake.

"It'll have to be in an area where we can control the meeting." Jake rubbed Sami's arm and returned the stare as if he could read her brother's thoughts.

Matt leaned his elbows onto the table, his intense gaze fixed on Jake. "We have only two things to offer as bait."

Jake nodded. "It's the only thing guaranteed to get all the players out in the open."

Sami looked from Jake, then to Matt, then finally back

to Jake. They'd made their decision. She clenched her hands in her lap to still their shaking. Her heart sank with the realization of what they planned, even as she asked, "What's the bait?"

"Not what, sweetheart. Who."

She tried to move away.

He held her still.

"No," she whispered.

Jake lifted her chin until her wavering gaze met his more steady one. "Your brothers are going to offer to turn Nicky and me over to the Kreshnins.

Samantha surged off Jake's lap. This time he didn't try to stop her. She stepped away and stared at him. "No! You can't do that. They'll kill both of you."

Jake hated to see her hurting. He especially hated being the cause of her pain. He reached for her hand. She took another step out of his reach. Damn. If her brothers weren't sitting at the table watching, he'd chase after her. Right now, he could only reassure her nothing bad would happen.

"Samantha, they're only going to *offer* to hand both of us over. Nicky will be nowhere near this meeting. He'll be with you. I promise."

"Oh, but you'll be right in the middle of it, won't you?"

He nodded, watching fear and anger flash across her face. The knowledge that his welfare mattered to her thrilled him. It also scared him to death. "Yes, sweetheart. It's important that I help close down this ring. It's my job."

"You could let someone else clean it all up. You don't *need* to be the one doing the dangerous stuff this time." She retreated a few more steps.

"I have to be there, Samantha."

"Why? Wasn't getting shot bad enough to nearly die once enough for you?"

The pain in her words tore at him. "To point out everyone I know to be involved in the extortion ring. It's what I've worked for the past three years, sweetheart."

Samantha marched to the door, grabbed her coat, then looked at all three of them. "Why don't you hang a sign around your neck, saying, here I am, shoot me?"

Jake watched as she fled out the door, cringing when it slammed shut behind her. He stood to go after her.

"Let her be alone for a while, Carlisle," Matt said from behind him. "It's her way. She always walks when she's upset."

Luke nodded. "She likes to work her problems out that way."

Jake sat in his chair, trusting her brothers knew Samantha better than he did. If she didn't return by the time they finalized their plans, he'd find her and make her understand how much he needed to be there to make sure Nicky's tormentors got the punishment they deserved and could never come after the kid again.

"What kind of weapon are you packing?" Matt asked.

Jake almost laughed. The guy worked like a bulldog with a bone, always down to business. Under different circumstances, they'd probably be good friends.

"A P-255 Glock."

Matt whistled. "Planning to put some big holes in people, aren't ya?"

Jake looked into the room where Nicky sat entranced by the movie. Then he glanced at the door Samantha had just stormed out. "Yeah. I guess I am."

* * *

Sami marched out through the trees surrounding the house. Her tennis shoes crushed the soaked leaves from autumn's annual shedding. Most of the early snowfall had melted during the day, leaving mud and soggy leaves in its wake. In another month or so, a snowfall of yesterday's size would linger for weeks.

Maybe she'd teach Nicky how to make a snowman then.

She exhaled long and slow. Who was she kidding? If they all survived this, the Child Protective Services would scoop him up right out of sight.

She slowed her pace, leaning against a semi-dry tree trunk to watch the inside of the cabin. Jake and her brothers still sat at the table making their big plans.

Only, their plan sucked.

He still had to be the lone wolf. He still had to put himself in harm's way. Couldn't he see how much she and Nicky needed him?

How had he done this to her? She hadn't asked him to kidnap her. It wasn't her idea to spend her days patching Nicky and him, get shot at and hide from police. And never had she planned on falling in love with him.

Sami waited for her breathing to catch up with her

heart and her mind.

Great. What a really stupid thing to do, Samantha. Fall in love with a man who is determined to get himself killed in the line of duty.

Sami turned and kicked the tree. She had no idea if her heart could handle being broken again. The scars still felt too new.

As the moon cast its light over the darkened forest, she watched her brothers file out of the cabin. They shook hands with Jake. Three hours before they'd tried to tear him apart. Now they acted like long lost buddies. Even growing up with her brothers, she still couldn't figure men out, much less make intelligent choices about them.

Hadn't her marriage proved that fact? Quiet, staid Michael should've been the perfect man for her. Yet, when she needed his strength to help her fight the leukemia killing their daughter, he'd turned tail and ran. Oh maybe not physically, but emotionally he sprinted out of their marriage. It just took his body a while to follow.

A shiver shot through her as she stood in the cold night air, watching her brothers climb into Matt's truck. She should've known they'd put their lives at risk to come help her. What had she been thinking to call them?

Jake stepped off the cabin porch as the truck pulled out. He made a B-line straight for her.

Oh yeah, now she remembered. Thinking had nothing to do with it. Her heart and her over-active hormones had taken control long ago.

"Samantha?"

He approached her like a lion tamer cornering a frightened cat. Oh he was smart all right. When she'd stormed out of the cabin, he'd been in great danger of getting his head bitten off. Now that she'd had time to calm down, he might only loose a finger or two.

Sami crossed her arms tighter around herself. "Done setting up your own suicide?"

"It isn't a suicide mission." He stopped inches from her. "But it's the only way to draw out all the main players."

"The plan sucks, Jake."

He just stood there, a foot away, patiently studying her, waiting for her to make the first move.

Why were men so cocky about life? She turned away from him. No way was she going to show him the tears that had started running down her cheeks.

She felt him step behind her. He wrapped his arms around her, drawing her back against his chest. A shiver shot through her. He was so warm, so alive. Sami leaned her head against his shoulder. A shudder ran through her as the tears poured out.

"Shhhhhh, sweetheart. Don't cry," he murmured in her ear.

A second shudder, then another wracked her body. Jake turned her, kissing her softly, cradling her face in his hand. "It's going to be okay, Samantha. I swear it."

He smothered her face in soft, gentle kisses. Sami couldn't stop her crying, despite the tenderness he poured over her.

"God, Samantha, you're killing me. Please stop

crying." He led her slowly to the cabin, lifting her into his arms at the door and carrying her inside. He sat on the leather couch, holding her tight in his lap.

Slowly, the heat of the fire in front of her, and the warmth of Jake all around her, seeped into the cold emotional cave she'd slipped into. She relaxed against him, listening to his heart beat against her ear as he held her cradled in his arms.

"Sami?" Nicky's small voice penetrated the mist of emotions still swirling around her. "Why do you cry, Sami?"

She fought to smile reassuringly at him. "I think I'm just a little tired, Nicky. Women sometimes cry when they get that way."

"You are not scared?" The little boy peered at her.

His perceptiveness startled Sami. She struggled to sit up from Jake's lap. It took a minute for him to release her so she could slide to his side. She drew Nicky beside her, wrapping her arm around his shoulders. "Nicky, I'm not going to lie to you. Yes, I'm scared. I don't want anything bad to happen to you or Jake."

"Jake is Big Partner, Sami. He not let Boss Kreshnin hurt us."

She hugged Nicky close. "You're right, Nicky. We can trust Jake to take care of us."

If only she could trust him to take care of himself. Sami peeked at Jake. He reached out to touch her cheek, his eyes held their own promise.

"You okay now, sweetheart?"

She simply nodded, fighting a second, less intense

volley of tears that threatened.

"Let's get some food and rest then. Tomorrow's going to be a big day."

Sami agreed. She just prayed it wasn't a bad one.

CHAPTER TEN

Sami finished tucking the covers around Nicky. She smiled down at his sleeping form. The little boy still had one hand clenched around the book they'd discovered on the shelves flanking the fireplace. He'd fallen asleep while she read to him from *Treasure Island* by Robert Louis Stevenson.

"He's probably dreaming of pirates and buried treasure," Jake said from behind her.

She turned to see him standing in the doorway to the bedroom. Starting at his sock-covered feet, she let her eyes take in every inch of him. His jeans hugged his hips and powerful thighs, leaving nothing to her imagination, including the bulge of his desire. Naked from the waste up, her makeshift bandage, spotted with dried blood, covered his left shoulder. The firelight cast shadows across the golden skin and hard planes of his chest and abdomen.

She licked her lips, remembering how his skin had tasted earlier.

He cleared his throat, and she lifted her eyes to his face. Heat and desire met her gaze.

"You said you wanted to check your stitches?"

Heat filled her cheeks. She knew he could see she'd been thinking about something totally not related to his wound. She swallowed and approached him. Stopping mere inches from him, she reached up to remove the bandage.

Her fingers shook. She clenched them once, before opening them to try again.

Cursing herself for acting like a novice who'd never seen a half-naked man before, she forced her mind to function as a nurse. Jake was simply another patient in need of her attention.

Yeah right and the pope was simply a catholic priest.

Determined not to hurt him, she pried the tape loose from his skin, then peeled back the gauze. "I knew it. That little wrestling match with my brothers tore one of the stitches in front." At least it wasn't as bad as she'd imagined. "I'll still have to check the back."

"Will it have to be replaced?" The rumble of his deep voice next to her ear flowed over her like a warm bath.

"It's already clotted over, so no. Which is a good thing, since we left all of my suture supplies back at my apartment. Besides after twenty-four hours suturing it now would only introduce more bacteria to the wound." She gently prodded around the wound to be sure no pockets of fluid were trapped beneath the skin. "Okay, turn around."

"Yes, ma'am." Following her command, his shoulder and arm grazed across her chest as he moved.

Her nipples hardened in response and sent a new tremor of desire coursing though her. Her gaze shot to his face, and the cocky smile tipping the edge of his lips told her the contact hadn't been accidental.

She returned the smile, then peeled the tape away a little less gently than she had before.

"Ouch."

"Oh, I'm sorry. Did that hurt?" she asked with feigned innocence.

He chuckled. His back and shoulder vibrating beneath her fingers. "Yes, it did. But then I think you knew that."

"Want me to kiss it and make it better?" The purr in her voice surprised her. She'd only meant to tease him, not seduce him. Or had she?

He turned his head, and all the teasing was gone from his face to be replaced by a tense stillness in the hard planes beneath his several days-old beard. A smoldering heat darkened the blue of his eyes. "Yes, I think you should."

She held his gaze and leaned forward until her lips met his shoulder. The heat of his skin beneath her lips thrilled her, and she pressed closer, letting her tongue slip out to sample what she'd been craving moments before.

"Mmm. Nurse, I like your beside manner."

She slowly pushed back and focused on examining the back of his gunshot wound. "There's only one torn back here, too. Overall, I'd say you're a very lucky man."

He continued to watch her over his shoulder. "Yes, I think I am."

The underlying meaning of his words made her blush again. "I'll put some ointment on it to help it heal better and keep it clean."

She moved around him into the bedroom, glad to put a little distance between them. Despite the intimacy they'd shared that afternoon, being near this half-naked man had her nerves on edge. Scooping up the tube of anti-bacterial ointment, she turned only to slam into his hard body.

He grabbed her by the elbows to steady her. "I thought it'd be easier for you to do it in here."

She swallowed at the suggestion. What did he want to be easier, for her to cover his wound with salve? Or strip him naked and have her way with him?

"Sit."

He followed her order, sitting on the bed, with his legs spread in the casual way men had of taking up more space than necessary, virtually trapping her between the bed, his thigh and the nightstand. She arched a brow and looked at him.

He grinned.

Okay. Two could play this game.

She opened the salve, squeezed and squirted a long row of the semi-greasy medication onto her fingertip. With her left hand resting on the top of his shoulder, she leaned over him to work the salve onto his back wound first, letting her breasts press into his chest and upper arm.

He sucked in his breath and she hadn't even touched him with the ointment. She bit her cheek to hide her smile. It was nice to know that after all these years she could have that affect on a man, especially this man.

Gentle, so not to really hurt him, she rubbed the ointment around the wound and between the stitches. "Since I used dissolvable suture, I won't have to remove them in a few days. They'll fall out on their own."

"Nicky's too?"

Her heart flipped again at the concern for the boy's welfare present in his voice. "Yes, Nicky's, too."

She finished, and pulled away from his body, turning to put more ointment on her finger. He grabbed her wrist mere inches from his skin. "What? I promise to be gentle."

"Come here," he said, as he guided her around his knee to stand between his spread thighs. He released her hand and settled his hands on her hips, moving her closer until she was wedged in against him. "Mmm, that's much better."

"Can I begin now?" she asked with a little laugh.

"Yes, nurse. Please make me feel better."

His double meaning made her heart jump a beat and her cheeks burn. "You know I've had lots of male patients say that to me over the years."

"You know why, don't you?"

"I'm sure I'm not going to like the answer. This is my chosen profession after all. But okay. Why?" she asked as she smoothed the cool ointment against his warm skin.

He moaned slightly. "There are two theories on why. The newest one is that we all watched those student nurse porno flicks as teens."

"Really?" she asked as his hands smoothed their way over her hips and down to cup her butt.

"Yes. It was a favorite of most of the fraternities on campus." He slid his hands forward to the clasp of her jeans and popped the snap. "The theory continues that we all fantasize our nurse is dressed in white stilettos, white hose and garter belt, silk panties and a skirt so short we can see the creamy curves of her ass when she walks or bends over."

Sami tried not to laugh at the cartoonish image he painted. His hands working down her zipper helped to distract her.

"There's one problem with that theory tonight."

"And that is?" She slipped her hands to his shoulders to balance herself and looked down into his dark blue eyes.

"You're too overdressed for my sexy nurse fantasy. These jeans will have to go." He shoved them down, his hands caressing her hips and ass before sliding over her thighs. With trembling legs she stepped out of them, still holding onto his shoulders.

"Mmm," he murmured as he slid his hands back up her flesh to cup her ass cheeks. "That feels so much better."

Sami swallowed hard, fighting her own urge to moan. "Wh-what is the second theory, professor?"

"Oh that is the one I prefer. It's the caveman theory."

"The caveman theory...of nurses...fantasy?" she stumbled across the words as his hands slipped up to her waist, lifting her sweater with them.

"Yes," he lifted his hands, pulling her sweater up to her breasts and cupped them beneath it. His thumbs idly rubbed back and forth over her nipples. "Back when men were hunters for the food and protectors of their women on a daily basis, they looked forward to a soft, comforting woman to come home to and have their wounds soothed."

"Ah, the tender ministrations of a woman to the big warrior." She trembled as he kneaded her breasts through the silk of her bra.

"A tender angel of mercy to comfort him in his hour of need." He lifted the sweater over her head. "Oh, baby. I've been thinking of seeing you like this ever since I laid these out for you to wear yesterday."

Clad only in the wisps of blue silk that made up her bra and matching panties, she looked down to see him staring in near reverence at her body. For the first time she felt not just sexy, but seductive. She couldn't remember feeling this desired by any man, ever.

The look on his face and his slow bewitching words had her so hot, she thought she'd melt into a pool of butter.

"Jake."

"Yes, sweetheart?"

"I can't take anymore."

He grasped her by the hips and pulled her closer until he could grind her against his hard erection straining at his fly. "I'm afraid you'll have to. I intend to enjoy every second of this."

Unable to stifle the moan this time, she tightened her grip on his shoulders.

"That feels so good, doesn't it, Sami?"

The first time he'd ever used her nickname and he said it with such passion. Her heart swelled with emotion. "Yes, so good," was all she managed to whisper.

He slid his hands up her sides and around back and fumbled with the clasp of her bra. For a moment she thought she'd have to help him, when suddenly he had it free. He swept it forward, releasing her breasts, then pulled it up her arms as she relinquished her hold on him. He tossed it to the floor and grasped her by the wrists before she could latch onto him again.

"Do this for me," he said and gently pushed her arms backward until her hands met behind her head.

Posed in such a submissive fashion, she felt so exposed, vulnerable. At the same time she felt worshiped, because the look on his face was the kind she'd dreamed of seeing on a lover's face only in her dreams. Was this how super models felt? "Is this part of the caveman theory?"

"Actually, I think this part came many centuries later. This is the knight of the realm being offered the fair maiden theory."

"I'm not sure I've heard this one either."

He wiggled his brow, then bent forward to kiss one hard nipple. He smiled as she shivered. "You see the knight came home after vanquishing the enemy in battle.

The young maiden tended his wounds, bathed him, then offered him her wares in recompense for his chivalrous deeds.

"A gift for the victorious hero returned home?" She gasped as he drew the other nipple into his mouth and sucked. His tongue flicking over the sensitive peak.

"A soft comfort to ease the aching need of his bruised and battered body." Slowly he slipped his hands down her sides and over her hips, his fingers hooking in the scrap of silk. With one sure tug he drew her panties off her body.

From the tips of her toes to the top of her head, she'd turned to kindling for the fire. Each touch of his hand, each lick of his tongue, ignited the flames of her need higher, until she thought she would die from its intensity.

Her legs no longer able to hold her, she fell full force into his body. She dropped her hands to his head, dragged her fingers through the thick blonde hair and lowered her lips to his. With all the passion he'd unleashed in her, she kissed him, her tongue sweeping in to taste him. Cinnamon. Spicy. She wanted to devour him.

A deep moan rumbled from Jake's chest and he pulled her tighter against him, one hand cupping her luscious ass, the other holding her by her thick mass of dark hair. He took control. Forced her to tip her head, his tongue pushing past hers. He flipped her around, then onto her back against the bed covers. He followed her down, his weight forcing her to relinquish to his power.

He'd wanted to go slow. To make her beg. To imprint

this moment in his mind forever. Now he'd settle for nothing less than total surrender. Like it or not, she belonged to him.

The need to bury himself deep inside her nearly possessed him. He released her lips to lick down the sultry length of her neck. His hips pressing down between her spread thighs. Her moans filled the room and she arched her back as he feasted on her breasts, sucking, licking, and biting each tight nipple.

Still lower he moved, letting his tongue trace the path over her soft stomach, down over the feathery hairs covering the apex of her sex. His hands spread her thighs wide, opening her soft folds. He latched onto her clit and began to suck.

"Oh, my God." Her hands gripped his head, her hips thrusting up to offer him more.

He slipped his tongue out to take what she offered. She tasted like sweet honey.

She spasmed around his tongue, and he drew more of the nectar from her body until she collapsed back onto the mattress still quivering from her orgasm. Anxious not to be away from her, he lifted his body away from hers to stand by the bed. He unfastened his jeans, and stripped for her pleasure as she watched him with sex-laden eyes. He reached into the drawer for the second condom he'd had with him, then covered his straining cock with it.

Once more he lowered his body onto hers. Her arms wrapped around him as he sank deep into her swollen warm flesh. Home.

It was his last coherent thought as he moved in and

out, deeper and faster with each thrust. The need to claim her driving him. She wrapped her legs around his hips. His arms strained as he drove them forward. Pounding against her flesh. Working deeper.

Beneath him, he felt her clench. Her body spasmed once more around him.

He thrust again and again. His body tightened.

He lost the ability to hold himself above her. Collapsing onto her as the last thrust had his own release shoot through him, his mouth covered hers in a kiss, smothering both their moans of completion.

They lay exhausted, a pile of tangled limbs. Their ragged breathing the only sounds breaking the room's silence. Sami released her grip on his shoulders and slid her hands down the depression between his back muscles along his spine.

"Mmm. Don't stop," he murmured against her neck, his beard scratching her skin.

"That was incredible." She wanted to stay this way forever. Even his weight on top of her felt like heaven. Too bad the reality of t heir situation would intrude all too quickly. If they didn't guarantee Nicky's safety all their lives would be forfeit. "Oh my God! Do you think Nicky heard us?"

Jake chuckled, then pushed his weight onto his elbows. "It's a little late to think about that, don't you think?"

"Maybe I should go check on him." She peeked around Jake to see the bedroom door was closed tight. When had he done that? When he'd followed her into the room? Why hadn't she noticed? Because the man had a way of distracting her beyond reason.

Jake's face softened. He lifted one strand of her hair, sniffed it, then tucked it behind her ear. "I'll go check on Nicky. We'll leave the door open for the rest of the night."

"Maybe I should sleep out there. In case he needs me." She struggled to sit up.

"Stay." He pushed her back on the bed. "He's used to being alone, Samantha. He'll get us if he needs us." He kissed her with a gentleness that surprised her. "Besides, I want to hold you tonight."

When she hesitated, he kissed her again. "Please?"

The mother in her wanted to be available to Nicky. The woman in her desperately wanted to stay cuddled close to Jake. The time they had together was so fleeting.

Her decision made, she cupped his face between her hands and returned his kiss. "I'll stay here."

He grinned like a kid at Christmas and pulled away from her. Grabbing his jeans he pulled them on, then swaggered to the door.

Just like a man to feel so cocky after making love.

She reached over and pulled on the shirt he'd discarded.

"What are you doing?" He stood in the doorway his lips pressed in a thin line, looking none too pleased that she was dressing as if she meant to leave his bed for the night.

Knowing the idea displeased him sent a little thrill through her. She hated to think this attraction between them was only affecting her.

"I thought I'd put something on just in case he calls out during the night." Finished buttoning it up, she scooted back under the covers, leaving room for Jake beside her. "Is he okay?"

"Sleeping like a log." He climbed into bed and drew her flush against his side, his arm curled around her shoulders. "Samantha, we need to talk."

Dammit. Coming from a man, that statement was never a good sign. She reached up and placed a finger to his lip. "It can wait 'til morning, can't it? Can't we just put the world out of our minds and stay like this?"

"This isn't reality."

"I know. I just want one night. Please?"

He studied her in the dim moonlight filtering through the curtains. He leaned in to kiss her again, then pushed her head down on his uninjured shoulder. "Go to sleep, Sami. I'll keep you safe."

* * *

The next morning, Sami stood out on the cabin's front porch breathing in the cool autumn air. Next week was Thanksgiving, and in a month Christmas would be here. She hoped they'd all be around to celebrate the holiday.

A flash of bright orange passing through the trees on the road leading to the house caught her eye. She leaned to the side of the deck for a closer look.

Her pulse quickened.

The orange formed into the shape of an insulated hunter's flack jacket as it drew near. She watched for a few more seconds. A large rotund man wearing camouflage pants and shirt beneath the jacket, along with a matching camouflage baseball hat, stepped onto the gravel drive leading to the cabin.

She sucked in her breath.

In his hands he carried a rifle.

She opened the door and called inside as calmly as possible. "Jake, could you come here?"

"What's up, sweetheart?" Chewing a piece of gum, he stuck his head out the door, his cinnamon flavored breath tickled her skin and teased her nose.

She pointed to the path. "We have company."

He stepped out in front of her on the porch. "It looks like a lone hunter. It's deer season, isn't it?"

Sami gripped his arm. "I'm a city girl, Jake. And no one in my family goes hunting. I haven't a clue when any hunting season starts or ends."

"Would there be any other reason this guy would come up here?" He reached for his holster hanging on the chair just inside the door. He casually slipped the handgun from it, then laid his jacket over the holster to conceal it from anyone standing on the porch.

Oh, my God. Sami glanced at the approaching man once more, her heartbeat pounding in her ears. "I don't think anyone lives up this way, but Uncle Victor told me that there is a caretaker who looks after the security of the cabins during the off season."

"Go inside with Nicky and stay away from the door." Jake handed her the car keys, deadly seriousness in his eyes. "If anything happens, you get Nicky out of here and to your brothers, okay?"

Her heart jumped into her throat, and she nodded.

"Just act like we're a family on a vacation, sweetheart," Jake whispered, then kissed her. He winked when he released her, then looked at Nicky. "Nicky, try to be quiet, okay?"

The boy nodded, his eyes as big as Sami's felt.

Jake stuck the gun in the back waistband of his jeans. One hand on the hilt, he stepped up to the first step as the stranger stopped just below the bottom one. "Hello?"

"Hey there. I'm Ralph Jones, the caretaker for the Bent Tree Cabin Resort." Ralph held out his hand, his rifle, in the other hand, pointed to the ground. "I didn't know anyone was up here this week."

Jake released the handle of his gun behind his back and shook the older man's hand. "We got in a few days ago."

"Really? I was up here on Thursday. Didn't see anyone." Ralph studied Jake a minute, then tried to peek into the cabin from the doorway. "The residents are supposed to contact me ahead of time when they're coming during the off season. In case there's a problem or an accident."

Sami stepped out onto the porch beside Jake and slipped her arm through his. "That would be my fault, Mr. Jones. My uncle warned me I was supposed to let you know we were coming, but my husband surprised me with this anniversary trip for our family..." She trailed the words off, then smiled at the caretaker trying to look slightly embarrassed by her breech of etiquette.

Ralph chuckled. "Well, I can understand that little

lady. My wife gets that way when I surprise her, too." He stepped back. "Y'all just give me a holler if you need anything. I'm just a mile down the road."

"Thanks, Ralph, we will." Jake stepped back a step toward the door. He continued to watch the other man lumber down the road and disappear into the woods.

"I thought he knew who you were." Sami's voice trembled.

His arms came around her and he held her tight as he leaned back against the door. "I know. I did, too. But he seems harmless enough. Just a man doing his job."

"Should we leave now?" The reality of their situation sank in once more and her fear for his and Nicky's safety grew by the moment.

"I don't think so, but to be on the safe side, I think we'd better gather up our stuff and pack the truck for a quick escape, just in case he or someone else returns. Otherwise, we'll stick to the plan to leave tonight. Your brothers aren't expecting us until later."

She nodded and started to step away from him.

He tightened his grip and stared into her questioning eyes. "Thanks for coming to my rescue." Then he lowered his lips to hers in the softest of tender, yet seductive kisses. Then he released her. "Now, does your uncle have any nails around this place?"

"Why?"

"I need to do a little repair work."

"Probably out in the shed by the generator." She let her fingers caress his stubble covered cheeks, then moved away to gather their things. When she lifted up the files

Luke had brought them, a loose piece of paper floated out to land on the floor at her feet.

"What's this?" She picked it up and stared at a pencil sketch of Jake on a wanted poster.

He peeked at the picture over her shoulder. "Your brothers found that on the internet. That's the same picture they flashed on the TV two days ago."

"What if that hunter sees this on the television when he goes home?"

"Then I suspect we'll have company." He turned away from her to resume gathering up the rest of his files.

"Jake?" Sami reached around him and touched his face. "We could change your appearance a bit, with a shave and hair cut."

He laughed a harsh sound. "Sorry, sweetheart. We don't have time to stop at the local barber's."

"I could do it for you." Before he could protest she hurried off to the bathroom and returned a few minutes later with a man's shaving kit in one hand, a towel over her arm and a pair of scissors in her other hand. "Uncle Victor left these here."

"I can do the shaving myself, Samantha." Jake reached for the shaving kit.

She held it out of his reach. "I know, but you need to rest that shoulder. You shouldn't be lifting your arm above your head for a while. Besides, I've shaved my share of patients, you know. Now, sit."

With those words, last night's conversation about nurses and male patients, and where they had ultimately ended up, ran through his mind, and he was instantly aroused. Since he couldn't argue with her logic, he sat anyway. Changing his appearance might buy them some time later on. Who knew how long it would take to get the Kreshnins?

Samantha lathered cool shave cream on his face. Her fingers felt like soft feathers on his skin. With efficient movements and skill she worked the razor over his cheeks, chin, neck and upper lip, carefully scraping the beard from his skin. Every stroke sweet torture for Jake, who couldn't ease his need to touch her more intimately while Nicky sat on a chair beside him watching her every move.

When she finished the shave, she settled a warm wet towel on his face, soothing the tender skin.

"Now time for a hair cut," she announced, combing her fingers, then a comb through his hair. As she clipped his hair with the scissors, Jake fought the urge to moan. While she worked she wrapped sweet domesticity and gentle sensuality around him. A man could get very used to this.

"You look funny, Big Partner," Nicky giggled, snapping Jake out of his mental fog.

He winked at Nicky, then rubbed his own chin. "Did Sami do a good job, little partner?"

Nicky laughed and held up a mirror. Jake looked in it and realized, she'd gotten his hair quite short, but overall it looked good. Now he resembled a businessman, instead of the street-wise loading-dock worker he'd been for three years. More importantly, he barely resembled the sketch of the wanted man in the news picture.

Jake stood at the kitchen window. The full moon hung high in the dark clear night. He scanned the forest just beyond the path to the door.

Nothing.

Samantha had just finished putting more of the medicine-smelling ointment on his wounds. She and Nicky sat in front of the fireplace bundled in their coats, playing checkers in the only light still illuminating any part of the cabin, a flash light.

In preparation for their departure, Jake had closed down all the lights and turned off the generator. His truck was parked in the trees out back, so that anyone just driving by would think the cabin was empty again. The plan was for them to leave as quietly as possible in one more hour, then travel north to an empty house near Matt's home. Once they were safe inside, Jake would contact his old partner, Doyle.

He turned to look at Sami and Nicky. After his shave and hair cut, she'd cut Nicky's, too. Her dark head bent next to his, the pair giggled as they shared a secret joke. She'd make such a good mom for the boy.

Jake ground his teeth in quiet frustration. If they all lived long enough to get them out of this mess, maybe he could convince the social workers to let her be the kid's foster mom. She deserved to have kids.

A vision of her with a brood of his kids filled his mind. He shook his head and turned to keep watch at the window once more.

Who was he kidding? His life hadn't changed in any

way. He still had a job that put a family at risk. No matter how deeply she touched him, he could never ask her to put her life, and their children's lives in danger daily. That was one lesson he'd learned as a kid.

With determination he fought this sudden urge to have things he'd long put out of his own reach. His mission was to get the Kreshnin organization and whomever worked for them put away before either Nicky or Samantha got hurt. Then he'd walk away. No promises, no regrets.

A flash of moonlight on metal out on the approach road caught his attention. It flashed again. Two vehicles moved slowly through the night. They turned off their headlights as the turned onto the gravel road.

Dammit! That hunter, Ralph Jones, must've contacted someone in Columbus' police department the minute he got home. The hairs on Jake's neck stood up. These guys weren't approaching like police. It felt more like an ambush.

"Samantha, get Nicky into the back room, and stay low!" He watched her obey his order without question, taking Nicky into the back room, both crouching beneath the bedroom window.

He pulled his Glock out of its holster, cocked a round into the magazine, then focused back on the two cars that stopped about fifty feet from the cabin. Car doors opened, and six men climbed out. Dressed in dark clothes they carried weapons in their hands that looked like assault rifles in the moonlight.

Uttering a few curses, he crawled toward the back

room. That was enough for him, he was getting Samantha and Nicky out of here.

Jake crawled faster, landing in the backroom, and shutting the door. Samantha had her hand over Nicky's mouth, both their eyes huge with fright.

"Quick, out the window," he quietly ordered, as he stood and pulled out the screen and opened the window.

"You're coming, too?" she asked as he boosted her up and onto the window frame, then held her hands as she swung out the window and down to the ground.

"Get Nicky to the truck. I'll be right behind you."

Next came Nicky. Just as Samantha grabbed him from below, a loud burst of gunfire sounded at the front of the house.

Glass shattered.

Bullets ripped into the cabin walls from three feet off the ground and higher.

God, he prayed no one had circled the cabin and was waiting for them back there. If so, he could be sending Samantha and Nicky to their death.

Once Nicky had joined Samantha on the ground, and they were running toward the truck, Jake fired a few shots into the back room's door just to keep the hit-squad's attention focused inside the house and away from the woods. Then he hauled himself up onto the window ledge.

The front door crashed open. Heavy footsteps sounded on the main room's wooden floor.

He swung one leg over the window frame, then the other, holding onto the ledge for one moment before dropping to the ground.

In that one moment, the bedroom door was riddled with bullets. Shattered glass peppered Jake. Pain seared through his left arm and the right side of his head as he released the window and dropped to his feet.

Crouching for only a moment, his vision blurring briefly, then cleared. He hurled himself toward the woods.

"They're out back!" one gunmen shouted in a thick Slavic accent, as he riddled the ground at Jake's feet.

Throwing himself behind a tree, Jake took a calming breath then aimed his gun at the window, letting off several shots. The gunfire stopped.

Then two men rounded the cabin to his left.

Jake dropped to his stomach and fired rapidly at the dark figures. One never got off a shot. The fire from the other hit the branches above Jake's head, then stopped as Jake's bullet found its target. Russian curses filled the night.

Movement to his right caught his attention. Jake rolled a few feet in that direction, and let off a serious of shots, then dashed further into the trees weaving his way toward the truck.

Samantha had the passenger door open and the engine running. The minute he slammed the door shut, she threw the truck in gear.

Jake clenched Nicky against his side with one arm, and gripped the door handle with the other hand as Sami wove the Suburban expertly through the forest. Bullets ripped into the trees surrounding them. A brief glance out the back window, showed three dark forms perusing them into the woods.

Jake prayed no bullets reached the car as Samantha concentrated on maneuvering through the trees, heading who knew where. The headlights flashed off one tree after another. Each time they nearly crashed into one, his heart slammed into his chest.

Samantha missed one particular tree that popped out of nowhere by mere inches. Jake let out a curse and clenched his eyes shut. The nose of her truck plummeted, then careened back upward.

He looked up in time to see them speeding toward a ditch separating the countryside from the highway.

"Hold on tight, Nicky." Jake released his grip on the door handle and wrapped both his arms around the little boy, turning toward Samantha, his body virtually blocked the space between Nicky's body and the dash board.

Samantha stepped on the gas. The truck dove over the ditch. Time seemed to stop as they flew through the air. Then suddenly, the front tires slammed down hard on the pavement, followed just as hard by the rear ones.

With superhuman effort, Jake fought to keep both himself and Nicky from bouncing all over the front seat. Somehow, Samantha managed to maneuver the vehicle safely onto the highway, speeding back in the direction of Columbus as Jake and Nicky righted themselves.

"Good, Jake! We do again, no?" Nicky's eyes twinkled with excitement.

God, he hoped not. Jake shook his head, willing for his heart rate to slow to somewhere near the speed limit.

"Not now, little partner. I don't think I could handle it."

"Besides, I don't think my insurance is up to it, either," Samantha said, all her attention on speeding them out of the area.

Jake stole a glance at her. Her knuckles were blanched white where her fingers gripped the steering wheel. Despite the dark, he could see the rise and fall of her breasts as she panted for air. She took several glances at the rearview mirror. Although she might give the appearance of cool, calm and collected, he suspected if he felt her pulse right now it would match his own.

"Are they behind us?" she asked as she glanced out the rear window again, straining to see anything moving in the dark behind them. "Is it a good sign no one is following us?"

"With luck, they'll take a few minutes to get in their cars and circle back around the long way. Cutting through the forest bought us some time." His ears rang and the road ahead wove oddly in front of him.

"And if they catch up with us?"

"They won't do that." He covered her hand where it held the wheel in a death grip. Her voice sounded strangely muffled to him.

"You don't know that."

He gave her a sheepish grin. "Hopefully they'll have flat tires when they get back to their vehicles."

"Those nails you asked me for earlier? I wondered what you wanted those for."

"A little added security never hurt." Jake loosened his hand on hers, leaning against the far door. He just needed to close his eyes. The throbbing in his head grew stronger.

Sami slowed down to just over the speed limit. "Where are we going?"

"We're supposed...to go to a house...near Matt's place," he paused, leaning his head against the passenger window.

"I know where Matt lives. Where exactly is the house?" Sami glanced at him, then back on the road. "Jake?"

It took a minute, but finally he answered. "I...don't...remember what...your brother...said."

"Jake, is something wrong?"

"Find...a place...to stop, Sami." The sound of him sucking in air filled the truck's cab. "I don't...feel too...good."

"Jake? What's wrong?" She tried to concentrate on the road and look at him. "Jake?"

When he didn't answer, she reached over Nicky's head to grab Jake's arm. Her hand settled on something sticky and wet.

"Jake?" Panic welled up inside her. "Jake, were you shot again?"

Oh God, what did she do now? She needed to get him someplace where she could stop his bleeding. What she wouldn't give for a tourniquet and a sterile OR room right now. But hospitals were out. They couldn't go back to the cabin. All her relative's homes were being watched. And they'd get caught for sure if they went to her apartment.

Besides, she needed some place now, not an hour away. She glanced at Jake's pale face. The quicker the better.

CHAPTER ELEVEN

"Big Partner is sleeping, Sami?" Nicky asked in a small voice beside her. Fear edged his words. He'd already lost everyone in his life.

She wrapped her arm around the boy's shoulder and gave him a brief hug. "I think Jake got hurt in the gun battle, Nicky. But I'm going find a place somewhere so you and I can help him get better, okay?"

Nicky nodded beside her.

A road sign popped up in her headlights ahead marking a county road turn off. She had no clue if there was a place to stop on it. It didn't really matter. They had to get off the highway before Jake bled to death or their attackers caught up with them.

Time for an executive decision.

At the county road she turned left. Traveling slowly

into the dark countryside, she glanced from side to side, looking for any building that looked abandoned. It didn't have to be fancy. Even a barn or old gas station would do right now.

"It is dark here, Sami," Nicky whispered beside her.

"That's just because it's night and everyone is asleep now, Nicky," she tried to reassure him, although she felt a little creepy, too. "Why don't you watch the road and see if you can find an old house for us to stay in?"

Nicky liked that idea, and sat forward on the truck's seat. That was one person's fear relieved.

Unfortunately hers only grew worse. When she glanced at Jake, the dark cab prevented her from seeing him. She laid her hand on his chest. It rose and fell easily, although a little fast for her taste.

"I'm…still…here, Samantha," he whispered.

Was he having trouble breathing now? God, she hoped not.

For the first time since Aimee died she prayed. *Please God, find us a hiding place.* Her heart couldn't take losing Jake. Not now. Not after just finding him.

"There Sami!" Nicky pointed to a drive, just as Sami drove past it.

The kid must have eagle eyes. Vegetation had grown over the entrance, almost blocking it out. No wonder she'd missed it. She put the car in reverse, backed to the entrance, and turned in, slowly moving along the grass and gravel drive. Ahead lay a small cape-cod type house. No cars in sight. Good.

Please don't let there be anyone home. Ten feet from the

door, she stopped the car and studied the house. The porch looked to be crumbling from dry rot. Loose shingles slid off the roof's left side. And the upstairs window had a hole in it, a thick tree branch lay through it.

Sami amended her prayer. *Please don't let there by anything living inside.*

"Nicky, you stay here with Jake," she ordered as she reached into the glove compartment for the flashlight Matt always insisted she keep there. Having an over protective brother on the Highway Patrol force meant she'd been drilled repeatedly about roadside safety, as well as always keeping an emergency kit available and ready. For once she appreciated Matt's obsession with preparedness.

Taking a deep steadying breath, she climbed out of the truck and walked to the front door, careful to step over the crater in the left side of the porch.

Wonder what fell through there?

Better not to ask. You might not like the answer.

The doorknob didn't budge with her first attempt. Holding the flashlight with her teeth, she gripped the knob with both hands and tied again. It finally turned with the extra effort. As the door creaked open, Sami flashed the light inside, sweeping the main room from one side to the other.

Cobwebs filled the ceiling's corners and window frames.

Ick. Dirt and dust covered the wood floor and old couch in front of the fireplace. Thankfully nothing moved.

This would have to do. And with a fireplace, maybe she could get them all warm for the night.

Hurrying back to the truck, she shut off the engine, grabbed the duffel bag and slung it over her arm. Then she helped Nicky out of the truck. "We're going to have to stay here tonight."

"It is scary, no, Sami?" He took the quilt she handed him from the back seat, his voice etched with uncertainty.

She hunkered down beside him, taking his small shoulders in her hands. "I'm not going to lie to you, Nicky. It looks frightening, because no one has lived here in a long time. I'm scared by it a little, too. But I'm more scared of not making Jake better. And right now, that's the most important thing. Right?"

Nicky nodded.

Sami hugged him. His courage seemed to know no bounds.

She hurried over to the passenger door to help Jake out. When she flashed the light at the window, her heart caught in her throat. Light sparked off the shards of glass in a cut on his head. He'd slumped against the door, blood flowing from his forehead down over his eye, cheek, jaw and neck. It looked terrible. Knowing most face and head wounds looked worse than they actually were because they bled so profusely didn't make her feel any better.

This was no stranger needing her help in the ER. This was Jake.

"Jake," she whispered, opening the door carefully and reaching in to support his head. "Please, please be alive."

She cradled his head against her chest. Feeling the warmth of his skin against her hand, she felt for his pulse. Rapid, but not weak. Shock hadn't set in yet. She flashed the light at his left arm. A jagged piece of glass protruded from his heavy denim jacket. With any luck it hadn't hit a major artery.

"Jake?" She lifted his head to get a better look at him. "Jake, can you hear me?"

His eyelids blinked, then opened. She flashed the light in his eyes. Reactive and equal. Good. At least there wasn't any obvious neurological damage.

"Head hurts," he whispered and clenched his eyes against the flashlight's beam.

"I bet it does. You may have a concussion." She handed Nicky the flashlight. "You're going to have to shine this on the path in front of us. Do you think you can do that?"

"I can do, Sami." He immediately flashed the light at the ground.

Sami pulled Jake's arm around her shoulder. "You're gonna have to help me get you inside. Do you think you can walk?"

"Will try," Jake whispered, then he lurched out of the truck.

She nearly crumpled under his added weight. Over the years, she'd caught many a fainting patient, so her knees automatically gave until she could handle him. Then she slowly lifted with her thighs. The man was all muscle— hard, heavy, muscle.

"Sorry," he mumbled, and she felt a little of his weight

leave her.

"It's about ten feet. Just don't pass out until we get inside."

He tried to move without her and they almost landed face first on the gravel. She held on tight and dug in her heels to stop their forward movement.

"Hey, no way can you make it without me, so we best do this together. Got it?"

He grunted in reply.

They took an unsteady test step and both remained standing. "Frankly, Jake, this lone wolf act of yours..." she muttered as they took another step, "...is beginning to tick me off."

They stumbled across the mud and grass covered gravel drive to the porch, where Nicky stood holding the light for them.

"Put the quilt on the floor near the fireplace," Sami instructed as they squeezed through the cottage's main door.

The boy hurried to spread out the quilt on the dusty hardwood floor. Once it was in place, Sami struggled to help Jake down, without injuring him further.

"Damn," he hissed as he fell back onto the floor.

"God, I'm so sorry." She helped him move to a more comfortable position. A sound from the corner drew her attention. Nicky stared at Jake with frightened eyes. She motioned him to come sit beside Jake. "Stay with him, Nicky. Talk to him, and don't let him go back to sleep, honey. It's really important."

If Jake really had a concussion like she believed, the

last thing she needed for him to do was lose consciousness.

Sami ran back to the truck, then pulled it around the rear of the house, So it couldn't be seen from the road. Then she grabbed the remainder of the water and food supplies they'd packed earlier in the day. Finally, she opened the rear of the Suburban and pulled out the roadside emergency kit Matt had insisted she always carry with her, especially since she'd started working the evening shift.

Something hooted. A mournful howl followed by faint barking far off in the distant night. A shiver ran over her. <u>Great</u>. Just what she needed. Visions of every horror movie her brothers forced her to watch as a kid flashed through her mind. She ran back into the cottage as if the hounds of hell nipped at her heels, slammed the door closed, and leaned against it, panting for a minute.

"Sami? Is something out there?" Nicky whispered from beside Jake, who was struggling to sit up.

"Is it…the Kreshnins?" Jake asked, reaching for his holster and looking a little on the confused side.

"No. No one's outside." She rushed to kneel beside them. Pressing her hand to Jake's chest, she gently stopped him from rising. "I just got a little scared is all. I told you. I'm a city girl, born and bred. The country sounds just spooked me."

Jake let the gun drop to the floor and collapsed back onto the quilt, his eyes closing with exhaustion for his efforts. "Thought something…was wrong."

What wasn't wrong?

215

The men hunting down Nicky were somewhere out there trying to find them. The only place she'd found to spend the night was this dilapidated building straight out of an Alfred Hitchcock movie, in the middle of who-knows-where, surrounded by who-knew-what kind of wild animals. They had no heat, no water and very little food. And to top it off, the man who'd finally gotten through the wall surrounding her heart, was trying very hard to bleed to death on her grandmother's antique quilt.

Shoving her desperate thoughts aside, Sami focused on the matter at hand–patching up Jake. Again. She set her supplies on the quilt next to him.

"Let's get you out of this coat, so I can see how badly you're injured."

With great effort and little grace, he leaned forward to let her work his coat and shirt off his right side. The blood from the gash on right side of his head, which had slowed considerably, had flowed down his face and neck to soak clean through the collars of both pieces of clothing. She worked the coat off to the left side, but stopped when she eyed the four-inch piece of glass protruding from his arm.

"This is going to hurt," she murmured as she grasped his arm in one hand and the glass shard in the other.

Her eyes held his for a moment, then he nodded.

"I'm sorry."

She pulled steadily. The shard ground its way back out of his arm, the shirt and coat sleeve. Jake sucked in air through gritted teeth, filling the room with a hissing sound.

Working quickly, she jerked the coat and shirt off the remainder of his injured arm. A gash about three inches in length lay along the distal aspect of his upper arm, crusted over with dried blood and oozing new from her removal of the shard. At least no artery spewed blood from the wound.

From the duffel bag she pulled a piece of clean gauze and taped it to the site for a temporary bandage. Then she focused her attention to the gash on Jake's forehead, just beneath the hair line.

"Nicky, can you hold the flashlight like this?" Angling the flashlight, she showed him how to shine it at the wound, but not directly into Jake's eyes, then searched through her backpack for her make-up case and the pair of tweezers she kept there.

She opened a bottle of water and soaked one of the gauze pads. Gently, she washed as much blood as possible from around the site, without causing more bleeding to occur. Splinters of wood and shards of glass littered the laceration.

"Do you remember what happened back at the cabin?" she asked as she worked.

"You two...were out the window. I'd just climbed over the edge...when the bad guys...burst into the back room. They shot the place up...pretty bad." He reached out to hold her by the wrist. "I'm sorry about...the damage to your...cabin."

She gave him a reassuring smile. "Don't worry about that. It can all be fixed."

With a shaky smile of his own he released her hand

and relaxed back on the quilt.

Taking a fresh gauze pad, she wiped the blood from the side of his face. "I'm just glad we all got out of there before they started shooting." Finished cleaning him, she picked up her tweezers and leaned closer.

"Wished we'd been a little faster." He winced when she began pulling out the pieces of debris from his wound. "I remember pain...in my head and arm as I let go of the ledge. Thought I was gonna blackout for a second when I hit the ground."

"Looks like you got hit with part of the window."

He gave a harsh laugh, then winced again. "Felt like it, too."

"I'm going to have to clean both these wounds." She lifted the bottle of peroxide, then leaned over and kissed him softly.

"What was that for?"

"An apology. This is going to hurt."

* * *

Chuck Berry's *Mabeline* played on the cell phone in Petrov's office. The former KGB man usually loved hearing the decadent western rock and roll song. This time he cursed the interruption in his native tongue, then pushed the half naked blonde off his lap. He hauled his body off the leather couch and reached for the irritating piece of Western technology,

"Da."

"They got away, Petrov," Ivan said on the other end.

"How did you miss him? The Shadowman said they were at the cabin. All you had to do was kill them."

Petrov considered throwing the phone at the wall, but the cost of replacing them was starting to add up.

"Brother, Carlisle is slippery as eel. We had him cornered, but he escaped out back of cabin with the woman and Nicholai."

Ivan paused and Petrov had a feeling his brother wasn't telling him all the bad news.

"What else is wrong?"

"Three of our men are wounded. Sergei is bringing them to Danitskov."

Danitskov had been a doctor back in Russia. Petrov had paid to have all the doctor's family transported to America. In return the doctor fixed any or his men's injuries whenever needed and without asking any questions.

"And Carlisle?" The damn American was costing him money, time, respect, and now men. Petrov wanted to hit something. He eyed the girl and leveled a backhanded slap to her face. Petrov smiled. *Oh, that felt good.*

"There was blood on the windowsill he went out," Ivan continued. "Carlisle must be injured. Ilya and I searched the area. There is no sign of them. They just disappeared like smoke."

Petrov growled.

At the sound the girl tried to scoot into the couch's corner and cover herself. He leveled a glare at her and signaled her not to move any further. She released her blouse and froze, like a little frightened schoolgirl. Her cheek had turned red from his hand. The site made him stiff once more.

"What do you want me to do now, brother?" Ivan asked through the static on the phone.

"Get back here. We'll have Shadowman find him for us."

"The Shadowman will be angry we missed."

"Too bad. He has much to lose if Carlisle and Nicholai are not found."

Petrov turned the phone off, laid it on the table and poured a tumbler of Bourbon and stared at the girl trembling on the couch.

Her fear pleased him. He slapped her again, this time making sure he got her mouth. She tried to bolt, but he grabbed her by the arm and flung her back onto the couch. Her puny efforts to flee excited him. Maybe he wouldn't have to send her to the stables just yet. There was still some spark left in her for him to break.

First things first, though. He swallowed half the whiskey in the glass, then flipped his phone over, punched the numbers and waited.

"Don't tell me, your men missed again," the cold voice on the other end said without greeting.

"Your information was bad," Petrov lied. He didn't want the Shadowman to know they'd missed the target. The man's arrogance already irritated him. If he weren't so useful, he'd put a bullet through his head tonight. "The cabin was empty as Soviet banks. I think Carlisle has taken pigeon and gone into foxhole. I cannot...how do you Americans say?...waste him until you find him."

"The cabin was a long shot," the Shadowman said. "I've already taken steps to squeeze the net around them tighter."

"You will do this how?" Petrov took another swallow of bourbon and reached down to cup his growing erection as he stared at the girl's swollen and bloody lower lip.

"In this country, police don't like cop killers, especially if it's one of their own. The morning paper will carry the story that Carlisle killed his captain."

"Why will they do this? Too many know he did not do this thing." Petrov opened his fly and pulled the girl to her knees in front of him.

"I've learned one thing in this business. If a story is leaked to the media the right way, the television and newspapers can make anyone guilty of anything." The Shadowman gave a harsh laugh. "Once the local and state police know he's a cop killer, they'll flush our prey out into the open. If we're lucky some hot-headed cop will do the deed for us."

The other man's icy tone cooled Petrov's own anger. Even during the last days of the Soviet rule in Russia, he'd met few men as ruthless as his partner in this new country. He'd give Cossacks a lesson in barbarity.

* * *

Jake watched the flames flicker and dance across the wood in the fireplace. After Samantha had patched him up—which had hurt like hell, just like she'd promised—she'd dragged some old boxes and newspapers into the room from other parts of the house. He'd talked her through the process of making sure the fireplace's flue was open. Which resulted in her getting covered with

221

soot.

He smiled at the memory. She'd come out looking like a raccoon, one very pissed-off raccoon.

Teaching her to build a fire with the old paper and the wood from one of the crates had been less hazardous. Then she'd fed them a makeshift meal of cold pop-tarts, cheese and fruit, making a game out of the process to ease Nicky's fright.

The woman's resourcefulness and calm efficiency amazed him. Jake knew she'd been frightened earlier when she'd run back into the house. Yet she'd put her fears aside to get down to the business of fixing him and taking care of all of them.

Now she sat, leaning against one of the empty crates, using it as a backrest. While the kid lay tucked in close to her other side, wrapped in a blanket she'd had in her emergency roadside kit, Jake lay with his head in the soft pillow formed by Samantha's crossed legs beneath him. Her fingers ran gently through the hair on his uninjured side as she talked to keep him awake.

If it weren't for the headache, the queasiness in his stomach, and the fact they were on the run for their lives, a guy could get used to this,.

"How'd you learn to handle that truck so well in the forest?" he asked, watching the flames jump and the wood crackle in the fireplace.

The sound of her soft laughter flowed over him and warmed him as much as the fire.

"That's my brother Dave's fault."

"How?"

"When I was learning to drive, he'd just graduated from the police force. He, Matt, and Luke all went to the driving course and practiced all the maneuvers." She chuckled again. "Of course, I had to do everything they did."

"Of course."

"Just making it through the hair-pin turns wasn't enough for them. They made me drive the course in reverse. Then they flooded the course with water, and I had to prove myself on that. Finally, they took me off-roading and made me learn to drive a standard in five-inch deep mud."

"Nice brothers you have."

"Oh, they didn't stop there. When winter came along, they dragged me back out to the course, and I had to do it all over again, this time in snow and ice." She smoothed his hair, and ran her fingers through it once more. "At the time, I thought they wanted me to fail."

Despite the throbbing in his head, he turned slightly to look at her. "I bet they're proud to have a sister who drives like a dare-devil."

She smiled down at him, her fingers tracing his cheek. "After I proved to them I could drive better than most rookies, they decided to put me through their own what-to-do-in-the-worst-case-scenario course."

"What was that?"

"Matt took a worse-case scenario course after he joined the Highway Patrol. He said he wanted to know what to do if an alligator ever got loose in Ohio." She grinned at him. "So the next thing I know, he's taking me into a quarry and teaching me how to get out of a flooded car, or dragging me to the fireman's training grounds to teach me how to get out of a burning building."

"Is he nuts? You could've been killed." Jake tried to sit up, but she stayed him with her hand on his uninjured shoulder.

"The point was to make sure I never would be. My brothers love me. They showed me the only way they knew how, without being sappy."

Jake settled back into her lap, his hand lightly stroking the firm muscles of her calves. "You're driving skills have come in quite handy the past few days."

For a few minutes, he listened to the fire crackling in the hearth. Its heat warmed him. Samantha's hand gently stroking his back and head relaxed him more. Weariness crept over him even though his head still throbbed. He'd love to close his eyes and just go off to sleep.

"How did your mother die?" Samantha asked, just as he was drifting off.

Damn the woman. She *would* ask the one thing that was guaranteed to wake him up, and the one question about his past he wanted to avoid. If he didn't answer, maybe she'd think he'd gone to sleep.

"Jake?"

Samantha's persistence gave new meaning to the word. However, considering how she'd bared her secrets to him, could he do less? Could he show her the same courage she'd shown him? He'd carried the reason behind his decision to remain alone around a long time. Maybe it was time to tell someone.

Not just someone. Samantha. Maybe in telling her, she'd understand why he couldn't offer her anything more than what they shared right now.

He inhaled deeply and exhaled slowly.

"She was murdered."

Silence hung in the room. He knew Samantha well. The silence wouldn't last long.

"How?"

The tenderness in her question teased his memories out of the dark cave where he'd buried them long ago. "My father was working on a case against a car heist and chop-shop ring. His division wasn't making much headway against the crew, so he went undercover to see if he could get the leaders."

He ran his hand over the stubble on his chin. Once started, the words just seemed to pour out. "Somehow they found out he was a cop and followed him home one morning. Joe and I were in school. The crew's leader decided dad would suffer more if they went after my mom, and at the same time, they'd send a message to all the other cops on the case. Mess with us, and your family isn't   safe."

"When I came home from school that day, Dad was distraught. He carried on like a wild man—screaming and waiving his service revolver. Finally, two of his police friends carted him off to the hospital in the back of a police cruiser for his own protection."

Samantha leaned down and kissed his forehead. "I'm so sorry, Jake."

Memories washed over him like a tidal wave.

Kindly Mrs. Davis from next door had tried to herd Joe and him off the school bus and into her house, away from the prying eyes of the other neighbors and the crowd of reporters. They'd gotten pictures of both of them. One callous woman even shoved a microphone in his face for an interview.

Desperate to protect his younger brother, Jake had fled back onto his own porch, drawing most of the crowd with him. That's when he saw her. He'd stood there staring in through the screen door paralyzed with shock at his mother's lifeless, pale body lying on the living room floor in a pool of blood on the gray and blue print rug. Two men in black suits lifted her and laid her on a stretcher.

The police weren't the only ones who'd learned their lesson that day. When an officer closed his mother's unseeing eyes and pulled a course woolen blanket over her face, he'd understood the message loud and clear. Cops couldn't afford to let anyone get close enough to become targets.

The day he'd joined the force he'd started building his world of isolation—no family, no close friends. No one was let inside who could be used to hurt him.

Until now.

He shoved the memories back in their dark hole. Needing to be connected with Samantha, he reached up and entwined his fingers with hers where they lay on his shoulder. He stared across her lap at the dark haired boy sleeping innocently on the rug beside them.

The Kreshnins, and whoever was pulling their strings,

might not know it yet, but they now had two powerful weapons to use against him.

CHAPTER TWELVE

Jake stood in the doorway watching Samantha help Nicky read from the magazine she'd pulled out of her backpack. The late afternoon light filtered through the room and cast them both in an odd old-fashioned light. They looked out of place, almost as if they'd been carried back a century to a more peaceful place and time—a mother   teaching   her   child   to   read.

He turned from the domestic scene, shoved his hands into the front of his jeans and headed around the back of the cottage where the truck sat hidden. No matter how right it felt to stay here in hiding with Samantha and Nicky, he had a job to finish. Not only did his case hinge on what happened in the next few hours, but more importantly, their lives depended on it.

With care, he inspected the car for any damage from their escape through the forest last night. Scrapes and nicks covered the bodywork, along with what he suspected were grooves from grazing bullets, one of which passed just above the gas tank.

Damn good thing Samantha drives like a professional stunt man. He didn't want to think what would've happened if he'd had to get them out of there. Not in the condition he'd been in last night.

Standing behind the truck, he hunkered down to study the wheels and suspension. He was no expert on truck frames, but after their action-movie ride, he'd bet a month's pay it sustained some kind of damage.

Even though he'd kidnapped her and scared her bad— man he regretted that—she still saved his ass four times now. Now not only had his actions gotten her involved in a situation that might still cost her life, but he'd probably ruined her car. He rubbed his hand over his face in frustration. One more thing he owed her, a new car. He prayed this one survived until they'd gotten out of this mess.

Two battered, holy sneakers appeared next to him.

"What you do, Big Partner?"

Jake turned to see Nicky squatting down bedside him, looking beneath the truck. He grinned at the seriousness in the boy's expression. "Trying to see if Sami's crazy driving broke anything on the truck."

"She fun driver. We fly though air." Nicky grinned up at him. "Sami good driver, no?"

The way she'd gotten them out of the ambush proved how good a driver Samantha was, if a little frightening. "Yes, she is." Jake ruffled Nicky's hair.

"I'm what?"

Samantha's shoes stepped in on the other side of him.

Jake shifted his gaze slowly up from her feet, over her shapely legs clad in jeans, the round curve of her hip resting against the truck's side, across her navy pea jacket where her hands stuck in the pockets, finally stopping on her face with its curious grin and sparkling eyes.

Beautiful.

Sexy.

Home.

He wanted to tell her she was all those to him. But if he admitted it, he figured the fates would somehow play havoc with her life just to take her away. No matter what, he wouldn't put her in anymore jeopardy, not if he could prevent it.

"You're good driver," Nicky happily announced from beside him, saving the moment.

"Yep, that's what we just said." Jake grinned at Samantha as he slowly stood, closing the distance between them for a minute.

"I'll just bet you did." She nodded toward the ground, then studied him with that clear gaze of hers. "How do things look down there?"

"I'm not a mechanic, but everything looks like it's still holding together." The urge to drag her into his arms gnawed at him. Instead, he moved around her, and climbed into the truck's cab. Turning the key in the ignition, he switched the radio to a news station.

Commercials played as Nicky scrambled into the passenger side of the cab. Samantha stood between the driver's door and Jake's knee.

"What are we listening for?" she asked, her brows

drawn together and a little of the sparkle gone from her eyes.

"To see if we're still on the police's radar." He idly rubbed his hand over her hip. She lightly caressed the bruise the window frame left on his right temple. Her fingers felt wonderful, gentle and cool.

"They already have a kidnapping bulletin on us. What else could they do? Put out a report about the raid last night?"

"At this point, I wouldn't put anything past whoever is in the Kreshnins' pocket."

"Do you have any idea who it might be?"

He captured her fingers in his hand, and without thought brought them to his lips. "My best guess is someone high up in the local police department."

"Do you have any contacts there?"

"Before I joined the FBI, I had a few, including my old partner Doyle."

"That's who we're going to contact once we get back in Columbus?"

He nodded.

"We go for ride now, Jake?" Nicky asked from behind him.

"No, little partner. We have to wait until dark."

"Why?" Samantha and Nicky asked simultaneously.

"Because…" Jake stopped as the commercial ended and the news reporter spoke.

"New details on the kidnapping case of the little Russian immigrant boy, Nicholai Gregorian."

"That's me!" Nicky bounced up and down in the

passenger seat.

Jake settled him with a hand on the back of his neck. "Yes. Let's listen to what they have to say."

"In a related incident, a source places both the kidnapped boy and his alleged captor, Jacob Carlisle, at the scene of Saturday's shooting death of FBI Captain, Thomas Bridges. This reporter has learned that Carlisle killed Bridges in a shoot out before absconding with the Gregorian boy."

"That's not true." Sami leaned into the truck and turned up the radio volume. "You didn't shoot him."

"We both know that. Someone is using the shooting to turn up the heat on us."

The reporter continued. "Wanted by both federal and local police, Carlisle was last seen leaving the scene of the crime with a woman assumed to be his accomplice and now learned to be a local nurse, Samantha Edgars."

"Dammit." Jake slammed his fist onto the dashboard. "They're playing hardball now."

Samantha drew her brows together, her lip pressed in a thin line. "But after last night's raid, we knew they had my name. What's so different with this announcement?"

He stared out into the quickly fading light. "Before this, you were pretty much anonymous to the local and state police. I'd bet anything on it. Now you're in more danger than ever."

"And that means?"

The hesitation in her voice hinted how scared she'd suddenly become. Knowing he'd put this terror in her life, his anger doubled.

"What it means is now we don't have just the Kreshnins and federal agents on our trail. Now we have pissed off local and state law enforcement agents, who think they're looking for a couple of cop killers. And they've broadcasted your name all over the news, which makes you and your family as much a target as it does me." Seething, he stood, and gently moved her out of his way. Then handed Nicky out, before climbing back in the truck and closing the driver's door. "Get our things together. We're leaving as soon as I get back."

"Where are you going?" Samantha asked. Her brows drawn together in confusion, she pulled Nicky by the shoulders away from the truck.

He held up her cell phone he'd fished out of her backpack earlier. "Down the road to make a phone call to your brother. Our plans have changed."

Before she could argue with him, he put the truck in gear, dust and gravel flying behind him. His enemies had done the one thing they shouldn't have. They'd put Samantha in the path of a bullet meant for him.

He was damn tired of playing defense. They wanted to play hardball by endangering Nicky, and now Sami? He'd show them hardball. When he got done with them, they'd wished they'd never started this game.

* * *

Sami stood on the porch, her quilt wrapped around Nicky to keep the stinging cold wind, which blew in on the storm clouds just after dusk, from freezing the boy too badly. Her flashlight scanned the truck that approached the cottage from the drive.

Jake was back.

About damn time.

The past half-hour, waiting for him to return, had been sheer torture. Every known wild animal on the North American continent had set up camp outside the cottage, she was sure of it. However, staying in the dark, cold cottage to face creepy, crawly things hadn't been an option. So, she told Nicky stories about Daniel Boone and Davy Crockett hunting in the forests, while they sat huddled together on the dilapidated porch. True to his male orientation, the boy now wanted to become a frontiersman—or at least go hunting and fishing in the woods.

She just hoped whatever phone call Jake had to make was worth the anxiety it put her through. Otherwise she'd save the Kreshnins the trouble and just kill the sexy hunk herself.

He turned the truck so it faced the road, before stopping. Wasting no time, she threw their things in the back after Nicky climbed in and scrambled into the safety of the vehicle. She barely had her seatbelt fastened when Jake peeled down the gravel drive again, sending rocks and dirt flying behind them. Once he turned onto the paved highway, he slowed to within the speed limit, but remained silent.

Sami held onto the door handle, with one arm around Nicky. She glanced at Jake. His lips pressed into a thin line, the muscle along his cheek twitched beneath the day-old stubble. He'd closed down again, turned back into bad cop.

"Was there a problem with Matt?"

"Nothing he can't handle." He barely ground the words out through clenched teeth.

"Do you know Davy Crockett, Jake?" Nicky asked before she could push Jake for more information.

The question, so out of the blue, surprised Jake. Sami watched him switch gears from hacked-off-stud-man to patient father figure in a blink of an eye.

"I know who he was. He died a long time ago."

Nicky nodded with enthusiasm. "Sami say he live in woods and hunt wild animals. I want to live in woods and hunt animals when I get bigger."

"I don't know about hunting animals, but I think you'd like camping."

Sami heard the hesitation in his voice and knew he was thinking the same thing she was—*if Nicky lived long enough to get to go camping.*

As they drove out of the rural countryside toward whatever fate held in store for them, she listened to Nicky and Jake discuss all the details of camping, hunting, and the wild frontiersmen who helped settle America. With each passing mile her heart grew heavy. Nicky loved his new country and soaked up every detail she or Jake told him. After all the trauma he'd suffered, he deserved to find some peace and happiness, not be on the run for his life at the ripe old age of nine.

The conversation in the truck died down. Nicky rested his head on her shoulder. She rubbed her hand up and down his arm, enjoying the weight of him pressed against her side.

The coughing wracked Aimee's body, shaking her from head to toe. Sami hugged her closer in the huge bed. Michael, claiming to need his sleep because of a busy day in the morning, chose to sleep in the guest bed, like always.

"Mommy," Aimee whispered once the coughing stopped, "Can I go to Davy's birthday party tomorrow?"

"We'll see how you feel tomorrow, sweetie." She smoothed her daughter's dark hair off her sweat drenched face. Thank goodness the fever finally broke. She slipped her hand down Aimee's face to the pulse at the base of her neck and counted. One hundred. About normal for a child Aimee's age. Good. She let her hand rest there, enjoying the feel of her daughter pressed against her side.

"Uncle Dave said we're gonna go ice skating. I want to skate like those girls on TV. Can I?" She coughed again, only not quite so violently.

"You mean like the Olympic skaters we watched the other day?"

"Yes. They jumped high and spinned all around." She moved her head to look up at Sami. Her eyes appeared even larger in her pale face.

Something brushed against Sami's fingers with Aimee's movement. "Once you're feeling better, maybe we can sign you up to take some skating lessons. Would you like that?" She felt along her collarbone. Something round. Hard. A swollen lymph node? Not unusual with an infection, especially with bronchitis. You're making more out of it than it is. Stop being the nurse, just be her mom. Yeah, but this was the third bout of bronchitis and ear infections Aimee'd had this winter.

"Can I wear a shiny costume?" Aimee slipped her arm over Sami's abdomen and toyed with the satin button there.

"Yes. We'll buy you a shiny costume. What color do you want?" *Sami let her arm slide down her daughter's shoulder to the top of her arm.*

"Pink." Her favorite color.

"Pink it is."

Aimee's breathing became slower, deeper. She slept, again.

Sami stroked her shoulder and upper arm in a soothing manner. Her finger met another round engorged lymph node. She searched her memory for everything she knew about infections. Did lymph nodes only enlarge around the area of the infection? Or did they enlarge all over the body? Damn, she wished she'd paid more attention to that part of her nursing classes.

Like any nurse worth the name her mind immediately jumped to the worse possible scenario. What were the symptoms of cancer? Weight loss. Aimee lost a lot of weight this winter from all her illnesses, but surely only because of the multiple. Another symptom—easily prone to infections.

Fatigue. There wasn't a day gone by that Aimee didn't need to nap or just plain fall asleep after an hour of playing. Pallor. She looked down at her daughter's pale, pale skin resting against the dark green of her pajamas.

No! Stop this. She's just a little under weather. All kids get sick in the winter. Take her to the doctor tomorrow. Let him tell you you're being an over protective mother and seeing more than is there.

ACUTE LYMPHOCYTIC LEUKEMIA. The diagnosis stood out in her mind like a flashing neon sign the moment they'd come out of the doctor's mouth—as if they advertised something. They had. They'd announced the end of their normal life and a battle they'd never been able to win.

Sami glanced down at Nicky. His battle wasn't a done deal. At least with Jake, her and her brothers on his side, the kid had a fighting chance to live a happy life. She was glad. He deserved so much goodness to come to him. He was lucky Jake was one of the good guys.

Even if Jake chose to close her out once more, she was glad he didn't refuse Nicky's attention. The two of them were made for each other. Nicky deserved a father, someone to guide him and love him. Jake needed someone to force him to love and care for him, a son, a family.

She shook her head, trying to clear the image of she and Jake sitting around a campfire with half a dozen children, the oldest of which was Nicky. But the vision played over and over in her mind as the tires bounced on the cracks in the highway's decade-old asphalt.

Weary from the constant threat to their lives and not sleeping in her own bed for days, she sighed.

A moment passed. Then Jake covered her cold hand in his warm one, squeezing it for a moment, then lacing his fingers with hers. The act meant to comfort her, touched her to her soul and yet saddened her at the same time. She tried to blink back the tears that jumped into her eyes.

He offered comfort, but he wasn't planning on loving her, or staying with her. For some unknown reason he believed he didn't have the right to love or have a family. She ached to convince him otherwise. If anyone deserved a wife and children, it was him.

Jake felt her fingers relax slightly in his, but not enough to signal she wanted him to release his hold on her. He hated to admit how good it felt to hold her hand. When he reached out to touch her, he'd only meant to reassure her and ease her fears. Funny thing the moment he took her hand, his own body had relaxed, too. The anger at their situation almost completely gone.

What was it about this one woman that affected him so deeply? Maybe the stress of running for their lives or the resulting Adrenaline rush that caused all these powerful feelings. Whatever the reason, for now he'd indulge himself in having her near him. When all this ended and his loneliness got too much for him, he'd pull out his memories of Samantha.

He chanced a glance at her in the dark truck cab. With their fingers still entwined, she used her other hand to stroke Nicky's head. Her dark hair fell over her shoulders, almost covering the side of her face as she stared out into the dark countryside.

Neither gorgeous and statuesque, nor petite and cute, Samantha fit the every-guy's-sister category. Most men wouldn't take a second glance at her on the street or in a bar. Given different circumstances he doubted he ever would've noticed her, either. That would've been such a waste, too. These last few days he couldn't imagine getting through them without her courage, stubbornness or passion.

His body tightened in response to thoughts of her passion. In self-preservation, he released her hand, fixed his gaze once more on the road ahead and eased himself closer to his door.

He felt her eyes studying him again. It took all his will power to keep his mind on driving. He knew his actions confused her. Hell they confused him, too. When she turned her attention on Nicky once more, Jake let out the breath he'd been holding.

Signs for the I-75 entrance flashed on the side of the highway.

"Can you get your cell phone our of your bag?" he asked her, a plan formulating in his mind.

"Uhm, yeah." She pulled her backpack onto her lap. Searching through it, she produced the phone. "Why do you want it? I thought you said the FBI could trace the signal back to us."

"I'm counting on it. Don't turn it on until I tell you."

He maneuvered the truck onto the interstate.

"You're heading south, Jake. Columbus is the other direction."

"I know, sweetheart." He grinned at her. "We're going to play fox to their hounds."

"Huh?"

He couldn't resist chuckling at her confusion. "We're going to cover our tracks and throw them off our scent."

"Oh! Make them think we're heading toward Cincinnati and my family."

"Right. Then we'll double back into Columbus."

* * *

Thirty minutes later, they eased in behind an eighteen-wheeler pulling off the highway and into an all-night diner's parking lot. Jake pulled into a slot and waited for the trucker to head inside.

"Watch me from the window." He retrieved her baseball cap from the back seat and pulled it down over his face. "When I stretch my arms over my head, call your brother, Matt. Tell him about the ambush. Then tell him we're on our way to Cincinnati and to meet us there to discuss plan B." He leaned closer and indulged himself in one long kiss. Then he got out of his side of the truck. "And Samantha, leave the phone on. Got it?"

"Ambush. Cincinnati. Plan B. Phone on. Got it."

"Oh, and one more thing."

She looked at him curiously. "What?"

"What do you like on your hamburger?" He grinned at her.

She shook her head. "Leave it to a man to think of food right now. Cheese, mustard and lots of pickles."

Trying to appear casual, he shoved his hands into the front pockets of his jeans and sauntered into the diner. He straddled a stool at the counter three seats away from the trucker who was busy studying the menu. The trucker ordered a slice of pie and coffee, asking the waitress to fill his thermos.

When the waitress approached Jake, he ordered three cheeseburgers, fries and milkshakes to go. He pulled the sports section over and read the results of Sunday's football games, watching out of the corner of his eye as the trucker ate his pie. When the waitress returned with his bag of food, Jake stood and stretched, hoping Samantha saw his signal. Then he dodged the trucker, who was headed to the john, and paid for their food at the register.

Samantha still held the phone against her ear when Jake tapped on her window. He signaled he wanted to talk for a minute. They traded the bag of food for the phone.

"Matt? Yeah, they're both fine," he said still standing outside the car. Don't call this phone okay? Yeah, it isn't going to be clean anymore. Right. We'll contact you when we get there." He clicked the disconnect button, but left the phone on to receive calls, then looked at Samantha. "Do you have any tape in that bag of yours?"

"I'm a nurse. I always have tape," she explained as she rummaged in her bag once more. She fished out a roll of hospital tape, the kind that tears easily but sticks to everything, and handed it to him.

He jogged around the back of the Suburban to the rear of the eighteen-wheeler. Then he secured the phone to the bottom of the big rig. Whistling, he shoved his hands back in his pockets and approached the driver's side of Samantha's car, stopped and kicked the tires to give anyone watching the impression he was just a weary traveler who'd been inspecting the car. He slipped back into the driver's seat and took the burger Samantha handed him.

"That poor trucker is going to have a heart attack when the FBI pull him over." She giggled, then bit into her sandwich.

Jake scooped a drop of mustard off the corner of her lip with his finger. "Yeah, but it will be a great story for him to tell his kids and grandkids."

"What is this called?" Nicky asked, eyeing the cold drink in his hand with doubt.

"It's a chocolate milkshake," Jake explained. "Try it. I bet you'll like it."

He took a tentative sip, then grinned at both Samantha and Jake. "Da. I like."

The pleasure on his face and the enthusiasm with which he tackled the all-American meal touched a spot deep inside Jake. The kid had lived such a hard life in the few years he'd been on the planet. Yet, he still had an innocence about him Jake wanted to protect.

Once this case had ended, where would Nicky go? To some foster home, probably. Would they treat him well? Take him fishing and camping like he so badly wanted? Would they teach him about his country, how to hit a curve ball? Would they love him? Or would it be another nightmare he'd have to learn to survive?

Samantha brushed Nicky's hair out of his eyes as he took another long sip of the shake. "Don't drink it too fast or you'll get brain-freeze."

"Brain-freeze?" Nicky stopped slurping, his eyebrows pulled down in a deep V.

"It's something my brothers used to get all the time. If you eat or drink ice cream too fast, you get a headache right here." She laughed and pointed to Nicky's forehead.

They belong together—Nicky and Samantha.

Jake watched the two of them. He couldn't remember a time when he enjoyed being with anyone as much as he had Samantha and Nicky. He ought to just keep driving—take them as far away from this mess as he could. In another century he would have. But as an FBI agent, he knew there really wasn't any place left for them to hide.

They had to face the people hunting them. The sooner, the better.

They finished their meal in companionable silence, watching the trucker return and pay for his dinner. As the trucker passed where they were parked on his way to his rig, Jake stretched his arm over the back of the seat, toying with a strand of Samantha's hair. He rubbed the silky strands between his fingers.

"Do you have any idea where we're going once we get back in the city?" She wrapped her lips around the straw and sipped on her drink. Jake tamped the urge to taste her again.

"Your brothers and I decided to contact my old partner."

"Doyle?"

Jake nodded. "We planned to contact him in the morning. But now, it looks like you, Nicky and I are going to drop in on him for the night."

"What's Doyle like?"

"You know Joe Friday on the TV show Dragnet?"

She laughed. "Don't tell me he's that much of a straight arrow?"

"Worse. Doyle makes Friday look like Barney Fife."

"Oh no." She laughed harder.

Nicky looked from one adult to another. "This is good guys, Jake? This Barney Fife and Friday?"

Jake rumpled his hair, winking at Sami. "Sure are Nicky. And so is Doyle. He's going to help us catch the Kreshnins."

"Good. Boss *Kreshnin vnyabrachneye ribynoek.*"

Jake laughed and put the truck in reverse. "That he is, little partner. That he is."

Samantha drew her eyebrows together in question. "What did he call Kreshnin?"

"The Russian equivalent for bastard."

She nodded her agreement with Nicky's assessment.

They headed back North to the city.

* * *

Jake drove through the dark residential section of Clintonville in which Doyle resided. When Doyle's wife of twenty years had decided to get in touch with her feminine side, divorcing him to live with her lesbian lover, Jake had helped his old partner move into this house.

All the homes sat back from the curbs of the quiet, tree-lined streets. Many of them were built in the 1920's and 1930's at a time when the area boasted to be a very upscale part of the city. Due to the trend of home remodeling that gripped the north-side community in the seventies and eighties, many professionals invested in and still lived in the homes.

Several years ago, after joining the Bureau, Jake contemplated looking for a home here, too. Even though he'd decided not to have a family, the investment potential seemed like a sound choice at the time. Then the undercover assignment fell onto his desk and he put all his plans on hold.

Scanning the street for unmarked police cars or utility vans out of place this late at night, Jake passed Doyle's house three times. Finally, reassured by the lack of obvious surveillance around Doyle, Jake turned into the alley behind the house.

He drove past the back of Doyle's place, parking the truck between two giant fir trees.

"Everything looks quiet," he said to Samantha as he turned off the engine. "You and Nicky stay here, while I go check it out up close."

"No, Big Partner. We go with you." Nicky's eyes widened and filled with tears.

"Hey, little partner, you'll be fine here with Samantha." He patted Nicky on the shoulder. "I'm just gonna go make sure the coast is clear."

"You come back *skora*?"

Jake nodded with great solemnity. "I'll be *skora*, quick. But you have to promise to do something for me while I'm gone. Okay?"

Nicky leaned closer. "What something I do for you?"

Jake caught Samantha's eye as he whispered to Nicky. "I need you to guard Sami while I'm gone. Don't let anything happen to her. Do you think you can do that for me?"

"Da. I do, Jake." Nicky nodded very solemnly. The fear in his deep blue eyes lessened.

With a squeeze to Samantha's hand Jake eased the door of the truck shut. The soft crunch of gravel beneath his feet broke the stillness of the night. Jake prayed no dogs would announce his presence in the alley before he got a chance to reconnoiter the situation at Doyle's.

Nothing stirred in the alley or the bushes lining the back of Doyle's yard. Jack eased the gate open, cursing the almost imperceptible creak from the slightly rusted hinges. He left it propped open with a brick he found lying next to the drive. If everything checked out ok, he didn't want to have the gate creaking back and forth when he brought Samantha and Nicky from the truck.

He hurried to the side of the house. Standing on the balls of his feet, he peered inside the kitchen window. True to form, neat as a pin, but no movement. The clock on the wall showed eleven-ten. Doyle was such a creature of habit. From eleven until eleven-thirty each night he sat in front of the news.

Jake worked his way to the front of the house, glancing into one of the living room windows. Yep, there he sat, drinking his nightly glass of milk. Jake bit down on the smile that played along his lips. Three things you could count on in life, the sun rising in the east and setting in the west, the moon going through its cycles, and Bill Doyle drinking warm milk in front of the channel ten news each night.

With quiet speed, Jake returned to Nicky and Samantha. She thrust one of the two backpacks at him when he opened the passenger door. God love the woman. She hadn't waited for his return, but used the time to pack everything they needed to take with them. Jake locked the truck, then taking Nicky's hand and signaling them to be as quiet as possible, he led them to Doyle's rear door. He tried the doorknob.

Locked.

Samantha motioned for him to move out of the way. With a brow raised in question he inched back just enough to allow her to squeeze between him and the door. The warm scent of her vanilla shampoo wafted up to him. Her shoulder brushed his chest. Distracted by her nearness, he almost missed her actions.

She'd slipped the edge of a credit card into the door-jamb equal to the height of the door knob. With a wiggle or two, the door quietly popped open.

"I learned that from Matt, too" she whispered.

Reaching around her, Jake pulled her behind him. He motioned for them to follow him in the house. He closed the door with a soft click.

Another click sounded from the corner of the room. A gun being cocked.

The trio froze.

"Adding breaking and entering to your offenses, Rookie?" a gravel edged voice asked.

CHAPTER THIRTEEN

"Hello, Doyle." Jake edged Nicky and Sami behind him, then with both hands up where Doyle could see them he turned to face his old partner. "How did you hear me outside?"

Sami peeked around Jake into the dark room. A lean figured man with a military haircut stood in the far corner of the room. The light from the hallway cast him in dark planes and angles, and the glint of light shone on wire rimmed glasses.

"You still crash through a surveillance like a bull in a china shop." Easing the hammer on the gun back into place, Doyle slowly lowered his weapon. "Who's that hiding behind you? Your accomplice and kidnap victim?"

Jake lowered his hands. He stepped aside to pull Sami forward. "This is Samantha Edgars. She's an innocent person I kidnapped out of a parking lot. Now she's mixed up in this mess and it's my fault."

Sami wanted to pinch him. He might have kidnapped her, but she'd chosen to help him. The fault for *their* dilemma didn't lie at his feet. It belonged completely to the people who shot him and tortured Nicky.

Doyle didn't say anything in response to Jake's confession. He stood with his arms crossed, waiting like a schoolmaster for his pupil to finish presenting him with the facts.

"And this," Jake put his hand on Nicky's neck, urging him forward, "is Nicholas. He's the reason we're here."

Doyle studied Sami and Nicky for a long moment, then nodded as if they'd passed some silent test. "Let's go into the den and get comfortable. Then you can fill me in on how you got yourselves into this pile of manure." With an odd rotating of his left leg and hip he limped past them, leading the way down the dark hall to his den.

Sami hesitated with her mouth open to ask the thousand questions flashing through her mind at warp speed. As if reading her thoughts, Jake silenced her with a finger to her lips and a shake of his head.

"Later," was all he said. And with a not-so-gentle nudge, he pushed her down the hall behind Nicky and Doyle.

This tendency of his to force her to do things without question, like patch up knife and gun wounds, jump out of windows and follow strangers, irritated her to her toes. One of these days she'd get even with him for it. Just before she stepped into the den, she paused and stuck her tongue out at him.

"Is that an offer, Samantha?" He lifted an eyebrow in that cocky arrogant fashion of his.

She really, really wanted to slug him. And if he pushed her one more time, she might just do it. Narrowing her eyes in warning, she gritted her teeth and marched into the den.

Not really sure what she expected out of detective Doyle's den, the high-tech room that greeted her didn't quite fit what she'd imagined. Two computers, a fax, and copiers lined one wall and corner. Dark plantation shutters covered the single window, preventing anyone from observing the room's contents from outside. Two phones, an answering machine and a police scanner sat on a corner desk. And against the last wall stood a large screen TV with two overstuffed wingback chairs and an ottoman arranged in front of it.

"How is the private security business going these days, Doyle?" Jake asked, leaning against the doorjamb.

"Not the same as putting the perps behind bars, but I have enough work to keep me busy." Doyle punched a button on the remote and a video game popped onto the big screen. He handed Nicky a small hand-held controller. "Why don't you sit here and play, while I talk to Jake and his lady friend."

"Her name is, Sami," announced Nicky as he scrambled onto the ottoman, his attention completely focused on the video game. For the first time since Sami met him, Nicky finally looked like any other nine-year old.

"Sit here, young lady." The older man turned around one of the wingback chairs for her, and then one for himself. "Rookie, you can sit in one of the computer chairs if you want."

"Thanks, Doyle." Jake pulled out a chair, turned it backward so he could straddle it, lean forward and rest his injured arm across the seatback in front of him.

As Jake explained their dilemma to his old partner, Sami's trained nurse's mind noted how exhausted Jake's face appeared with its drawn features and dark smudges beneath his eyes. A bruise had formed on his forehead where he'd been hit with the window debris the day before. The white butterfly strips she'd used to close it looked ghoulish against the purple and green skin.

His slumped body posture spoke volumes. He needed rest and wanted this to end. For a brief moment his eyes shifted to Nicky. In that unguarded instant she read both a longing and deep worry.

Funny, in less than a week she could read this intense man's thoughts so easily at times. In all the years she'd lived with her ex-husband, she doubted she ever had such insight into his mind or feelings.

"And now you need my help." Doyle's gravely voice penetrated Sami's reverie, bringing her back to the conversation.

"I hate to ask it, old man, but I have nowhere else to turn. The most important thing is to keep Nicky safe." Jake ran his hand through his hair. The muscle in his jaw flexed repeatedly.

He hated asking for help. She wondered if he hated asking Doyle in particular or just anyone in general. If she hadn't phoned her brothers on the sly, she knew he never would've agreed to their help.

"What do you need from me, Rookie?" Doyle propped his left leg carefully on the ottoman.

Jake hesitated a moment as if gathering his thoughts. "I need a conduit to both the feds and the Kreshnins. You have a pretty extensive snitch network. Any chance one of them could get to someone in the Kreshnin organization for us?"

"They're a pretty closed group, those Russians, Rookie."

"Believe me, I know that. It took me nearly three years to infiltrate even their outer edges. I met Petrov Kreshinin the month before this whole mess blew up in my face." Absently Jake rubbed his shoulder.

Suddenly curious, Sami straightened. "When did this murder take place?"

"Back in September. Why?" Jake leaned one arm on his chair, the other stroking his beard.

"How long before this raid did you hear the boy had witnessed the murder?" Doyle picked up on Sami's train of thought.

"The week before." Jake's hand gripped his knee, the knuckles tightening. He inhaled deeply, his eyes narrowing in anger. "Whoever tried to ambush me didn't want me to talk to Nicky."

"And between patching his wounds, the fever and being on the run, you really haven't had a chance to find out exactly what he knows, have you?" Sami asked.

Doyle slowly nodded. "Seems to me it'd be a good idea to find out exactly what your young friend saw that night."

Jake sat next to Nicky. "Little partner, take a break from the game a sec and help us with a problem."

"But the gorilla's winning." Nicky hunched lower over the controller, his finger flying feverishly over the buttons.

Jake reached between his arms to push the pause button. "Now, Nicholai. This is important. The game will still be there when we're done talking."

Nicky slumped on the ottoman, his lips pursed and his eyebrows drawn downwards in a scowl. Sami hid her own smile at the kid's first American snit. She wondered how Jake planned to get the information out of him now.

Jake sat cross-legged on the floor in front of the ottoman. He flicked Nicky's shoelaces a few times. "Lil' partner, I'm tired of all this running around, how about you?"

Nicky nodded, his fingers trying to catch Jake as they played shoestring tag.

"You remember the night you saw Boss Kreshnin hit the man on the head and put him in the car trunk?"

"Da," the boy muttered.

"Do you remember if anyone else was there?" Jake leaned closer.

Nicky nodded, seeming to shrink further in his seat.

Sami scooted to the edge of her chair, anxious to hear what he'd seen, but worried the memories might hurt him. "Can you tell us who?"

"Who was there, Nicky?" Jake laid a hand on the boy's knee.

"Boss Kreshnin, and Ivan."

Jake glanced at Sami and Doyle. "Malenki Ivan Kreshnin is the younger brother of the Boss. Nicky, was anyone else there?

"A little man. He was very…how you say? Mad."

Jake squeezed Nicky's knee reassuringly. "Do you know his name?"

Nicky shrugged. "He was Madson."

"Madson?" Jake turned his head, and quirked an eyebrow at Doyle. "Do you know a Madson on the force?"

The older man thought a few minutes, then shook his head. "Unless he's new the last few years. The name isn't one from the old days, that's for sure."

"Maybe he's a transfer in, or from a division neither one of you are familiar with," Sami suggested.

Jake shook his head this time. "Doyle sat on the Fraternal Order of Police benefits committee before he retired. You knew everyone on the force then, didn't you?"

"Not personally, but we did see each file of every member. The name Madson doesn't ring a bell." Doyle lifted his left leg off the ottoman with practiced care, then limped to his computer. "I downloaded the old files into my hard drive just before I left the force. Come over here, Nicky. Let's see if anyone pops up you recognize."

Nicky's eyes widen as images flashed onto the computer screen. He hopped off the ottoman and ran to pull the chair Jake had vacated up beside Doyle. Jake joined them with a third chair to the side.

Watching them, anguish filled Sami's chest. All three shared something special. Nicky was an orphan now. Doyle had his electronic cave for company. Jake spent his life living a lie.

They were all loners.

Shaking off the sadness, she wandered down the hall to the kitchen. Flicking on the light she found the coffee maker and filters. It would probably be a long night.

Looking out the closed slats of the kitchen blinds, she watched the clouds flit past the moon, thinking about the lonely existence of the men and boy in the other room. It hit too close to home for her peace of mind.

Ever since Aimee died she'd found herself more and more isolated. Oh, she didn't blame it on anyone in particular. Although Michael's leaving didn't help the situation much. No, she knew she had only herself to blame.

Her grief had moved in like an indolent relative, parked itself in her life and took over every aspect of it. She'd made it her best friend. Daily, she had breakfast with it, took it everywhere with her and at night it was the last thing she thought about before exhaustion set in. She'd lived with it so long every joint and muscle ached from it.

Finally she'd had enough. As a trained professional she should've recognized how low she'd sunk and how dangerous her decision to end her pain had been. If she'd seen these symptoms in a patient she would've moved heaven and earth for an intervention by family members or psychiatric professionals.

But what happened when you were the patient? What did you do when the loneliness and grief felt like an anvil lying on your chest? How did you stop from taking the only solution you thought open to you?

That's how she'd hatched the plan to double fill the sleeping pill prescriptions she'd gotten the docs to write for her. When she'd left the ER that night, she'd known within twenty-four hours all her pain and loneliness would have ended.

Only she hadn't planned on Jake Carlisle invading her life and forcing her to snap out of her depression.

A half-smile pressed past her lips. Since the big lug shattered her depressed existence, she hadn't had much time to wallow in her own self-pity. And Jake hadn't steered away from the topic of Aimee's leukemia once he found out, either, unlike her family and co-workers. They all acted like she'd burst into a million pieces if she heard her daughter's name or spoke of Aimee's death.

Maybe the time had come to let Aimee rest. Her daughter deserved to know peace. God knows she'd suffered enough for it.

Sami's skin tingled.

Without turning around, she knew Jake stood in the doorway watching her. She drew her hand over her eyes, pinching the corners at the bridge of her nose to prevent the tears that threatened. Exhaustion played havoc with her emotions.

"You okay?"

His baritone voice rumbled over her. A shiver ran up her spine, this time from pleasure and not fear.

"I'm just a little tired, that's all." Sami busied herself setting out coffee mugs. She opened the door of the refrigerator in search of milk. "Any luck with the pictures, yet?"

"It's a long shot at best. If the guy worked on the force in the past ten years, Doyle should have a file on him somewhere. At least I feel like we're doing something about it for once, instead of just running and hiding."

"Or being shot at." Sami couldn't hide the shudder that ran through her.

He moved behind her, wrapping his arms around her. Still holding the milk as if it had some miracle cure inside to the problems they faced, she gave into the need to feel the comfort of his body and leaned against him. His scent filled her senses. Would she ever smell cinnamon again and not think of him?

"I wish I could promise that there won't be any more shooting," he whispered against the top of her head. "But I won't lie to you. I don't know anymore than you do at this point. Except, remember we're all well trained. Have faith in your brothers, Doyle and me to finish this thing."

"I can't bear the thought of telling my parents any of them are dead. It's the worst thing in the world to know you out lived your child." Another deeper shudder ran through her. Like a knight protecting his lady, his arms tightened around her to ward off the pain and worry that beat at her.

"Shh, sweetheart, let's not borrow trouble just yet. If it comes to the point you have to tell your parents bad news, I'll help you do it. Until then, let's think only positive things about the trap. Okay?"

Sami nodded. His words made sense. For a few more minutes she stood letting him hold and comfort her. Deep inside she felt a peace she couldn't ever remember feeling. It thrilled her. It scared her.

Somewhere she found the strength to break the bond with him and resume making them coffee. These feelings would have to wait until after they'd assured Nicky's safety. If, by some miracle, they all escaped this mess fairly unscathed, and these newly awakened emotions remained, then she'd explore them. If Jake let her.

"You need some help with that?" Jake stood a few feet away from her. Yet not so far away he couldn't assist her if she needed it. She realized he needed the distance, too

Sami shook her head. "Do you or Doyle like cream or sugar?"

"No, old cops learn to drink it black." A rueful smile split his lips. "We grab it on the run, despite the jokes about donut shops."

A snicker escaped her. "My brother, Dave, gained a lot of weight right after he got married. When I kept mentioning donut shops and cops to him, he got mad and worked out until he lost all the extra pounds."

Jake shot her a curious look. "How often did you mention it to him?"

"At least daily, by e-mail and phone."

"You two going to talk til that coffee gets cold?" Doyle yelled from down the hall.

Jake reached for two of the mugs. "The old man loves his coffee."

"How did he hurt his hip?" Sami whispered.

"A little more than five years ago I was recruited into the FBI and left the force. Doyle took on a new partner, a kid out of college who was studying to be a lawyer." He studied the dark liquid in the two mugs in his hand. "The kid never could keep his mind on being a cop. He and Doyle went out on a call late one night. Doyle chased the perp down an alley. The kid was supposed to block the exit with the car."

"Only he didn't?"

"The kid wasn't fast enough. When the perp shot out the alley, Doyle's partner knew he'd fouled up and gunned the gas."

Sami cringed. "And Doyle was right behind the suspect."

"Broke the old man's leg and hip right at the socket joint in four places, virtually shattering it."

"Did he have a total hip replacement?" Sami picked up the last mug of coffee, the one doctored heavily with cream and sugar, and the glass of milk for Nicky.

"With the best surgeon in town. That's the only reason he isn't in a wheelchair, but the damage was so bad, that Doyle had to take disability and early retirement."

Jake stepped aside to let her pass her body brushing against his as she squeezed through the doorway. The intimate contact reminded her of how they spent the night before. Suddenly she wished she had a cold glass of tea instead of hot coffee.

"I bet he just hates it." She led the way down the hall, then paused a few feet from the den and lowered her voice to a whisper. "What happened to the cop who hit him? I hope he isn't still on the force."

Jake narrowed the space between them, his breath warm against her skin. "The guy's mother was some bigwig downtown. She got him removed from the force without even a citation to his record."

"That doesn't seem fair."

"Well, the guy's mama got him out of hot water, but it did cost them a few bucks. Doyle did receive a mighty big boost to his retirement fund."

She lifted her brows in surprise. "He took it?"

Jake nodded toward the den then grinned down at her. "I'd say he's invested it well, wouldn't you?"

"All that equipment?"

"The house, and the start-up fund for his PI business."

"You two done whispering out there?" Irritation laced Doyle's gravelly voice from just inside the room.

Jake lowered his voice even more. "Don't let him know I told you all this. He's touchy about it." Once more he nudged Sami into the room, but this time she didn't mind quite so much.

* * *

By two in the morning, Jake knew Nicky couldn't pick out the guy known as Madson from the file pictures Doyle had on line. If the guy that betrayed him was on the force, he didn't exist on Doyle's computer system.

"Nye photographia, Jake." *No more pictures, Jake.* Nicky whined, his head lying on his arm on the computer desk. He'd regressed to speaking in Russian, a sure sign of his exhaustion.

"Eta vashnee, Nicholai." *It's important, Nicholai.* Jake rubbed his hand over the boy's dark hair and neck.

Doyle pushed away from the computer. "We're all worn out, Rookie. How about we tuck this little fella in bed for the night. We can start again in the morning." He pushed Nicky's chair to the side. "Besides, Miss Sami is out cold."

In the wingback chair, Samantha lay curled in a ball, her feet tucked daintily beneath her, and her face pressed into the side of her arm. He doubted she was as comfortable as she looked.

He shook her awake, then lifted Nicky in his arms. "You still have that room with the twin beds upstairs, old man?"

"Same as when you helped me move it in." Doyle stopped at a panel near the front door and pushed a sequence of buttons.

Jake didn't remember seeing an alarm system when he reconnoitered the place earlier. "Why didn't you have the alarms on when I first came in?"

"I've been following the news," Doyle said as he led them to the bedrooms. "When I saw the crap hit the fan with Bridges' death, I knew you'd be coming to see me sooner or later. Even you sometimes need the help of old friends you can trust." He stepped into the first bedroom at the head of the stairs. "Working together is gonna be like old times."

Jake showed Sami to the bathroom, then carried Nicky into the bedroom with the twin beds. Setting Nicky on one, he pushed it against the wall. Then he shoved the second bed from across the room next to it to make one large bed. He sat on the edge of the bed, brushing back the sheets and tucking Nicky inside them.

"Where am I sleeping?" Samantha asked quietly from the doorway.

"In here, sweetheart." Jake stood and removed his jacket. He pulled his gun from the holster on his shoulder. He checked it and laid it on top of the beside table. Then he dragged the table to the outside of the new sleeping unit. He wanted the weapon within his reach. "Nicky near the wall, you in between, and me between you and the door and window. Tonight we sleep as one big happy family."

"Or one very scared one." Samantha laid her coat on top of Jake's, then sat to take off her shoes. He stopped her.

"Leave them on." Her eyes clouded with concern, her lips firming into a thin line as she understood his message. "Just in case."

She wiggled onto the bed and tucked the blankets around herself and Nicky. Jake turned off the lights then climbed in next to her. He stretched out on his back, then flopped his right arm above his head and listened to them breath in the dark.

A few minutes passed.

Samantha's hand slipped into his right hand where it lay between them. "Just in case," she whispered.

After a few minutes her hand relaxed in sleep, but still he held onto it. In the dark of the night, as the old house settled around them, and he listened for the sounds of someone, anyone, who might want to harm them, he wondered about the strength of this woman beside him.

Since the moment he grabbed her, she'd been in danger, tied up, shot at, in hiding. Yet except for the one attempt to escape before she knew his need for her, she hadn't uttered one complaint.

Doyle's words were so wrong.

If they managed to emerge unscathed from this mess, nothing in his life would ever be like old times.

* * *

The soft shuffle of Doyle's feet on the hall floor and down the stairs brought Jake instantly awake just before dawn. He lay on his side, his back to the door, curled quite comfortably around Samantha's back. She, in turn, had one arm draped protectively around Nicky.

Just like a family.

For a moment he gave into the fantasy. Pushing back the veil of her dark tresses lying on her neck and shoulders, he kissed the sleep-warmed flesh of her shoulder. Slowly he kissed his way up her neck to nibble lightly on her ear lobe.

She rewarded his efforts by pressing her bottom against his decidedly interested groin.

"Mmm…" she purred.

With a groan, Jake released her ear and pushed himself away from her all-too-tempting body. He cursed himself as ten times a fool for indulging in tasting her when he couldn't promise her anything now and maybe not later, either. Too bad his body didn't seem to understand the situation like his mind.

"Jake?"

The come-back-to-bed softness in her voice called to him. He closed his eyes, fighting the urge to curl around her once more.

"Go back to sleep, Samantha. I need to talk to Doyle before he heads out."

Without looking back, he snatched his gun off the bedside table. Slipping it into his holster, he pulled the holster onto his shoulder. Like a tourist fleeing a grizzly bear in Yellowstone park, he nearly ran out of the room. He prevented the door from slamming shut on his escape from the room, barely. Once out in the safety of the hall, he slumped against the wall, rubbing his hand through his thick hair, then down over the fresh stubble of his beard.

Things were going to get hairy today. He needed to keep his wits about him. He needed to focus, not on Samantha's soft curves, but on closing down the crime gang and discovering the identity of Madson. If he didn't do both, Nicky and Samantha would never be safe.

A few minutes later, Jake found Doyle in his den, studying a computerized map of the city's old industrial district. Several red X's dotted the map. Jake straddled a chair again. Squinting, he tried to decipher Doyle's plan.

"What's all this, old man?"

"The red X's stand for empty warehouses. Places empty and ripe for an ambush."

With the mouse, Jake highlighted in blue an area northwest of the city's business district, but south of the University's grounds. "Most of this area is controlled by the Kreshnins. Any warehouses inside that area is a death trap for us."

"We need to stay inside the city limits or we risk pissing off the suburban police forces." Doyle circled the spot northeast of I-71. "I used to patrol here after you moved to the feds. Some sound buildings sit empty here. And my network is still pretty active in that area."

"Can you think of someone who has enough contacts to get word to the Kreshnins that Samantha's brothers want to hand me over to them?"

Doyle leaned back in his chair, rubbing his hip out of habit. "Do you want to follow the drug or the extortion connection?"

"I'd like to keep the drug gangs out of this, if possible. Too many loose cannons for my peace of mind."

"Extortion it is. We'll need someone they might've used as a bagman or number runner, then." Doyle nodded his agreement. "I'll do a walk around downtown while the businesses are opening. I've two guys in mind that might be able to help us. How do you plan to contact the little lady's brothers?"

"Luke is going to leave me a message on e-mail. We'll have to coordinate this carefully. I'm pretty sure the feds are watching them."

Doyle wrote both letters and numbers on one of the plethora of sticky pads lying on his wall length desk. "This is the code to the computers. I need to be off to see a man about a mouse trap."

He limped out the door, parka in hand. A few minutes later, Jake heard the rumble of the old Chevette pull out of the drive and the garage door close behind it.

The old man was a throwback to the foot patrolmen at the beginning of the twentieth century. There wasn't a person he'd met on his patrol rounds that he didn't remember something about. The homeless and the business proprietors alike counted on him to help them with problems. In return they kept their eyes and ears open for information that might prove useful on one of his   cases.

If anyone could get a message through to the Kreshnin gang, it would be Doyle.

Jake clicked on another of Doyle's computers bringing up the search engine he used for messages. The time had come to see what Samantha's brothers had found out. When he typed in his code, a little envelope popped up, telling him he had received messages. The one marked Fairy Tales caught his eye. He clicked on it and a coded message appeared.

"Is there any word yet?"

The soft sleepy sound of Samantha's voice caressed him from behind.

Damn. He'd hoped to read the message before she found out. If it contained bad news, he wanted to protect her from it, or at least prepare her first. Now he prayed it said nothing.

Stealing his features, he swivelled around in the computer chair. The anguish in her eyes, and the way she had her arms wrapped around herself, twisted his gut.

He motioned for her to sit on his knee. "Matt and I agreed to this before they left the cabin. It's in a code that looks like one of the myriad of jokes and chain mails that are circulating through cyberspace."

A strained sound, halfway between a laugh and a sigh escaped her. "Dave's wife, Judy constantly overload's my e-mail with those things. We call her Queen of the forward button."

Samantha leaned closer to peer at the message. Jake willed his body not to think about the softness of her bottom sliding along the length of his thigh.

"The three little pigs?" she asked with a hint of a smile.

Good. She'd gotten the joke. Her sense of humor hadn't died under all the stress.

"Luke decided on that, since they're all in some sort of law enforcement." Jake scanned the mouse the length of the note quickly. "Good news, sweetheart. They're both safe at home."

She tilted her head sideways, one eye brow lifted in puzzlement. "How do you know that?"

"Let's read the whole thing." He ran the cursor down the screen as he read. "Two of the three little pigs went hiking in the forest and met the three bears. The papa bear turned out to be a friend, the mama bear was mean to the pigs, and the baby bear was very smart." He chuckled. "Seems your brothers thought you should've been nicer to them."

"That *was* nice." Her lip lowered in a half pout, half frown. "What else does it say?"

"The second little pig went home to prepare for the wolf and talk to the first little pig. The first little pig is mad because he didn't get to go on the hike. But is glad he get's to come play at the big party."

"Dave's mad because they didn't tell him they were coming to find us. But he's coming tomorrow, right?"

Jake nodded. "The third little pig went to play with his computer. He promised to give Papa Bear an invitation to the big party." Jake indulged himself a minute by rubbing his hand along Sami's hip and thigh. "Matt spent the night at home and Luke went looking for information."

"The big party? That's the plan for meeting the Kreshnins, isn't it?" Her muscles stiffened beneath his hand.

He continued to gently rub her thigh, in the only comforting way he knew. "I know you're worried about this meet, but if everyone does their part, Nicky will be safe by morning."

She lifted her head to stare away from him. He gently grasped her chin and pulled her face around to look at him.

"Samantha. It's the only way."

The anguish and desperation in her eyes tore at his heart.

"Why not go to your people at the FBI? Surely they can stop the Kreshnins' man on the police force."

"We don't know that it is the police, Samantha. It could be someone in the federal government. Besides, my cover was so deep for the past three years, that I don't know anyone I can trust there anymore." The urge to comfort her fought with his need for complete honesty between them. He stroked a finger down the curve of her lower lip. "Until we know for sure, we can only trust your brothers and Doyle."

She nodded, then inhaled deeply. "I haven't felt this way in a long time. I couldn't stand it if something bad happened tonight."

"I swear to you," he held her hand tight. "You and Nicky will be safely tucked right here in Doyle's war room. Nothing bad will happen to either of you."

Her eyes softened. She cupped his face with both hands. "Don't you understand? I'm not worried about Nicky or myself."

"It's all going to work out all right, sweetheart." This time Jake looked away. He couldn't hear what she said so plainly without words. He eased her off his lap and strode across the room to the computer with the maps on it. "I'm tougher than you think."

Her hand touched his shoulder from behind, branding his wound like a hot iron. "You aren't indestructible, Jake."

It took all his determination to focus on the maps Doyle had marked and not take her into his arms. When he heard her footsteps on the stairs above, his hand touched the same spot on his wounded shoulder where hers had touched. "If you only knew how vulnerable I've become, sweetheart."

In self-defense, his mind zeroed in on the area he and Doyle determined they should set the trap. He hoped the old man knew what he was doing.

In the meantime, he picked up Doyle's phone and dialed a number only his captain and he used. Time to involve his only contact at the DA's office. If something happened to him, he wanted to know Samantha and Nicky would have someone to watch over them.

* * *

Heated air from the underground sewers rose like gray specters as it hit the cold morning air. Doyle parked his non-discript brown car in the downtown parking lot. He eased his body out of the driver's seat, stood next to the car and waited for the cramp in his hip to release its grip on his joint. Even though walking the downtown streets gave him a sense of deja vu back to his patrol days, his crippled leg always brought reality crashing in.

When Jake landed on his doorstep last night, anger and relief had flooded over Doyle—anger that his old partner still hadn't asked for help when he found himself in this situation at the beginning, relief that Jake finally came to him for help when he needed it the most. Now, Doyle had a chance to show the Rookie he could depend on friends for help.

Jake deserved some happiness.

Doyle rubbed a hand over his hip. He'd always liked Jake, but after his accident he'd learned just what kind of a man he was. From the time he awoke in the hospital recovery room after his accident, until his last physical therapy treatment, the kid had encouraged and nagged him by equal turns, until he'd been capable of walking without anyone's help. Even though some debts could never be repaid, he meant to try. He had a feeling the little lady and boy back at his house might just be the key to Jake's future.

Doyle started off to search the small downtown businesses' alleys and backdoors. He needed to find a semi-bookie, part-time truck driver, full-time loser, named Lyle.

Downtown buzzed with a life of its own in the early morning hours before the lawyers, businessmen, and secretaries commuted to work. While restaurant supply trucks dropped off fresh produce and frozen meats every morning, garbage trucks picked up the previous night's refuse, and store-owners shooed the homeless from their doorways where they'd curled up for protection from the cold night winds.

This was the underbelly of the teaming metropolis. People here saw things, knew things, heard things. Just the kind of information Doyle gathered and filed away for future use.

It took several blocks, but when he turned the corner onto Main, just east of High Street, there stood Lyle, talking to an even more disreputable looking guy. Lyle wrote something on a piece of paper, then took the man's money.

Doyle hesitated just long enough for Lyle's mark to move on down the road before approaching the worm. If anyone could weasel information to the Kreshnins, it was Lyle. The guy had more tentacles into the outer edges of the city's crime scene than a set of Siamese octopuses.

Doyle edged closer in the gray morning light, trying not to send his prey skittering off into a back alleyway. Even though all his contacts knew he'd retired early from the force, occasionally for some damn reason they took it into their heads to make him chase them. Today, neither he nor his hip were in the mood.

Just as Lyle turned to climb behind the wheel of his paper delivery truck, Doyle snagged his arm with his firm grip. "Good to see you so industrious this morning, Lyle."

The snitch stiffened, trying to pull away before he realized it was Doyle who had him cornered against his truck, and not some other low-life meaning to put an end to his existence.

"Oh, hey, Doyle. Long time no see." He glanced up one side of the street, then down the other, making sure no one saw him speaking to the detective.

"Long enough to see you still haven't given up making book on the streets." Doyle pressed his informant into the side of the truck, blocking them from view by cars passing by on the street. For once he was as anxious as Lyle not to be seen talking to him.

"Hey, you know me man, just trying to make a livin'." He moved his hands in a jerky, twitchy fashion. "What cha doin' out here this early, Doyle?"

"Funny you should ask, Lyle. You're the reason I'm here."

His eyes widened. "Me? I ain't done nothin'. I swear it, Doyle. Ya got the wrong guy, man."

"Oh, I've got the right guy, Lyle. You're going to do me a favor, or I'm going to inform the watch commander I have reliable information that not only did you know the murders at the race track last month were going down, you had a hand in them."

"Hey, I ain't got nothin' to do with that, Doyle."

Doyle let his meanest smile slide over his face. "You know that and I know that. But if you don't do exactly like I say, I'm going to let the local cops harass your sorry hide for it."

The little weasel shuffled his feet and nodded like an old time minstrel show dancer, more than willing to cooperate. "Okay, okay, Doyle. Whatcha want me to do?"

"So glad you asked, Lyle." Doyle released his hold on the semi-slimeball, keeping him hemmed in close to the truck while he gave him the specifics to pass on to the Kreshnins. Then with a warning to follow the instructions to the last detail, he let the snitch take off.

Now, he needed to search out the old factory he'd just set the ambush in.

* * *

The private office number blinked its silent call. Madson lifted the receiver. "What now?"

Every minute that Carlisle and the kid remained on the loose, his stress level doubled.

"Such impatience, my friend. Especially when I have such good news for you."

The thick Russian voice rumbling on the other end of the line irritated him more. Perhaps he needed to rethink his connection with Petrov. His private Swiss accounts had more than enough money for his purposes. Severing ties with the Cossack was a tricky deal at best and dangerous at worst.

"Tell me your people found Carlisle and the kid." He

rubbed his hand over his forehead as the throbbing started once more. With a brief glance at his office door to assure himself it remained closed, he leaned back in his chair and closed his eyes.

Another chuckle filtered across the line. "It seems our mole has plucked a bird with brothers anxious to hand him to us."

"How did you get this information?" A warning tingling started between his shoulder blades and inched up his spine. The throbbing turned into a drum solo. "Is it reliable?"

"The source is known to my people. We deal with him on occasion. His information is most reliable."

"What do the woman's brothers want in for handing us over Carlisle and the boy?"

"Revenge. Seems little lady's big brothers don't like idea of Carlisle kidnapping her. They want to meet us. They say to turn him and the Nicholai over to us."

"Why don't they kill him themselves?"

Petrov chuckled into the phone. "They don't want dirty hands. You Americans are so afraid of a little blood."

He ignored the insult. Kreshnin still thought he was an invincible KGB agent. "Where do they want to meet? Can we control the situation?"

"The address is not in my area, but my people can cover all exits. The question, my friend, is do we let anyone walk away?"

Something about this meeting felt like a setup, but if he played his cards right, maybe he could work it to his advantage. He could get out of this whole mess with the kid and Carlisle dead, and the added bonus of the lady's brothers and Petrov Kreshnin all silent as well.

"No, Petrov. No one leaves there alive."

"Da. That is what I thought, too."

No matter what, the kid couldn't be allowed to give testimony against him. Too many things depended on the kid's silence.

CHAPTER FOURTEEN

Sami churned the wooden spoon through the homemade cookie batter with a vengeance, pushing all her anger and worry into the spoon's rhythm.

"Stupid man, thinks he's invincible," she muttered as she reached for the oats and poured them into the batter. "Well, he can just suture his own gunshot wounds from now on. I'm through playing human repairman."

She bit her lip, blinking back the hot tears that threatened to make her cookies more moist than necessary. She reached for the cup of raisins, tossed them in and resumed stirring. "I'll go crazy staying at home, not knowing if everyone is okay. But at least he has sense enough not to drag Nicky anywhere near this ambush."

With a final swipe at the mixture, she shoved the spoon hard into the bowl. Turning to check if the oven had finished heating, she ran smack into Jake's solid form.

She tried to move around him, but his arms held her in place like two vice grips. Embarrassment flooded her. "How much did you hear?"

"Not much before you swore you weren't going to play human repairman for me anymore."

She kept her eyes fixed on the third button of his navy blue shirt. If she saw the amusement in his voice mirrored on his face, she couldn't be held accountable for hurting him.

"Samantha?"

"You're in my way, Jake. I have cookies that need to go in the oven." She pushed against him, but he held her fast.

"It's going to work out alright in the morning, I promise."

"You don't know that." The warmth of his body and the comfort of his arms eased her fears just a little.

He slipped a finger beneath her chin, forcing her head up. Concern and tenderness etched lines around his eyes. "Doyle staked out the warehouse for escape routes, this morning."

His hold on her tightened. His jaw clenched in that stubborn male way of his, and steeliness crept into his eyes.

"The Kreshnins are going to pay for what they did to Nicky."

"How do you know the Kreshnins won't try to set their own trap?"

"I'm counting on it, sweetheart."

"You're counting on it?" She pushed hard against his

chest, and this time he released her. "You're planning on getting killed aren't you. It doesn't matter to you one iota if you live or die in this battle, does it? You don't care if someone else might miss you, do you?"

"It's never mattered to anyone else before, Samantha."

She turned her back to him, bending to pull out a pan for the cookies. "Well, this time it's different," she muttered, half-hoping he wouldn't hear.

"Why is it different, Samantha?"

With determination, she focused on plopping spoonful after spoonful of cookie dough onto the pan, then shoved it into the hot oven.

"You'd make me beg?" Hope and desperation edged his voice.

She tried to ignore it. Her fingers gripped the spoon tightly in her hand. Couldn't he see how his words lashed at her like a whip against her naked flesh?

Her mind and body wanted to screech, *I don't think I'll survive losing someone else I love,* but the words remained unspoken between them.

Her heart clenched with pain as his footsteps retreated down the hall's hardwood floor, then faded away.

She gazed out into the stark winter landscape of Doyle's backyard. The naked trees appeared mournful and forlorn against the steel gray sky. The scene matched the despair creeping in at the edges of her heart.

Sami gripped the edge of the sink tightly, pressing all her frustration and tension through her arm muscles down into the counter top. Dammit, she wouldn't give into the fear now. When she had nothing to do but wait, then she'd deal with her fear.

Determined, she dragged out another baking pan and filled it with globs of dough. Just like she did at work, she'd stay busy. The more she moved the less time she'd have to worry. It was one of the reasons she chose the job she did.

Of course, she'd perfected working and worrying when Aimee became ill. The longest days of Sami's life had been after Aimee's death. There had been nothing to do but blame herself for not saving her daughter. Every day since then she fought the battle to stay busy enough to keep the pain and memories at bay.

"Sami?" Nicky asked from the doorway behind her.

She forced a reassuring smile onto her face as he joined her. "Hey there, Nicky. Do you like oatmeal raisin cookies?"

"I never had them, Sami. Are they as vkoosnee, delicious as Russian cookies?"

"I don't know. I've never had any Russian cookies." Sami removed the first pan of cookies from the oven and replaced it with the second. "You sit at the table while these cool a minute and I'll see if Doyle has enough milk left for us to have cookies and milk. Then you can decide for yourself how good they are."

"This is American children's custom, yes?"

"When I was a girl about your age I would help my mother bake cookies all the time. My big brothers would gobble them up almost as fast as we could make them." She found enough milk for two glasses. Pouring them each one, she set a plate of soft, chewy cookies between them. The smell of cinnamon, oats and hot raisins wafted up from the plate.

Nicky took one, sniffing it for a minute then sinking his teeth into the treat. "Mmm, good, Sami."

Returning his smile, she took a bite of her own cookie.

"Mommy, these are my favoritist cookies," Aimee said from her perch on the counter as she handed her the box of raisins. "Does they have o'meal-raisin cookies in hebin?"

"I don't know, sweetie." She smiled at her daughter, then poured a cup of raisins into the batter. She stirred the gooey concoction while keeping an eye on Aimee who was determined as always to help with the baking. "Why do you ask?"

Aimee didn't answer for a minute and Sami could almost see the little gears in her head turning as she formulated her answer.

"Coz," she finally replied, "Grandpa Walt would be sad if he couldn't have o'meal-raisin cookies no more."

She stopped stirring a moment to study her daughter. Michael's father had passed away just this past summer. Aimee talked about him in heaven frequently as if she were trying to wrap her four-year old brain around the concept. "Honey, heaven is a nice place for your Grandpa Walt to be. I'm sure they have all his favorite foods there, even oatmeal raisin cookies."

This seemed to appease Aimee who didn't ask any more questions while they dropped spoonfuls of cookie dough onto the baking sheet. It wasn't until they were seated at the table later eating samples of their work with glasses of cold milk to wash them down that she returned to the subject.

"Mommy, can I go to hebin to see Grandpa Walt? I could take him some cookies."

"No, sweetie, we can't go see Grandpa Walt right now."

"Why not? I miss his blurby kisses"

Walt had always smacked his lips on his granddaughter's belly or arm and made wet kisses. Aimee had loved them.

She pulled her daughter onto her lap and hugged her tight. "Years and years from now when you're old like Grandpa Walt was, then you can go to heaven and see him."

Sami blinked back a tear as she sat at Doyle's table remembering the innocent conversation she'd shared with her daughter. How wrong her prediction had been. Two months later Aimee's leukemia had been diagnosed. Less than a year later she'd gone to heaven to be with her grandfather.

"I used to make these cookies for my little girl."

"Did she like them?" Nicky said after gulping down nearly half his glass of milk.

"Yes, these were her favorite cookies." Funny, for the first time in a long time she had remembered something about her daughter not really associated with her cancer and death. Maybe time and distance could be a healer. She looked at the boy sitting next to her. Maybe it takes people to help you get over the pain, too. "Aimee loved to help me bake all kinds of things like you did today. But her favorite snack by far was banana bread."

"Banana bread?" Nicky gave her such a puzzled look she imagined he saw yellow-banana shaped loaves of bread in his mind.

Sami laughed and took another cookie. The ripe bananas on the top of the refrigerator caught her eye. "Tonight we'll make banana bread while Jake and Doyle are gone. I bet you'll like it as much as Aimee did."

Nicky paused in the middle of drinking his milk, setting the cup on the table. He slumped in his chair, his lips pressed together and his eyebrows drawn down in a scowl.

"What's wrong, Nicky?" She knew his sudden mood change had nothing to do with her baking.

"I want to go with Jake and Doyle tonight, not sit around like baby. Big Partner will need me to...catch Boss Kreshnin."

Sami sat in her chair to think how best to handle this mini-Russian revolt. "You of all people know how sneaky Boss is, Nicky. Right?"

The boy nodded despite his belligerence.

"Then Jake, Doyle and my brothers will need all their wits about them to stay focused on catching him, right?"

Again the boy nodded. This time his shoulders relaxed a bit.

"Now, if you and I were to go with them and somehow got in their way, they'd try to protect us. That would give Boss the advantage he might need to get away."

Nicky twisted his lips from side to side.

"Or worse, Nicky. It might get Jake or one of the others killed." She set her elbows onto the table, folding her hands in front of her. "That's not what you want to happen, is it?"

The boy shook his head, then muttered, "No."

"Neither do I. The best help we can be right now is to stay here out of the way."

"That's what Big Partner say. He say I have to stay here to protect you."

"To protect me?" Oh the big bad undercover FBI agent hadn't really said that, had he?

Nicky nodded and reached for another cookie. "He say from worry."

Sami ground her teeth together and fixed the rear of the house with an evil eye, which she hoped Jake felt, preferably right between his shoulder blades. She shoved her chair from the table, scooped up the plate and refilled it with cookies. As she stomped her way to the computer den, anger replaced the fear she'd been fighting all day over the man and his stupid macho plan to get killed.

Two heads lifted from scrutinizing the blue prints spread on the table before them when she stormed into the room. She stopped just opposite them and hurled the plate of warm cookies onto the blueprints. The cookies jostled a moment, crumbs sliding over the side.

"You don't need to worry about me, Mr. I-don't-need-anyone. I can take care of myself. And Nicky, too, for that matter. So you just go get yourself blown to pieces. Just try not to take one of my brothers with you."

She turned on her heel and marched out of the room, her spine ramrod straight.

"She'll do fine," Doyle muttered, his attention already on the blueprints.

"Yep, she'll do fine." Jake bit back the smile that threatened to creep out. He reached for a cookie and took a bite.

Damn, the woman could bake! From now on he'd invent

things for her to get anxious about, if it meant she'd bake more cookies like these.

He stared at the door where she'd disappeared.

A future with Samantha.

The idea didn't scare him. That surprised him. Maybe, when this mess ended, he'd see just how comfortable it felt then. With determination, he pocketed thoughts of the future out of his mind. He had to survive tomorrow's battle first.

"The building is five stories high." Doyle drew Jake's attention to the problem at hand—trapping the Kreshnins. Doyle pointed to spots along the edge of the first floor. "These are the obvious points of penetration, the front door, side door and rear loading dock."

"They'll be crazy to only come in at those places."

"That's why we're going to let them set their own point of operations."

Jake nearly choked. "Are you nuts? We'll be sitting ducks, Doyle. Despite what Samantha thinks, I don't plan to just go in with guns blazing. I sort of planned on living a while longer."

"Relax, Jake. We already have some of our defenses in place. Lyle may be one of my informants, but I know better than to trust him from here to the front door. As soon as I gave him the message to deliver, I visited the old factory. I added some new features to the building's structure."

Jake stared at his old partner. "What kind of additions?"

The left corner of Doyle's lips lifted slightly. "Seems

the SWAT team lost some plastique a few years ago after a drug raid. No investigation ensued over it for political reasons."

"Mind showing me where you booby trapped the place?" For the first time since he discovered Nicky tortured in the restaurant's storeroom, Jake felt like he had the upper hand.

Doyle pointed out each spot he'd wired with the plastique explosive. He also pointed out a few more tricks he'd set throughout the building. With their plans set, Jake sent a final message to the brothers via e-mail. Dave and Matt would set up outer perimeter surveillance, while Luke took care of some audio-visual support.

Jake waited for Samantha's youngest brother to acknowledge his message. Despite what she thought, he'd already learned he needed to depend on others. The time with her taught him that.

* * *

"Nicky, I need you to come talk with me some more," Jake said after they finished dinner.

Sami took a deep breath. She knew what he was planning. All three adults had decided they needed to record Nicky's testimony, as well as all the information he had on the Kreshnin clan's activities in case the planned attack the next day went South.

"But I go play video games again, Big Partner," Nicky shuffled his feet with his head down.

Jake put his arm around his shoulders and steered him into Doyle's living room, where they'd set up a video camera and tape player. "You can play them later, I promise. I was hoping you'd help me make a movie instead."

"A movie?" This information brightened Nicky's face.

"Sort of, but you're going to be the only person on it."

Nicky drew his brows together in confusion. "I not know how to act."

Jake sat him down on the couch, then took the chair next to it. "That's okay. All I want you to do is answer questions as I ask them. The questions are going to be about all the things Boss had you do. I want you to tell the truth and tell me everything you can remember about each question. Do you think you can do that?"

"Da. I can do it."

"Let's talk about the night the man was put in the trunk of the car. Okay?"

"I already told you. Madson helped Boss."

"I know you did, but this time you need to tell the camera."

Sami watched from the doorway as Jake led Nicky through the events the night Ivanovich was killed. It still amazed her how Nicky could tell the same exact accounting of the events. Nothing changed. His voice never wavered. It was as if he read it from a script. Maybe that's the way his brain worked. Like a script of events or a laundry list.

"Very good, Nicky," Jake said when the tale was finished. "Now, we're going to do something a little different. Do you remember all the times Boss sent you to collect money for him?"

"Da. I go same places every month. You know this,

Big Partner. You go with me." Nicky squirmed in his seat a bit.

Jake laid his hand on the boy's knee, instantly stilling him. "That's right, I did. That's one of the ways we became friends, wasn't it?"

Nicky nodded and Jake sat back in his chair once more. "Tell me who each person was and how much money they owed."

"Andropov, the baker...three hundred. Baranov, at the restuarant...four-fifty..." Nicky repeated the same list he had when he'd been fighting the fever. Only this time, he listed each man's occupation.

Sami listened, then realized what it was she heard. The words that had so innocently tumbled out of his mouth before now made sense. Nicky's memory held every piece of evidence against Kreshnins' extortion operation.

Twenty minutes later Nicky finished recanting every visit he'd made to the Boss' victims, as well as every time he saw someone injured. Apparently, if the victim was short on what he owed, the enforcer that accompanied Nicky would break a finger or pummel the man into remembering just how serious Kreshnin was. Sami burned with the desire to punch something. No child should witness such violence.

"Good job, Nicky," Jake said, and sat forward once more. "We're almost done, little partner. There's just one more question I need you to answer, okay?"

'Then I go play gorilla video game?"

"Yes, until Samantha says you have to go to bed, okay?"

"Okay," Nicky mumbled half-heartedly.

"Do you remember when Boss and Ivan would take you with them to special houses?"

"The ones with the ladies?"

Sami sucked in her breath. Oh God, they hadn't really taken a little boy to their sex-slave houses, had they? How deranged were these men to expose a child to something like that?

"Do you remember the names of the streets?"

"I can't say them, Jake."

"Do you think you could remember the words if you saw them?" Jake pulled out a map and laid it on the table in front of Nicky.

Nicky scrambled onto his knees and leaned over the table. "Here is one, number 1205," he said pointing to a spot on the map.

"Main Street," Jake repeated for the camera. "Very good.

Sami left the room and wandered into the den, unable to listen to anymore. Her nerves, already on edge nearly hummed from her anger. As much as she wanted to keep Jake, Doyle and her brothers safe, she realized now just how evil the men threatening them were. They had to be stopped.

"You know, once he's out of their hands, the boy will probably forget most of what he's seen or heard," Doyle's raspy voice said from behind her.

"He never should've been involved in this mess."

"No, but you and Jake are doing everything you can to protect him."

"It doesn't feel like enough."

"Sometimes all a person needs is someone to believe in them to change the course of their life."

Sami studied the older man for a moment. "Are we talking about Nicky now or Jake?"

"I'd say a woman could look a long time before she finds a man better than Jake or a boy smarter than Nicky." He fixed her with a steady gaze. "Wouldn't you?"

Before she could answer, Nicky came barreling into the room, landing right on the chair in front of the video games.

"Interview time is over?" she asked as Jake sauntered in behind him.

"Yep, he did real good." Jake handed the digital camera to Doyle. "Make several copies for us, old man. I want no chance of this stuff getting lost or destroyed." He turned to pull Sami into his arms. "You know what you have to do?"

"Yes," she replied, her heart in her stomach.

In the event that no one returned from the meeting, she was to deliver the information and Nicky directly to Jake's contact in the DA's office, Natalie Johnson. She was also to ask for federal protective custody for both herself and Nicky.

* * *

They stood in the kitchen loading the night vision gear and weapons they planned to use at the warehouse. In an hour dusk would settle on the city. The meeting was set for six a.m., but they planned to be in the warehouse all night, quietly observing the Kreshnins from camouflaged spots.

"Don't forget, Rookie. As soon as I give the cue that the explosives are going off, get rid of the night vision equipment. One flash from the plastique with those on and you'll be blinded."

"Got it, old man." Jake packed his gear into a SWAT team style duffle bag. "How do you get this stuff?"

"Let's just say I have my sources. You're better off not knowing."

A shadow passed over the room.

Samantha stood in the doorway, her silhouette blocking the light from the hall. With her face hidden by shadows, her concern showed in the way her arms wrapped around her torso in a hug. Jake suspected she wore her anger, as well. Once they were all safe, he'd face her ire.

"This is going to be a long night." Tension filled her voice.

"There's no other way." As much as he'd like to reassure her things would turn out good, he couldn't lie to her. "We need to be in place before the Kreshnins come in to set their trap."

"Luke never liked waiting as a kid. He'd open his Christmas presents as soon as he found them."

"Luke's not a kid anymore. He'll do fine."

"Dave's third child is due any day now."

Jake and Doyle exchanged looks. The older man zipped his parka and lifted his duffel bag. "I'll be waiting for you in the van." He paused at the door. "You remember the code to the alarm system, Sami?"

"Yes, Doyle. You be careful."

"Thank you, ma'am. You and the boy stay safe."

Jake finished loading his bag, zipped it and set it aside. His eyes on the darkened profile of Sami's face, he hefted on his own coat. "I won't promise we'll all come home unharmed, Samantha."

"I'm not asking you to."

He walked around the table and came to stand only inches from her. He cupped her face in his hands. His thumbs caressed the smooth skin of her jaw line. In the fading light he read the worry in her crystal green eyes. "What do you want me to promise?"

"Just try not to get any of you killed."

"I'll do my best to keep your brothers safe."

She gripped his hands in her softer ones, imprisoning him on the spot. "I want a repeat of what happened in the cabin, Jake."

He fought a hard laugh. "Sweetheart, we don't exactly have time for that now."

"Not now. Later. I want enough of you intact to give me another day in the cabin."

"When this is over, I'm planning on more than just a day with you there."

He lowered his lips to hers in a claiming kiss. He willed her his strength and took a big dose of her passion. Now that he'd found her he planned on sticking around long enough to explore their need for each other. He tried to convey that promise through his kiss.

With a determination he didn't know he possessed, he

pushed away from the warm seduction of her body and grabbed his gear. At the door, he paused. "Don't open this door for any cop or federal agent."

With that order, he stepped out into the dusk.

The prey had become the hunter.

* * *

Two blocks from the warehouse, a dark truck sat parked between two brick buildings, waiting for Jake and Doyle to appear. When they approached it, the head lights flickered three times, then once. The code Samantha's brothers had decided on. Jake backed the van in beside them.

Dressed from head to toe in dark camo gear, all three of the Edgars brothers climbed out of the truck's cab. Matt pulled two tarps out of the truck bed while Luke and the brother Jake hadn't met yet, grabbed their own bags of equipment. The group secured the two vehicles and camouflaged them from any curious passers by.

"You're the guy who dragged my sister into this mess?" Dave said by way of introduction.

"That would be me." Jake hefted his duffle bag onto his shoulder.

"You hurt her, and I'll make the hit team that shot you look like amateurs."

Jake nodded. Samantha's older brother didn't mince words. But he didn't plan to give the brothers a reason to seek vengeance on him. Not because he feared them, but because of Samantha's growing importance to him.

Darkness covered the city with the help of a cloud-filled, moonless sky. Jake handed everyone night vision goggles as they approached the warehouse. Stopping across the street from it, they slipped on the goggles and scanned the building's perimeter and the surrounding area. When they were sure no cars held occupants ready to gun them down, Jake and Dave circled the building to look for any obvious snipers or traps.

Assured the Kreshnins hadn't set up their point of attack yet, Jake motioned the others to join them at the warehouse's rear entrance.

The group slipped inside the metal door, and Jake signaled them to halt. He lifted his goggles and unrolled the blueprints on the floor. The others followed suit and knelt beside him. On the paper, Doyle had marked the areas where the small quantities of plastique were in place.

"None of these will cause more than flashes and minor structural damage, but try not to use them as spots of concealment." Jake pointed to the three areas marked in black. "These are the points of penetration. The idea is to let them enter, then block their exits."

"How many do you think they'll bring?" Dave had already loaded ammo into his rifle and slipped into his assault vest.

"Anywhere from a few to a whole team. Boss Kreshnin is known for overkill. He's the highly dramatic big Russian type. But I'll bet whomever is helping them may not want it announced to the world they're taking us out. That could play in our favor."

Luke stopped in the middle of pulling out several small cameras out of his bag of equipment. "Take us out?"

The others exchanged looks over his naivete. Jake knew the group's youngest member was out of his league when it came to planned ambush and despite his words to Samantha, he didn't want to lose her brother in a gun battle.

"Luke, your job's to focus on getting the evidence we need to put these guys behind bars. They'll want to kill me. Especially when they find out Nicky isn't part of the deal and that he isn't even on the premises. Your brothers are going to see that doesn't happen." He laid a hand on Luke's shoulder. "You just focus on your job, and leave the fighting to us."

Luke pulled out a Baretta, checked the magazine and pushed the clip into place, as quick as any expert marksman. "How about I just keep this handy then?"

Jake glanced at Dave and Matt. They grinned at him, then focused on memorizing the layout of the warehouse.

"I take it you know how to use that thing?"

Stupid question. Of course he did, his brothers would've insisted he learn, not to mention the Treasury Department, which controlled the IRS investigators.

Luke shrugged. "You worry about staying in one piece so Sami can give you hell when we get home. I'll worry about myself and my equipment."

Doyle and Matt set out a perimeter of ammo, easy enough for them to get to in the heat of battle, yet out of sight of their enemies. Dave upturned some old packing crates and storage barrels to make points of concealment. Jake helped Luke place the surveillance equipment.

Three tiny cameras, set at various heights and

distances around the center of the main floor would record the exchange between Jake and Boss Kreshnin. If everything went well, they would have the evidence to clear Jake and destroy the mafia's extortion hold on the Russian immigrant community, close down their drug and prostitution activities and convict Petrov of murder.

And if things didn't go well, then someone would have evidence of my murder, too.

Jake couldn't help his pessimism. For the first time in a long while, he wanted the kind of future every other man wanted. A home and a family *with* Samantha. With his luck, now that he knew what he wanted, his job would cost him everything. He sat back on his heels a moment watching the others work.

Four good men and one strong woman believed he was worth the effort to keep alive. He'd just have to prove them right. He hoped putting the Kreshnins behind bars was his best option. But if for one second he thought Nicky or Samantha would be in danger after this morning, he planned to take the Kreshnins out— permanently.

* * *

During the long periods of straining to listen into the dark for sounds of their prey's approach, thoughts of Samantha and Nicky infiltrated Jake's mind. Even though he was glad they were safe and sound at Doyle's, he wondered if they managed to actually get any sleep. Sitting in the dark, cavernous old warehouse he imagined Samantha curled around Nicky as protectively as she had been last night. God, he wished he was there now, holding her in the dark.

"Rookie?" Doyle's low rumble filled his ears. He'd stationed himself just outside the main entrance lying in the gully lined with bushes, saying with his hip, there no way he could move around inside with any kind of stealth. "We have bogies approaching from the north."

Jake glanced at his watch. Five o'clock. The Kreshnins played it true to form, arriving an hour early for the meeting. "How many, Doyle?"

"I count two vehicles, no make that three."

Straining, Jake heard the engines rumble low then stop. Eight car doors opened, and shut, one louder than the others. He eased further into the packing crate he was huddled inside. "Let them get inside and into their positions. Remember, we want them to relax and give us some evidence on film," he whispered into the mouthpiece of his communications set. "No one goes up to the second floor, Matt."

"Gottcha." Matt sat somewhere at the top of the second floor steps. The old service elevator had been disabled years ago. The task of keeping unwanted snipers from accessing the catwalk surrounding the main level fell to him. His other job was to act as sniper from above.

The front door creaked open. Someone tried the rear door, but Doyle had rendered it useless just after Jake's team gained entrance through it.

Voices whispered. Flashlights scanned back and forth throughout the first floor. Jake listened for Boss Kreshnin. If the big man didn't show, none of this mattered.

"Vsio kharasho khazyaeen." *The coast is clear, Boss,* someone said into a two way phone.

The front door opened again.

Two massive forms stepped inside.

Hollywood couldn't have cast two Cossacks better than Petrov Kreshnin and his little brother Ivan. The KGB had handpicked them from their village along the Ob River in the Ural Mountains during the height of the Cold War. Fresh from their parents to a state run school, their natural tendencies to bully others made them perfect material for the strong-arms unit of the secret police.

But Petrov and Ivan were no ordinary enforcers. They were smart enough to get out of the country when communism fell, setting up their own cell for extortion, money laundering, drugs, and sex in the one place they knew they could make a profit--America.

"Misha, Sasha, Vladik, spread out. Hide yourselves. We want the mole to show himself and the boy. Then we'll pounce, like the otter catching his little fishes, no?"

The big Cossack ordered in Russian, then laughed at his own wit.

Jake really hated all of Petrov's anecdotes from the old country. Everyday while he was in deep cover, he'd heard Petrov compare himself to some animal—bear, wolf, fox, even shark.

"Ilya," Boss switched into English, as Ilya spoke more American than old country Russian. "Up to the Eagle's nest with you."

A young blonde man trotted up the old iron steps to the second floor. The rusted metal cat walk creaked overhead as he made his way to a position, then a transmission over the two-way to Boss confirmed his position.

Jake wasn't worried. Matt would take the kid out before he became a problem.

Several more men dispersed throughout the main floor, and one stationed himself outside as a look out. All in all, Jake counted fifteen men, including the Kreshnin brothers.

He hunkered in his packing crate and listened for tale-tell sounds of the enemy's numbers shrinking.

* * *

Matt eased the bolt rifle's sling over his shoulder. Never taking his eyes of his prey, he slipped his Glock with its silencer out of his holster and crept along the bridge. Neither he nor his weapon, with its black matte finish, would show any light in the darkness. With a panther's sleek moves he worked his way closer and closer.

The young lieutenant, focused on the level below, had laid his weapon aside and sat watching the front entrance to the building. His mistake lay in the assurance they'd outwitted their enemy.

Matt trained the laser site at the gang member. He hated what he was about to do, but when it came down to his sister's life, Nicky's and Jake's, or this guy's, he'd do whatever it took to keep the others safe.

"Ilya, you are in place, yes?" The big guy's voice rumbled over the kid's walkie-talkie.

"Yes, Boss. I'm ready."

Matt waited for the kid to answer and pocket his communication device. He raised his arm until the laser site pointed at the kid's heart. Gently, he squeezed on the trigger.

A soft whiz, then a muffled pop sounded.

The kid jerked slightly, then slumped sideways. Matt crawled forward, easing the dead sniper and his gun away from the precipice. He refused to look at the kid's face.

Quietly, Matt slipped into the vacated spot. Legs hanging down he scanned the area below. He pressed the headset's mouthpiece to his headset closer to his lips, whispering to the others.

* * *

"One down, Jake. Two bogies in the center of the room. One to the left of you. Two flanking Dave. One about two feet in front of Luke. One stationed at each door."

Jake listened to Matt's whispered report in his ear. The guy worked quietly. So focused on the conversation between the Kreshnins, he'd almost missed the sound of the silencer above him.

"Is Madson going to join us this morning, Petrov?" Ivan sat on a crate cleaning his fingernails with a knife.

Petrov laughed. "The Shadowman has not stomach enough for what needs to be done. He leaves it to us to dispose of the cop and boy."

Jake glanced upward. On the side of Luke's camera just above his head, the faint green light showed the recording had begun. He'd just sit a while and let the gangsters hang themselves. Maybe he could even find out this Madson's identity.

"One bogey down to your left, Jake." Dave's voice rumbled through the headset. "Let me get the other one before you make your move."

"Brother, I like Nicholai. It is necessary to kill him? He is most useful with his little memory, no?"

A slap sounded on the other side of the room. Jake knew from experience, the larger bully had slapped Ivan in the head.

"Stupid! He can put us in American prisons. The brat must be silenced for good."

"Da. You are right as always," Ivan mumbled.

Jake could imagine the younger Kreshnin rubbing his head.

"And besides, if we do this right, Madson will be in our pocket, yes?"

A clicking sounded in Jake's ear, followed by Doyle's raspy voice. "Two bogey's down outside, Rookie."

Gray light started to filter through the grimy windows of the old factory. Jake flexed and released his hands, then rolled his head to one side, then the other, trying to loosen the cramping tension in his shoulders. Damn, he wished Dave would hurry. He wondered how many men were outside, but couldn't risk being heard asking Doyle until Dave was in position.

"I told you killing Ivanovich was not such good idea, Petrov. Madson should do more of his own work, not us. After Nicholai is no longer threat, what is to keep him from doing the double cross to us?"

"Because, I too know of Madson's involvement in

murder. There is more evidence than just brat's story. If cops get his car, he is dead man. Madson cannot touch us."

Jake's attention riveted to that piece of information. This Madson wasn't a cop. So who was he?

CHAPTER FIFTEEN

Sami and Nicky lay curled on opposite ends of the couch together. Early morning cartoons flickered on the television. For some reason, she couldn't make herself sleep in the bed they'd shared with Jake the night before. Instead, she'd made the night a camp-out in Doyle's living room. The all night movie marathon did little to ease her fear for Jake and her brothers, but it kept Nicky occupied.

"Sami?" Nicky mumbled from his side of the couch.

"Yes?" She lifted her head to look across the couch at him.

"Why Big Partner show me pictures of men last night?"

He sounded confused, even for someone just waking up.

Sami sat up. "Jake and Doyle wanted to see if you could identify Madson in any of the pictures, Nicky.

Don't you remember telling us that you saw him with Boss Kreshnin the night they killed the man?"

"But I not see Madson's face, Sami."

A shiver of apprehension slid down her spine.

"You told Jake you saw Boss and Madson dump the body in Madson's car, Nicky. Didn't you?"

"I saw Boss and other man put white-haired man in car, after they shoot him. But I not see other man's face."

Sami brushed his hair out of his face. "Nicky, why did you identify Madson as helping kill that man?"

"Madson is words on car, Sami."

Her confusion doubled, along with her fear they'd missed something important. "Where exactly did you see the words Mad son?"

"On metal plate at bottom of big black car."

Suddenly everything made more sense. It was no longer a case of just Nicky's word convicting this man. His car held DNA evidence that linked him to the homicide and Nicky could pinpoint which car to the police. Sami went to the kitchen, then returned with a piece of paper and a pencil. "Write exactly what you saw on that plate for me. Okay, Nicky?"

Taking the pencil, he wiggled around on the couch. He bit his bottom lip, concentrating as he printed out what he'd seen.

MAD*SON.

"You're sure about this?"

He nodded, handing her the pencil.

"Of course you are. You don't forget anything you see." His eyes grew wide with fright. Sami sat next to him, pulling him into her arms. She ran her hands up and down his arm as much to calm herself as to reassure him. "It's okay. When Jake and Doyle return they'll know what to do with this plate."

Damn it! If they'd known this yesterday, they could've run it through the Department of Motor Vehicles and found out who set Jake up in the first place. If she knew the codes to unlock the security on Doyle's computer, she'd look it up herself, but Jake had taken it with him. And she couldn't call her usual source for computer help—Luke—he was at the warehouse, too.

Great. Just when you need a man, where are they? Off playing cops and robbers with no way to contact them.

She couldn't shake the feeling they should've known this piece of missing information before they'd set up the ambush.

* * *

"Ready when you are, Jake." Dave's voice rumbled through his headset again. That meant he'd secured his side of the room.

Jake inhaled and exhaled, gripping his gun tight, then relaxing his hold. "We go after the charges." He slid out of the crate and eased himself into a crouch. He'd removed his night vision goggles with the first gray rays of light. Now he saw Petrov's back less than two feet in front of him. Ivan sat a few feet away. They both concentrated on the door, where two of their minions flanked it to ambush whomever came inside.

He glanced to his right to where two more men flanked the side entrance. "Matt? Can you see the rear door?"

"Two back there, Jake."

Including the five they'd already taken out, that made thirteen. Two more lay in wait somewhere in the building. The odds wouldn't get much better.

"Doyle. Now."

Jake closed his eyes, counting to ten for the delayed charge.

An explosion sounded at the side of the building, quickly followed by another at the rear of the building. Gunfire erupted from both areas, as well as shrieks of pain as debris from the now disabled doors fell on their enemies. Jake tossed two flash-bang explosives into the center of the room, turning his head away from the sense-numbing phosphorous light that filled the area.

Jake moved in behind Petrov, laying the barrel of the gun at the base of the big man's skull. "Move, and I'll blow your brains all over the floor."

Petrov lifted both arms and froze. "So the traitor shows himself."

Dave appeared behind Ivan, who held both hands to his eyes temporarily blinded from the explosives. Jake scanned the area. Matt or Luke had taken out the missing gang members, their bodies lying prone on the floor. Doyle had entered with the first explosions and had cuffs on one guy at the front door, the second lay unmoving at his feet.

"It seems you and your brother are out of options, Boss."

"You think you have game won, Carlisle, yes? But it is

not checkmate just yet. I have, how you say, ace in hole."

Jake locked cuffs on both his wrists. "You mean your inside man?"

The big man laughed. "You do not know who it is, no?"

"How about you fill me in? Exactly how does your man keep you out of jail?" Jake asked, watching Dave cuff the younger Kreshnin. Matt moved through the room, securing the wounded gang members. "He conveniently loses the evidence before trial? Or is he a cop who keeps the arrest from actually taking place?"

Doyle's voice rumbled through the headset again telling Jake he'd called in the local cops. He only had a few more minutes to find out the identity of Kreshnin's contact.

"He isn't cop, idiot. He has more power than that."

"Federal agent, then." Jake felt like a mole digging in the dark. Kreshnin didn't seem the least bit fazed about his   impending   arrest.

"Your FBI is joke. Tell me where you hide my little Nicholai. You have kidnapped my, how you say, ward."

"Nicky is safe. And he doesn't belong to you. He'll be in protective custody soon and his testimony will put you on death row."

"The boy won't see courtroom alive."

Jake resisted the urge to pistol-whip the bastard. He hauled him to his feet by the cuffs, shoving him toward the front entrance. "As soon as we get your partner in custody, the boy will give his story to the District Attorney. Looking at the death penalty should take some of the hot air out of you, Petrov."

Ivan laughed from behind them, just as they went out the door. "Nicholai's problem just begins with the DA, right brother?"

"Shut up, stupid!" Petrov growled at his brother.

* * *

Stationed across the street in his old Lincoln, the man had watched the procession of Kreshnin's guards into the building earlier in the night. Now in the daylight he heard the explosions, one after the other.

With any luck, they would all kill each other or the building would collapse and wipe them all out for him.

Of course that still left him the problem of the brat.

Through the gray morning light, he saw a figure slip into the main entrance of the building. Someone he hadn't seen since his earliest days on the force. His body moved in a herky-jerky manner with one bad hip.

Doyle.

He should have known! Carlisle would go to his old partner for help. The one thing they had in common, being former partners of Doyle. Only the old man tried to blame his injury on him as a rookie. It took all his mother's influence to get him cleared of any wrongdoing and out of the police force.

An idea popped in his head. Suddenly he knew where they had the kid stashed. First, he needed to sever his association with the Russians. They'd served their purpose. His Swiss account held six figures now.

Lifting his rifle he trembled with anticipation.

* * *

Jake pushed Petrov out the door. His eyes took a moment to adjust to the dim morning light outside the building. "Your contact is in the DA's office?"

The big Russian clamped his jaw shut.

Jake and Doyle exchanged looks. No wonder Nicky couldn't find the guy in the police pictures.

Dave pushed Ivan outside to join his brother.

A high pitched whine sounded in the air.

Boss' body jumped up and backward out of Jake's grasp. A dark red circle spread across the crime boss' chest, his eyes stared vacantly at the flakes of snow falling gently out of the gloomy sky.

A thud followed by another whine split the morning peace. Jake, followed by Ivan, Dave and Doyle all hit the dirt next to the dead man's body.

An engine roared to life across the street.

Jake scrambled behind a mailbox, his weapon drawn. He didn't have time to get off a single shot before the big black Lincoln peeled away from the curb.

He ran into the street behind it. Squinting, he read the licence plate on the car swerving down the snow-covered street.

MAD*SON.

"Rookie?" Doyle's low-gravelly voice caught Jake's attention. "Did that say MAD-SON?"

"Yeah, Doyle. It's a vanity plate. I wonder if that's what Nicky saw that night. The kid remembers details."

Doyle fished his keys out of his pocket and threw them at Jake. "If so, those two are in big trouble."

"How so?" Jake's heart skipped a beat then stepped

into double time.

"My old partner used that as his plate."

"The one who caused your injury? The one who left the force to join the District Attorney's office?" Jake yelled over his shoulder, already running to Doyle's car.

"The same one. And he knows where I live."

* * *

Snow fluttered down to cover the driveway and yard outside Doyle's kitchen window. Sami refrained from sighing as she handed Nicky a plate to wash. She wondered how the meeting with the Kreshnins had gone. Was anyone hurt? Did they find out information on the mysterious person who set Jake up?

This waiting would kill her.

Sami shook her head. She wouldn't think about death. Not now, not today. She'd lived in its shadow for far too long. Before she awoke in her car, bound and gagged, she couldn't remember the last time she wanted to live.

Ever since she'd felt alive. Intense sensations flooded her as she thought back over her time with Jake and Nicky. Not once did she have the urge to sleep forever. Now she wanted to grab hold of life and hold on with both hands.

Nicky slid the plate into the cupboard next to the window. "That is last dish, yes?"

"You got it, kiddo." Sami released the water in the sink, then wiped her hands. "What do you want to do now?"

"Another car race?" The excitement in his eyes made her laugh. Nicky mastered the NASCAR video game in

Doyle's den as quickly as any other nine-year old American. So far he'd beat her five games to one.

"Okay, but you have to be Dale Earnhardt, Jr. this time, and I get to be Jeff Gordon."

He jumped backward down the hall in front of her. "It not matter, Sami. I still beat pants off you."

"Oh, you think so, huh?" She started to chase him down the hall.

A knock on the front door stopped them in their tracks.

Sami laid her hand on Nicky's shoulder. "It's probably the paperboy or something. But just in case, you stay back here until I make certain."

His eyes wide with fright, Nicky nodded.

She gave his shoulder a reassuring squeeze, then headed for the door. Edging herself to the side of it, she peered out the peephole. She blinked twice before looking again.

Standing on Doyle's front porch in his long black overcoat, hands clasped behind his back, stood Thomas Madigan. The assistant district attorney, poised to break through the political foray into the mayor's race for next year, appeared very official outside the door.

Sami wasn't taking any chances. "May I help you?"

"Ms. Edgars? This is ADA, Tom Madigan. Detective Carlisle asked me to bring you and Nicholai to meet him at police headquarters. The Kreshnins gang has been captured."

Relief poured though her and she sagged against the doorframe. They were all right. Jake was all right.

Sami took a deep, calming breath. Surely, if the ADA knew all those details, Jake had sent him. God, all this intrigue had her seeing conspirators at every turn. She opened the door, and allowed Madigan into the house. "Pardon my hesitancy, but the past five days have been a bit harrowing, to say the least."

"I'm sure it has." He smiled that confidant, politically savvy smile she'd seen on TV so many times in the past several years. "And where is Nicholai hiding?"

Sami laughed and called Nicky. She put her arm around his shoulders. "This is Mr. Madigan. He's going to take us to see Jake and Doyle."

Nicky nodded his head shyly.

Madigan gave her another of those television-spot smiles. "Get your coats. We don't want to keep the others waiting."

Grabbing her coat out of Doyle's closet, Sami shook her head. The guy apparently didn't know the difference between reality and a campaign opportunity. As long as he took her to Jake and her brothers, she didn't care how phony he acted.

Before joining Mr. Madigan and Nicky again, she stepped into Doyle's den and retrieved the disc with Nicky's taped testimony on it. Slipping it into her purse for safekeeping, she shrugged on her coat and hurried to the door.

The cold wind whipped snowflakes around them as the trio stepped out onto the porch. Sami's sneaker caught on a hidden patch of ice. She stumbled, starting to tumble face first toward the concrete porch.

Two hands grabbed her by the elbows. From behind she felt herself steadied on her feet again.

His grip on her tightened. "Careful. We wouldn't want anything to happen to you now."

The DA's breath brushed her neck. A shiver of cold ran through her. Sami gave him a smile in thanks, pulling one of her arms out of his grasp.

He held onto her by one hand and Nicky with the other, leading them around to the passenger side. As they rounded the front of the car, Nicky froze. His eyes widened. Sami followed his line of sight down to the plates.

Her heart jumped into her throat.

MAD*SON.

"You're him!" That sounded stupid. Of course it was the mysterious man chasing them. Now it all made sense!

"That's right, lady." He gripped her arm tight, hauling Nicky against him with his other hand. "You and the kid are going on a little ride with me."

She struggled to get loose. "We're not going anywhere. Jake will be back any second."

Madigan gave an evil laugh. "The good detective has his hands a little full at the moment. Unless you want me to kill the kid right now, you'll do exactly like I tell you."

His eyes narrowed, the smiling placating politician gone. In its place stood the evil behind the mask. For whatever reason, he didn't want to murder them here in a neighborhood where he'd be easily recognized, but he would if he had to. She didn't doubt if for a second.

"Okay. I'll do whatever, just don't hurt Nicky."

He released his hold on her to jerk open the passenger side door. "Climb into the driver's seat from this side. No funny moves, or your young friend won't live to see the city limits."

Sami scooted across the leather front seat, glancing at Nicky to try and reassure him that they would survive this. She only wished she believed it herself.

Madigan shoved Nicky into the seat between them, not relinquishing his hold on the scared child as he shut his door.

"Now," drawing a gun out of his pocket, he pointed it at Nicky's mid-section. "Ease us out of the driveway, and drive toward High Street. We're going to take a little tour of the North side, then head out of town."

With care not to give Madigan any reason to get nervous, Sami followed his directions and headed down Doyle's street. The snow started to fall thicker. A drab brown Chevy approached them, almost swerving into the front of the car, but quick movements by Sami prevented a collision. She glanced up as the car passed.

Piercing blue eyes met hers.

Her pulse quickened.

Jake. Jake was here.

Sami focused her attention on driving.

Stay calm. No need to give Madigan warning that help just arrived.

For once her little voice made sense and she heeded it. In her rear-view mirror the Chevy did a U-turn in the road, its back end fish-tailing for a moment, then it followed them at a good distance.

"Turn left onto High street, Ms. Edgars. Stay within the speed limit. You really don't want to do anything to attract the attention of the police." He pulled Nicky just a little closer to his side.

His threat crept along Sami's spine. From the wild look on Madigan's face, she knew he wouldn't hesitate to kill the boy and her before a cop could get to the car. She had to do something. They weren't likely to live past the city limits, either.

To avoid the cars parked near the curb, Sami changed lanes. The car slid on a patch of ice. Sami gripped the wheel, fighting the urge to hit the brakes, remembering the advice Matt gave her years earlier.

Never hit the brakes. Always turn the wheel in the direction of the skid.

With calm rapid movements, she had the car back under control in seconds.

The snow started to fall faster.

Jake followed the big black Lincoln down High street. His heart pounded. He fought the rising panic. Somehow he had to save Samantha and Nicky from that mad man.

"Shit. Where is that son-of-a-bitch taking you, Samantha?" He gripped the steering wheel tighter, then forced his fingers to flex and relax.

He couldn't do anything to help them from here. Somehow he needed an edge, some way to tilt the scales to their advantage. But how? He felt so helpless.

The Lincoln slid toward a parked car. Jake sucked in a deep breath. Samantha maneuvered the car back into its own lane, narrowly missing the lime green Volkswagen.

His light turned yellow. Jake pulled through the light. He couldn't risk losing them. But he didn't want to alert Madigan to his presence, so he stayed a block behind.

If only something would happen to even the stakes. He could ram them from behind, maybe gain the edge by surprise. No that was no good. In this weather, he might cause them to wreck and seriously injure Samantha or Nicky.

Think, damn it. Frustration built inside him like a pot of pasta about to boil over. The advantage lay in Madigan's hands as long as he had Samantha and Nicky in his grasp.

A green pick-up pulled in behind him. Jake glanced into his rear-view mirror and recognized Matt at the wheel. Good. At least now he had some back up. But back up for what?

Samantha turned the Lincoln off High Street. Where was Madigan taking them?

"Turn here." Madigan directed Sami to turn onto the narrow and curved North Street. Lined with cars on both sides, barely enough space existed for her to maneuver between them. Some of the old cobblestones from the early nineteenth century had worn through the modern pavement. It gave the Lincoln's tires a little more traction, although it still slipped on the ice patches.

"Why are you doing this? You can't possibly believe killing us will keep your campaign hopes alive," she asked, trying to keep his attention focused on her, not behind where Jake followed them.

He gave a harsh laugh. "This isn't like TV movies, Ms. Edgars. No real confession just before the heroine is rescued. There isn't going to be a rescue, so you don't need my reasons. And as for my campaign, well, let's just say what the voters don't know won't hurt them."

"Can I at least know where we're going? It'll make driving a little easier."

"To a construction site big enough to hold you two and this car."

The guy was nuts!

North Street quickly turned onto Neil Avenue, at the most northern extent of the Ohio State University district. Sami wracked her brain for any memory of construction on campus. Nothing that big came to mind.

They stopped at the light.

"Now turn right and head west."

The tires of the Lincoln spun on a patch of ice beneath them, trying to find some traction. The car lurched forward, the rear-end fish-tailing for a moment as she turned onto Dodridge Street. Sami got control of the car, driving down the hill toward the bridge crossing the Olentangy River.

Madigan flexed and gripped his fingers around the gun handle. His mind raced gleefully.

It would all work out okay. He'd report the car missing as soon as he got back into town. With it buried under tons of steel and cement, decades would pass before the evidence surfaced. Once he had the kid silenced, and with the Boss dead, no one would know of his involvement with the Kreshnins.

Petrov and his people had served their purpose. Years ago, when he'd been the greenest of assistants to the District Attorney, he'd come across a case of extortion against Petrov. Cutting a deal to lessen the other man's offense to a virtual slap on the wrist had put him in a position of power. By keeping the gang out of the media spot light, and the cross hairs of the DA's guns aimed at organized crime, his efforts had been well rewarded.

He now had bank accounts of endless funds in both Switzerland and the Cayman Islands, totally untraceable to him. With that money he could make anonymous donations to his own political campaigns.

The public needed him. They were stupid lambs ready for the slaughter. He planned to lead them blindly through his plans. First the mayoral ship, then the governor's office. After that he only had Washington left to conquer.

No one, especially not some poor immigrant kid was going to stop him now.

The car swerved at the light, then the woman gained its control once more. Their speed increased as they descended the hill toward the bridge.

Watching Samantha maneuver the car over the ice and onto Dodridge Street, still following at a distance to prevent spooking Madigan, Jake would be damned if he'd let any harm come to Samantha and Nicky. They'd put their trust in him.

He needed something to happen though.

Anything. Just one thing to give him the upper hand. Then the bastard was dead.

He gripped the steering wheel tighter, focusing on his anger, not his panic and fears.

In front of him the Lincoln swerved once more on the slick road. This time it continued to slide. Just as it came to the bridge, the tail swung forward, the speed of the vehicle sending it through the old concrete structure and over the edge of the bridge.

Jake watched in horror as the car carrying the woman he loved and the boy he wanted as his own careened into the icy-cold waters of the river below.

CHAPTER SIXTEEN

Like in a bad movie, the car seemed to tumble in slow motion, head first into the icy waters of the river below. For a moment Jake stopped breathing.

"No!" The word tore out of his mouth as he stopped Doyle's car inches from where the Lincoln plunged over the side. He threw himself out of the car, then stumbled and slid his way down the snow-covered embankment.

He had to get to Samantha and Nicky.

They couldn't die. Not like this.

She couldn't die. He hadn't told her he loved her.

From the street he heard car doors banging and voices calling his name. His attention completely focused on the tail end of the car protruding from the river.

Dammit, he had to get to them. But where? What if he dove in and he missed them? He rushed into the water.

"Wait." A hand landed on his shoulder, pulling him

back.

Jake glanced at Matt, trying to jerk his arm out of the other man's grasp. "Let me go, Samantha and Nicky are in there."

"I know, Jake. Don't you think I want to dive in there, too?" His grip tightened. "She's my baby sister, for crying out loud. But give her a chance to get out. I taught her what to do."

They waited there, knee deep in the freezing water.

Time stood still.

The past few days flashed through Jake's mind. Samantha fighting with him, then helping him with Nicky. The light in her eyes when she laughed. The love in them as she played with Nicky. The haunted pain in them when she spoke of her daughter. Her ability to adapt to each new situation. The feel of her body pressed against his in passion. The taste of her lips, her breasts.

Suddenly, he didn't want to live without her.

Sami made herself lose control of the car. The back end swung around to the front. She felt the impact with the old concrete bridge before she saw it coming.

Madigan screamed beside her.

She pushed the electronic window button for the rear windows with one hand. With the other she reached for Nicky as the car tumbled downward, her arm helping to brace him against the impact. Her seat belt held them both.

Madigan hit the dashboard, then the window as his side of the car took the full brunt of the collision with the boulders lining the river bottom. His neck twisted sideways, his eyes, two glassy orbs.

A calm came over her. She knew what to do. Matt had drilled it into her head after the time he had to fish the elderly couple out of the Scioto River south of the city four years ago.

The icy water rushed in around them from the shattered front windshield. Gripping Nicky's coat, she released her seat belt and shoved him into the back seat. She gulped in air, fighting off the urge to panic in the freezing cold water. She scrambled into the back seat with Nicky.

"Take a big breath, Nicky."

The little boy swallowed in air, his eyes huge with fear.

"Can you swim?"

He shook his head no.

"Okay. When I shove you out of the window, you hold onto the car, okay? No matter what, you hold onto the car window. Jake is up there somewhere. He'll save us both."

With all her effort, she shoved the boy out the window, holding onto his coat, until she felt him floating next to the car. She glanced at the front seat, no longer able to see more than Madigan's dark form in the swirling, murky water rushing into the car and filling it from front to back. No movement stirred from the passenger side.

Sami wiggled out the opening. Her lungs burned from holding her breath. She kept one hand on Nicky as she pushed her head above the water. Frantically, she reached around Nicky, searching for the edge of the rear window of the car. If she couldn't secure them to the car until Jake came and got them, the current would pull them down river. The news frequently showed scenes of the river being dragged further down stream for bodies washed away from an accident.

And she wouldn't let this child die. Not this time. No matter what, Nicky would live. This time she'd save the child she loved. And she did love this little boy.

"Jake! Where the hell are you?" She screamed over the sound of the water rushing around her and the sirens arriving on the bridge above them.

Two arms encircled her and Nicky from behind. "Right here, sweetheart. Matt's here, too. You're going to be okay."

She felt him tighten his hold on her. His body pressed against hers holding them all tight against the metal frame of the Lincoln. His lips pressed into her wet hair. She shivered, from the cold or relief, she wasn't sure.

Oh man, did he feel good!

"I did it, Jake. I saved him. This time I saved him."

"I know you did sweetheart. But you have to let go of Nicky, so Matt can get him out of this freezing water." His hand gently pried her fingers loose from the death grip she had on the boy's coat.

Matt reached in and slid Nicky out from between Sami and the car. She watched, still gripping the edge of the rear window, as Matt half swam, half wadded to shore. Once Nicky stood next to him, the paramedics wrapping him in a thermal blanket, she released her hold on the window. She let Jake ease her around the tail of the wrecked car.

"Wait!" Pushing against him, she tried to go back to the rear window.

Jake gripped her tighter. "Samantha, he's dead. There's no use trying to get him out."

"I know that. The disc with Nicky's testimony on it is in my purse. I have to get it out and get it to the police. It clears you and puts Kreshnin away for good!" She struggled again, but it was no use. He held her pinned between the bumper and his body.

"Sami! You are not going back in that car."

"But Nicky's testimony, the Kreshnins," she said between chattering teeth and body wracking shakes.

He wrapped his arms around her. His body heat a blessing.

"Listen to me, sweetheart. Boss is dead, Madigan is dead, the gang is either half dead or in custody. That disc's not important enough for you to risk your life over. Doyle can make us a thousand copies. Nothing is more important to me right now than that you and Nicky are safe." He kissed her hard, then took a strong grip on her arm and shoulder. " Now, if you're done trying to play polar bear, let's get out of this freezing water."

They clung to each other, fighting the swift current.

"The car's trunk," she whispered as they stumbled over the rocky shore.

"What about it?" he asked once they too stood safely on the riverbank.

"It's got...Ivanovich's ...DNAinside," she managed to get out through her chattering teeth. "Tell Matt."

"I will, sweetheart." Then Jake pulled her into his arms. "I thought I'd lost you, Sami," he whispered against her ear, hugging her so tight she could barely breathe.

Sami shivered, her arms wrapped around his waist. The paramedics wrapped them into warm blankets. "For a...minute, I thought...you did, too," she said between shivers.

He pulled away for a minute, all the love and fear inside him there for her to see. "I love you, Samantha."

He didn't wait for her reply. His lips descended on hers in a kiss to convince her how deep his feelings ran. She clung to him. Letting him warm her from the inside out, her heart swelling with the need to return his passion with her own.

"Ahem."

Somewhere behind her, her brother cleared his throat. She didn't care. This was Jake. He was warm. He was hers. She'd been half-alive before him.

"Sami. Jake." This time Matt made sure they heard him. "You two may want to stay out here and freeze to death, but Nicky needs to get to the hospital to be checked for hypothermia. And the news vultures will descend on us any minute."

Jake broke the kiss off. "Your brother knows how to kill a romantic moment."

She giggled against his lips. "Not a romantic bone in the guy's body."

"Come on, let's get you out of the cold."

He led her up the slippery bank to the emergency squad. Swarms of cars and people blocked their ascent.

Lights from television cameras blinded her already bleary eyes. Two policemen stopped him from climbing in beside her.

"Jake Carlisle, you're under arrest for the death of..."

Sami started to climb back out of the van, only to have her brother step between her and the policemen.

Matt flashed his badge at them. "Carlisle is already in custody of the Highway Patrol, officers."

"He's wanted by us for the murder of Captain Bridges and kidnapping Ms. Edgars."

"Too bad, I arrested him before you, isn't it? While he's going to the hospital for medical attention, we can have our superiors decided on whose jurisdiction it is."

"Hey! What's to keep him from escaping?" The officers tried to muscle past Matt, who held his ground.

Matt shoved Jake into the emergency van beside Sami, winking at his sister, then shut the door. Leaning into Jake's arms, she watched her brother through the rear window and heard his parting words.

"Don't worry, Carlisle isn't going anywhere for a very long time. On that you can make bet."

"I'm not, you know," Jake whispered against her hair.

Sami wrapped her arms around him, closing her eyes. For the first time since he kidnapped her, she felt calm. And the first time since her daughter died, she felt at peace.

A shaky giggle sounded from the stretcher where Nicky lay bundled in warm blankets.

Sami opened her eyes and grinned at him. "And what are you laughing at?"

"I had first swimming lesson!" He grinned at them, one tooth missing.

Jake chuckled beside her. "Yeah, little partner, a crash course."

* * *

At the hospital, Samantha, in her element, took charge.

First thing, she ordered all news reporters kept out of the hospital. Secondly, she insisted on sharing a cubicle in the emergency room with Nicky. Then she convinced the house supervisor to let them stay in a semi-private room together.

Jake watched her in amazement as she bullied both the attending pediatrician and the social worker to get her way. His sweet, smart Samantha, knew how to turn into a hell-on-wheels mama when she needed.

Standing in a pair of green surgical scrubs one of her co-workers scrounged up for her, she currently had the hospital's social worker pinned against the wall, her finger in the other woman's face.

"I know damn well what the rules and regulations are regarding minors with no parents or guardians." She edged closer. "But I'll be damned if you are going to jerk this boy away from the one man he feels safe with. Not to mention, that I am more qualified than any foster mother to observe him for signs of infection or hypothermia. I don't care what strings you have to pull to get him left in my custody while he's in this hospital, you just do it."

Jake leaned over to Matt. "Should we interfere before someone gets hurt?"

"Nah," he shook his head. "Sami can handle her

own."

"I'm worried about the social worker."

"True. But I figure the more my sister vents her anger on that lady, the less she'll have for me, when I tell her I do have to take you to the police station for questioning until this mess is straightened out."

Sami stopped mid-sentence. Her gaze slowly turned to Jake and Matt.

The social worker took that as her cue to escape.

"You can't be serious, Matt." Samantha squared off in front of her brother.

Jake hated the fear that suddenly edged her voice, her hand resting over her heart. He wanted to take her in his arms and tell her everything was okay. But he wouldn't lie to her. More likely than not, he would face departmental charges at the least, possible kidnapping and child endangerment charges, as well.

"Jake?" She seemed smaller at that moment, frail and scared, something he hadn't seen from her ever, not once, even the day he kidnapped her.

"He has to do his duty, Samantha." Jake went to her and wrapped his arms around her. "I didn't play by the rules, now I have to face the consequences of my actions. You wouldn't ask anything less of me or your brother, would you?"

"Yes," she mumbled into his shirt.

Jake couldn't contain his laughter. "That's my Samantha, defiant to the end. No matter what happens, just know I love you, sweetheart."

She leaned back in his arms, raising those pale green

eyes full of love to him. "I love you, too, Jake. And if Matt lets them harm one hair on your head, I'll make his life hell."

"You mean you don't already?" her brother chuckled from behind them.

Before she could list how she planned to torment her brother further, a knock sounded on the hospital room door.

Jake recognized District Attorney, Brad Fallon. He was accompanied by a young woman Jake had met once before—Captain Bridges' contact in the DA's office and the person who'd set this whole investigation in motion—Natalie Johnson.

"May I come in?" the DA asked as he stepped into the room. "I know you have all been through a very trying ordeal, but I would like a few words with both, Detective Carlisle and Ms. Edgars before the reporters fight their way in."

Slipping his hand into Samantha's, Jake pulled her back to sit on the edge of Nicky's bed. The boy had talked for a few hours, but fallen asleep since then. Even Samantha's tirade against the social worker hadn't roused him. She laid her hand on his forehead, once more checking that his temperature felt normal.

"What did you need to speak with us about, Mr. Fallon?" Jake pulled Sami in closer, reassuring himself she was all right, just as she had reassured herself regarding Nicky.

The DA closed the door behind them, then cleared his throat and pulled at his tie once. "The District Attorney's office had no knowledge of Assistant DA Madigan's involvement with the Kreshnin crime family. At least until three hours ago, when your brother, David, announced the fact to the policemen who arrived at the scene of the gun battle in the old factory district."

Samantha started to say something, but Jake squeezed her side in a signal to wait and see what else the man had to say.

"As you can imagine, this has become somewhat of an embarrassment to my office." He cleared his throat again. "We were also the people who issued the arrest warrant for Detective Carlisle. Unfortunately it was at the request of Mr. Madigan, which has only added fuel to the fire."

"What is it you wish us to do to help?" Jake offered the man a bone, an idea forming in his own mind.

"If we told the same story, spinning it so the best possible light shone on all of us, and we somehow act as one unit on this with the reporters…"

"Jake has to be cleared of all charges," Samantha interrupted him. Jake's heart warmed at her quick defense of him. Her support would take some getting used to. "And no departmental repercussions, either. He had nothing to do with Captain Bridges' death. I'm an eyewitness to it all."

"So, your brothers informed me, Ms. Edgars." The DA had the political savvy to act chagrined, although Jake had a feeling the fiery woman beside him could take the man down a peg or two if she wanted. "And of course, not only will Detective Carlisle be cleared of all charges, he will be awarded a Medal of Valor for bringing down the newly emerging Kreshnin crime gang. Which Ms. Johnson, here has attested to the undercover work she and Bridges had involved Mr. Carlisle in."

"Then it's a deal," Samantha announced beside him.

"Hold on a minute, Samantha." Jake hated to take away her victory. Something more important than his career lay on the bargaining table.

Samantha grasped his hand in hers. "Jake, he's agreed to clear you, what more do you want?"

Jake fixed the DA with a determined eye. "If you want me to help you smooth this over with the press, you're going to have to give us a little help with Nicky."

Fallon nodded with great enthusiasm. "Of course, Carlisle. We'll see that he's placed in the best foster home we can find."

"Not good enough." Jake stood, making sure Fallon understood him completely. The man had a nightmare of a PR problem. Jake had the man over a barrel, and he wanted to be sure he knew that. "If you want my cooperation, and the cooperation of Samantha's family, then you'll cut through every inch of red tape and see that Nicky goes to live with Samantha. That she has clear access to adoption rights and no one, I mean no one questions the arrangement."

"Jake?"

She slipped her hand in his, but he didn't take his gaze off DA Fallon's face. He simply squeezed her hand for reassurance. "You fought to save him, Samantha. He deserves a mother willing to die for him."

A very happy politician's smile split the District

Attorney's face. He held out his hand to Jake. "It's as good as done, Carlisle."

Jake released Samantha's hand to seal the deal with the other man. "When you have the papers giving Samantha free and clear custody of Nicky, then I'll give the reporters any story you cook up. Until, then it'll be no comment."

"You drive a hard bargain, Detective. But you have me in a corner. The papers will be here this afternoon." With that, the wily politician excused himself.

"Matt, if you could excuse us." Jake nodded toward the door, and Samantha's brother took the hint.

"Jake? I thought you would want Nicky to come live with you." Samantha tilted her head in curiosity.

"I do." Jake turned to her, pulling her into his arms.

"I don't understand. How can you have him live with you, if I have custody of him?"

Jake kissed her softly. "If you marry me, then Nicky will be both of ours. Our son. Yours and mine."

The wonder that filled her eyes, as his words settled into her heart, surprised him. She hadn't expected his proposal.

"I mean if you don't mind being married to a loner cop, a renegade of sorts."

Sami stood on her tiptoes, kissing him hard. "You aren't a loner anything anymore, Mr. Kidnapper. We're a team now."

He pulled her tight against him, kissing her just as hard. "You taught me something very important."

"Mmm, I did?" she murmured against his lips.

"To do my job right and be a whole person, I need more than just myself. You showed me it's okay to lean on someone else."

She grinned at him. "You can lean on me anytime, Jake."

"Me too!" Nicky announced behind them, a semi toothless grin spread across his face. "We family now, Big Partner?"

The couple moved to his side. "If it's okay with you, Little Partner, we're going to make it official pretty soon."

A warhoop sounded from the little boy, which signaled the room's invasion from the hallway, where Samantha's entire family had waited patiently.

Jake shook hands with her father and was engulfed in the arms of her tiny mother. Dave introduced him to Judy, his very pregnant wife and their daughter and son. Luke took over the telling of the gun battle to anyone who would listen, especially the pretty young nurse in charge of Nicky's care.

Another knock sounded on the door. Doyle stood on the threshold, uncertain whether or not to intrude. Samantha slipped her arm through his and pulled him into the melee.

Jake shook his old partner's hand. "Thanks, Doyle. We couldn't have done it without you."

"I'm just sorry I didn't put it together sooner." He rubbed his hand nervously over the injured hip Madigan caused in the brief time he partnered Doyle, the one that cost him his career. "The boy and Sami never would've been in danger if I'd been on the ball."

"You sent me to save them, old man. I'll never forget it." Jake noticed everyone's attention on him. He pulled Samantha in tight against his side. "I hoped you could do me another favor."

Doyle nodded. "Anything you need."

"How about being my best man?"

Once more the room erupted in warhoops and hugs.

EPILOGUE

A blanket of snow lay over the rolling hills and barren trees of the land surrounding the cabin. The couple inside didn't mind the peaceful isolation as the wind whipped across the roof and rattled the windows.

Samantha snuggled against Jake in the big bed, gazing at the fire in the fireplace joining the cabin's main room with the bedroom.

"It was a lovely wedding," she murmured sleepily against his chest.

Jake slowly ran one hand up and down her back, raking his nails across her soft skin and firm muscles. "Yep. Well worth waiting for."

"We couldn't get married before the holidays were finished. I wanted Nicky to know what family means at Thanksgiving and Christmas. It's all new to him."

Jake chuckled. "He certainly has taken to your family like a duck to water."

"Our family." She leaned on one elbow, her eyes

staring intensely at him. "They're your family too, now. I even think my mama loves you more than me."

"She just loves the fact that your smile is so contagious these days. I plan on keeping it that way."

Samantha swallowed hard at the power of that promise. "Your kidnapping saved my life."

"Are you kidding? It almost cost you your life, not to mention Nicky's." He tried to rise, but she pressed herself on his chest, forcing him to stay down.

"Listen to me for a minute." She blinked back her tears. She needed him to understand how close she'd been. "When Aimee died, I was numb. I'd fought so hard and so long, there wasn't anything left for me to give. The depression I fell into lasted forever. Nothing mattered to me. I was a walking corpse. I lived in an emotional coma. My life consisted of work, sleep and work. I'd even started considering..."

She shuddered hard as some memory haunted her.

"Consider what?" he prodded her with his gentle question.

"I have something to show you."

She scooted out of the bed and padded naked across the room to her purse. The sensual scene of her naked in the firelight had him growing hard with need once more. When she climbed back in bed, he pulled her tight against him.

"The night you kidnapped me I'd just gotten these." She held up three slips of paper.

He'd had enough prescriptions in his life to recognize them. He held them up and couldn't pronounce the names. Concern crept along his spine. "What are these?"

"Sleeping pills." She swallowed hard. "I just wanted to go to sleep and end the pain. I'd finally decided to do something about my depression...if you hadn't come along and forced me back into the real world...the world of the living," a deep sigh escaped her, "I'd planned to fill those that night, and take them all."

"Oh God, Samantha." He pulled her tightly into his arms. "I could have lost you before I ever knew you existed."

"I just wanted to forget all my pain." She let him hold her for a few minutes, indulging in tears for the woman she left behind that incredible night.

"But then fate stepped in and sent you to rescue me." She wiped away the tears and lifted herself to smile at him. "You see, you saved me that night. You and Nicky forced me to put aside my own self-pity and face the fact that life goes on. You made me realize I wanted to live life, pain and pleasure, happiness and sorrow, all of it. But not alone. I want to face it all right beside you."

She wiggled onto his body and stretched out, staring into his eyes. "I love you, Jake Carlisle with all of my heart."

"I love you, Samantha Carlisle. You made me realize how much I needed others, and that it wasn't a weakness to depend on those you love." Jake brushed a stray lock of hair off her face. "So you don't mind that I dragged you out of a dark parking lot and forced you to help me?"

"I forgive you for that." Samantha pushed herself up, kissing him deeply.

"You forgive me for tying you up and gagging you?"

She entwined her hands in his, lifting them to kiss each one. "Oh I forgave you that the moment I saw Nicky." She straddled his hips with her thighs, luxuriating in the feel of the soft hairs of his abdomen against her own smooth stomach.

"Mmm." He pulled her arms up with his, so both their hands were above his head, her body stretched taut over the length of his. "Do you forgive me for tying you up that first night and scaring you with that knife?"

"Oh, yes. I hadn't awakened with such an erotic dream like that in years." She wiggled a little higher, loosening one of her hands away from his, then grinned at him. "There's only one thing I really need to get even with you for."

Jake lifted one eyebrow in question. "What's that?"

She watched his eyes widen as he felt the heavy metal encircle his wrist and heard the heavy click of the metal.

"I did want to discuss the handcuffs."

Laughter burst from him. He tried to wrap his other arm around her, but she fought to secure it with the other metal restraint.

"This is my fantasy, Jake Carlisle. You've just been kidnapped." She lowered her lips to his and slid her tongue slowly into his parted lips, tasting the fullness of his love. "And you are going to stay my prisoner..." she started kissing her way down his chest, "until I've had my fill of you."

As she slid her lips and tongue down his abdomen, Jake prayed she wouldn't finish with him for decades.

THE END

ABOUT THE AUTHOR

Suzanne Ferrell discovered romance novels in her aunt's hidden stash one summer as a teenager. From that moment on she knew two things: she loved romance stories and someday she'd be writing her own. Her love for romances has only grown over the years. It took her a number of years and a secondary career as a nurse to finally start writing her own stories.

A double finalist in the Romance Writer's of America's 2006 Golden Heart with her manuscripts, KIDNAPPED and HUNTED (Romantic Suspense), Suzanne has also won The Beacon Unpublished and the CTRWA's contests in the erotica categories with her book, The Surrender Of Lacy Morgan.

Suzanne's sexy stories, whether they be her steamy Western eroticas, her on the edge of your seat romantic suspense, or the heart warming small town stories, will keep you thinking about her characters long after their Happy Ever After is achieved.

Visit author Suzanne Ferrell's website at:
www.suzanneferrell.com

Other books by Suzanne Ferrell:

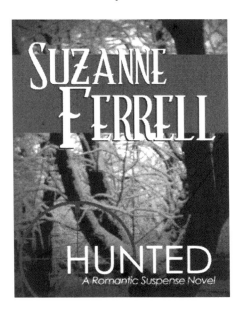

Hunted

In one fiery explosion Katie Myers' witness protection cover is blown. Unable to trust the Marshals who've been responsible for her safety, she's on the run from the cult leader she put on death row. In desperation she forces a near stranger at gunpoint to help her hide.

By-the-book patrolman Matt Edgars is shocked when the woman he's come to rescue points a gun at him and demands he help her leave a crime scene. The stark terror in Katie's beautiful eyes has him breaking rules for the first time in his career.

With a hit man on their trail, Matt must break down the walls Katie has built to guard the secrets of her past. If not the cult leader will fulfill his prophecy and take the one woman Matt has ever loved to the grave.

The Surrender Of Lacy Morgan

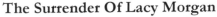

"Set in the Montana Territory, 1882, The Surrender of Lacy Morgan is a story of outlaws on the run, brothers seeking justice and an untraditional love story that had me saying "Ahhhh..." more than once. Ms. Ferrell has a very talented voice for writing gritty and vivid historical settings."
- The Long and the Short of It Reviews

"Suzanne Ferrell's cowboys are how the West should've been won...one dangerously sexy hero at a time."
- Jo Davis, Bestselling author of *Ride The Fire*

Made in the USA
Lexington, KY
08 May 2013